ESCAPE TO OAKBROOK FARM

HOPE COVE BOOK 2

HANNAH ELLIS

Published by Hannah Ellis
www.authorhannahellis.com

Cover design by Aimee Coveney

To Dua,
You deserve the world...
here's a book instead.

CHAPTER 1

The best man was looking at Josie curiously. He was obviously about to strike up a conversation and she wished he wouldn't. She'd had enough of making polite conversation with strangers at her sister's wedding. Finally, she'd found an unoccupied bench and thought she'd get a few minutes to enjoy her champagne in peace. Sam had casually sidled over and she smiled benignly up at him. They'd never met before but she'd heard his name mentioned often.

On a normal day he was probably pretty average-looking, but his suit was cut perfectly and made him annoyingly easy on the eye. Annoyingly because she'd only split up with her boyfriend a few days earlier and was keen to project her negativity to men in general, rather than just her ex, Jack. It was difficult when they looked absolutely delicious and gazed at you with sparkling green eyes.

"I'm going to have to ask." Sam took a seat beside her. "What's with the shoes?"

"Excuse me?" she said, taken aback.

"Your shoes… Did you forget to pack them or what?"

"No." Her tone was frosty. "My shoes are on my feet."

He looked slightly awkward. "Those are the shoes you intended to wear today?"

"Yes. Why?"

"No reason."

She glared at him. "If you have an issue with my shoes you may as well say it."

"They don't go with your dress."

"They're Converse," she said. "They go with anything."

His gaze roamed over the guests mingling in the hotel gardens. It was a lovely location on the Devon coast, very close to her sister's house in Hope Cove. The cherry trees in the hotel gardens were in full bloom, creating an explosion of pink. It was quite a sight with the fallen petals making a delicate pink carpet.

"You're wishing you never started this conversation, aren't you?" Josie was amused by how uncomfortable he looked. Everyone else who'd commented on her footwear had said they looked cute and much comfier than high heels. Josie couldn't stand wearing high heels and her sister, Lizzie, had eventually given in to her demands to wear her favourite trainers with the elegant silk bridesmaid dress.

"Not really." Sam adjusted his tie, the same shade of teal as her dress. Then he glanced at his shiny black dress shoes. "I'm wishing I'd worn a pair of trainers. My feet are killing me."

She beamed. "That was my argument. Why spend the day being uncomfortable just to follow convention?"

"It's a good point, and one I wish I'd brought up earlier."

"Go barefoot," she suggested. "The beach is right down there. People go barefoot at beach weddings. You'll probably start a trend. I'm sure everyone's dying to take off their fancy shoes at this point."

"You wouldn't thank me for taking off my shoes and socks. People would pass out."

6

"Keep them on then, please." She felt self-conscious as his gaze shifted back to her feet. "They don't look that bad, do they?"

"No. Just unusual. It's quirky."

An elderly lady wandered slowly over to them and Sam moved to let her sit between them. "Have you met my neighbour?" he asked Josie.

Annette smiled. "We've met before. At Lizzie and Max's house."

"The Boxing Day get-together." Josie thought back. Things had been difficult with her and Jack then as well, and he'd backed out of making the trip with her at the last minute. He never had been keen to spend time with her family.

"We're pretty much family now," Annette said. "I'm Max's aunt, you're his sister-in-law. What does that make us?"

"I'm not really sure," Josie said.

"Me neither." Annette glanced downwards. "I'm very envious of your shoes. They look very comfy."

"They are." Josie cast a cheeky grin in Sam's direction.

Annette patted his leg. "Get me a drink, will you? A tonic water. I'm parched." There was a short silence while he moved away. "He's lovely," Annette said out of the side of her mouth. "Single too."

Josie spluttered out a laugh.

"I'm just saying." Annette shot her a sly smile. "In case you're interested. Don't say I said anything, though – he's always telling me off for trying to set him up with women."

"I thought I was special for a moment," Josie said. "Now I find I'm just one more in a line of women you're trying to set him up with…"

She chuckled. "He's thirty-five; he needs to find someone. Max is finally settled. Just Sam now, and then I can die happy."

7

Josie's smile slipped and she glanced away. "I was sorry to hear about Wendy." Annette's partner had passed away a couple of months earlier. She'd had a hip replacement that refused to heal and led to a host of complications. Pneumonia killed her in the end. Josie had heard all about it from Lizzie.

"Thank you," she said quietly. "I've found today difficult, to be honest."

"I'm sure." Josie gently put a hand over Annette's and gave it a quick squeeze as they watched the party.

Sam reappeared with a glass of tonic water for Annette a couple of minutes later. "We're supposed to head inside," he said. "The dancing is about to start."

"I'll find a spot to sit and watch," Annette said, getting up.

Josie followed. "I'll join you."

"You'll have to dance with Sam," Annette told her. "It's tradition – the bridesmaid and the best man…"

"I don't think Josie likes to stick to tradition," Sam said, looking pointedly at her shoes.

"I just didn't want my feet to hurt. I didn't realise my footwear would cause quite such a stir."

"If you're worried about your feet hurting, maybe you shouldn't dance with me! I can't promise not to tread on them."

Inside, the three of them found a table just in time to watch the first dance. A jazz band played and the atmosphere was smooth and sophisticated. Everything had been planned to perfection.

"Lizzie looks gorgeous, doesn't she?" Annette said, pulling a tissue out of her handbag and wiping at her eyes.

Josie reached to pinch a tissue, nodding and trying not to let Sam catch her being so sentimental. What was it about the first dance at weddings that was so romantic? Lizzie looked radiant, and she and Max both beamed as they glided round

8

the dance floor. They could easily be the happiest people in the world.

"Come on then." Sam stood and reached for Josie's hand as the song ended and another began.

"Okay," she said with a sigh. She didn't want to seem too keen, but secretly she was desperate to get on the dance floor. She caught a whiff of Sam's aftershave when he pulled her close and closed her eyes as she breathed it in.

"Was Annette okay?" Sam asked. "She looked a bit tearful outside."

"She was just saying how hard it was today, without Wendy."

He looked in Annette's direction, flashing her a smile. "They were together almost sixty years," he said quietly. "I can't get used to seeing Annette without Wendy. They were always inseparable."

"It's so sad."

They were silent for a moment and Josie was aware of the feel of Sam's hand on her back. He'd obviously been joking about being a bad dancer and she definitely didn't need to worry about him stepping on her toes.

"Did Annette say anything embarrassing about me?" he asked. "She's so keen to set me up with someone, I swear she's going to start paying women to date me soon."

"There was no money mentioned," Josie said, grinning. "But she does seem concerned by your marital status."

"I think it gives her sleepless nights," he said. "I'm worried she's going to take out an advert in the local paper. I'll be in the classified section under *Free To a Good Home*."

She laughed at his cheeky grin as they moved with the music. "What would the advert say?"

"Thirty-five-year-old male," he said without pause. "Good-looking." He raised an eyebrow and grinned. "Charming, healthy, owns his own home... albeit in the middle of nowhere surrounded by a load of gossips and next door to an eccentric old lesbian! She could probably leave that last bit out."

"Sounds like she should be auctioning you off, not begging someone to take you…" The words came automatically and were quickly followed by a blush.

"That's you *and* Annette who think I'm a catch then."

"I'm not sure I said that."

The song ended and he gazed at her with bright eyes. "It's what I heard."

CHAPTER 2

Lizzie looked exhausted when she came to say goodnight. "It's lovely that you and Sam got on so well," she remarked. "I was worried you'd spend all day moping over Jack."

"He's nice." Josie's attempt at flippancy would have been more effective if she hadn't been grinning. She couldn't help it, though. It had been an unexpectedly wonderful day. And she definitely had Sam to thank for that.

"Every time I looked over you were dancing with him," Lizzie said. "I'm glad you had a good time."

"It was a lovely day," Josie said. That's what you're supposed to say about weddings, but it was true. "Annette is a lot of fun too."

"Poor Annette." Lizzie glanced around the room. "She's having such a hard time. Where is she?"

"She went up to bed a while ago."

"Lucky her. I'm worn out but I think it'll take me another hour to say goodbye to everyone."

"Get on with it then. I'll see you tomorrow."

Josie kissed her sister goodnight, then stepped outside for

some fresh air. It was a beautiful evening, and she gazed up at the starlit sky with the full moon shining brightly. The whole day had gone by without her dwelling on her breakup with Jack, but suddenly she felt gloomy. She was twenty-eight years old and had just split up with her boyfriend again. They'd split up four times in the past eighteen months, but they always ended up back together. She had no idea if it was over for good this time or not.

The other problem was that she was unemployed again. Her last job had only been a temporary position to cover maternity leave. It was a PA job in a small advertising company and she'd enjoyed it. They'd been happy with her too and would've kept her on if they could. It had been convenient since she'd never had any trouble getting time off for auditions. Acting had been her dream for a long time, although she was finally coming round to the fact that it probably wasn't going to work out.

She wasn't too worried about the job situation; she always managed to find something else. It just seemed like she had a lot of decisions to make. If her and Jack really *were* over, where was she going to live? She'd been living at his place in Oxford. She'd have to go and see him and either sort things out or pack up her things. Moving back with her parents would be fairly depressing.

"You okay?" Sam asked, appearing beside her.

"Yeah. Just miles away." She looked down at his bare feet. His tie had disappeared too and he looked far more casual. "I see you took my advice about the shoes."

"You made me dance too much. I'm in agony."

"I didn't make you do anything." She automatically followed as he walked away, through the gardens. "Where are you going?"

"Down to the beach. I'm going to soak my feet! Do you want to come?"

She nodded and they continued through the gardens together and out onto the coastal path beyond. Sam winced and hopped along the stony path. The short way to the sandy cove was lit by white lights on short wooden posts. Josie inhaled the wonderfully salty air as Sam headed straight for the shoreline, rolling up his trouser legs and groaning when the water washed around his feet. "That's amazing." He looked content as he wandered through the gentle waves. "You okay? You've gone quiet on me."

"I'm fine." She dug the toe of her shoe absently into the sand. "Just tired. Weddings are emotionally draining."

"All that romance in the air! It's exhausting."

She forced a smile but felt sad again. "In the last two weeks I've split up with my boyfriend and lost my job." And also lost the filter between her thoughts and her mouth apparently. Why had she said that?

"Sorry." An odd look flashed across his face but she struggled to read him.

"You already knew that, didn't you?"

He made a decent attempt at looking confused.

"Oh no." Josie's shoulders drooped as she sighed. "Someone told you to keep an eye on me? Who was it? Lizzie? Or Max? He's weirdly protective of me. Like he feels the need to do the whole big brother thing. I keep telling him a brother-in-law is different to an actual brother but he doesn't listen."

Sam smiled kindly. "They were both concerned."

"That's embarrassing. I'm so sorry. You didn't have to be nice to me just because they told you I'm a charity case."

"Between keeping an eye on you and looking after Annette I've had a terrible day." His eyes sparkled mischievously. "Really awful."

She couldn't help but smile, even through her embarrassment. "Did you just dance with me because you felt sorry for me? I feel like an idiot now."

"You don't need to feel like an idiot." He looked suddenly bashful. "I definitely wasn't dancing with you out of charity."

"Really? You promise?"

He looked right at her. "I spent all evening giving angry looks to anyone who seemed like they might try and cut in." He paused. "And being incredibly grateful that you split up with your boyfriend last week. I mean, I'm sympathetic and everything. But selfishly very glad. Although my feet might not agree."

Her head tilted to one side. "You're very sweet."

"Don't say that." He frowned and walked out of the water. "Women don't like sweet guys. It's an anti-compliment!"

"It's not," she insisted. "It's definitely a compliment."

"I'm not sure I believe you."

When he approached, she took his hand and pulled him closer, automatically reaching her arms around his neck. His hands settled on her hips and the heat seeped through the thin fabric of her dress. After spending most of the evening dancing in that position it felt almost instinctive. Except now they were alone on a beach with no music and she was dying to kiss him.

It was the emotions of the wedding taking hold of her. She'd only split up with Jack a couple of days ago. Now she was about to kiss a stranger on the beach. Her fingers trailed over the smooth skin of his neck and she pulled him to her, closing her eyes as their lips met. The gentle kisses felt so natural, but she was surprised by the butterflies that fluttered in her stomach before taking flight over her whole body. She felt as light as air, and it took a moment for her to realise he'd lifted her off the ground.

"I don't think I was supposed to kiss you," he said, when he set her back down. His words tickled her cheek.

"What were your instructions?"

"I was supposed to make sure you didn't sit in a corner looking miserable all day."

"In that case," she whispered, "I'd say it was a job well done."

CHAPTER 3

The sun streamed obnoxiously into her hotel room the next morning, but Josie woke with a smile on her face nonetheless. From the window she could see straight out onto the beach and the exact spot where she'd kissed Sam the previous evening. Lizzie and Max's wedding had turned out to be way more fun than she'd anticipated.

Her mood ebbed when her phone rang and she saw it was Jack. What did he want?

"How was the wedding?" he asked. Typical of Jack to carry on as though nothing had happened.

"Fine," she mumbled.

"Sorry I missed it. When will you be home?"

"To collect my stuff?"

He sighed heavily. "Don't be daft. It was just a stupid argument."

"A stupid argument that ended with you saying 'I'm not sure this is working out… maybe we're not right for each other… It might be best if we just split up'. It seemed like more of a breakup than a stupid argument."

"I was having a bad day."

Anger coursed through her. "So you split up with me because you had a bad day?"

"I didn't split up with you… I was just rambling."

"Was this all to get out of coming to the wedding?"

"You know I hate weddings. And family events. I panicked, that's all."

"You're pathetic, Jack."

"Yeah but you love me, right?"

She shook her head and gazed out of the window. If they hadn't actually broken up then she'd cheated on him by kissing Sam on the beach. Probably best not to mention that.

"I'll be back tonight to pick up my stuff."

"Not to pick up your stuff. Don't be dramatic. I'll see you later, babe."

She sighed. "Bye, Jack."

The conversation basically summed up their relationship. She did love him, even though she wasn't always sure why. He was infuriating.

Once she'd showered, she pulled on a pair of cropped trousers and a T-shirt. Then, after a quick blast with the hairdryer, she scraped her shoulder-length brown hair into a ponytail. She'd been blessed with flawless olive skin and never bothered with make-up.

Down in the restaurant, the wedding party took over one side of the room, and she scanned the tables before heading for the breakfast buffet. Sam was already there, sitting with Annette and Max and Lizzie. Josie's appetite disappeared when she saw him. What was wrong with her? It was only a kiss, for goodness' sake. No need to go all jittery and pathetic. She helped herself to breakfast and was about to sit down with her parents when Annette called out to her.

"Come and sit with us…"

Pasting on a smile, she walked over and sat at the end of the table.

"Max was just telling me you're unemployed," Annette said with an inappropriate grin.

"Good morning to you too!"

Josie caught Sam's eye and gave him a half-smile. He even looked good without a suit. She'd been convinced it was the suit and the champagne and the romantic atmosphere that had made him so attractive, but even in jeans and a T-shirt she couldn't fault him. He was a good build and had one of those lovely friendly faces. His light brown hair was smooth and soft. She knew because she'd run her hands through it when she'd kissed him. The memory brought heat to her cheeks and she looked away quickly.

"I've got a job for you," Annette said.

Max chuckled. "I don't think Josie wants to come and live at the farm and be your carer."

"Oh, be quiet." She slapped his hand and then turned to Josie. "Ignore him. I need someone to come and manage the dog kennels for me."

"I thought you'd closed down," Josie said, remembering a previous conversation with her sister.

Lizzie raised her eyebrows. "She has."

"Out of necessity," Annette said. "Not choice. But I want to re-open. It's too much work on my own, though."

"I don't know why you can't just enjoy retirement," Max said. "You should be taking it easy, not working yourself to the bone."

She scowled at him. "Just because I'm old doesn't mean I should sit around doing nothing and waiting to die."

There was an uncomfortable silence before Sam spoke. "No one said that. We just worry about you doing too much."

"What you should worry about is me not doing enough. I

hate being idle. I'm going crazy in that house on my own without Wendy and without the kennels. I don't know what to do with myself." There was another silence before she continued. "I've thought about it – I can employ someone to help me with the kennels. I can't manage everything on my own, but with some help the kennels could be up and running again in no time." She looked at Josie.

"I don't know anything about dogs … or running a kennels."

"I can teach you," Annette said. "I know everything. And Lizzie said you've had all sorts of different jobs. You must be very adaptable."

"I suppose that's one way of looking at it," Josie said, amused.

"You'd pick it up in no time."

Josie shook her head. Annette seemed to be serious about the job offer. "It wouldn't work, though… you live in… wherever it is… the middle of nowhere. And I live in Oxford." It occurred to her that she wasn't exactly sure *where* she lived. With Jack or her parents? She really did have a lot to figure out. She lived in Oxford, though, whether it was with her parents or Jack, and Oxford definitely wasn't commuting distance to Devon.

"Yes, Averton is a bit of a trek from Oxford. But it won't matter. You can come and live with me. I've got plenty of room. There'll be lots of perks: free accommodation and food – I'm a great cook – and no travel time to work. I can pay you a decent wage…"

Josie laughed. "It's a lovely offer, Annette. But I can't move to the countryside. I have a life. I can't just up and leave." Though if pressed, she'd have difficulty explaining what exactly she couldn't leave. Her non-existent job or her boyfriend who may or may not be her ex? Her life was a bit pathetic. She'd expected Max and Lizzie to jump in and help her out with putting an end to the conversation, but they were staying suspiciously quiet.

"It's good timing," Lizzie said, finally voicing her opinion. "And it might be good for you. A fresh start and all that."

Josie frowned, then noticed Annette looking at her expectantly. She really was serious. "You've caught me by surprise. I can't imagine living in the countryside."

"You don't have a job," Lizzie said. "This is perfect. What else would you do?"

Josie opened her mouth to speak. Because she *did* have a plan. She was going to take more acting classes and try to find an acting job. She'd worked on a TV show a couple of years before and loved it. She wanted to give her career in acting one last shot.

With everyone looking at her, her dreams of working in television suddenly felt silly. Lizzie had never hidden the fact that she thought it was a pipe dream and nothing would come of it. To be fair, she was probably right.

"I don't know what I'll do." Josie stood and the chair scraped noisily on the wooden floor. "Thanks for the offer, Annette. I'll have to think about it, obviously. I'm going to get a coffee."

Picking up her plate, she went and sat with her parents to eat in peace.

"Any luck with the job-hunting?" her dad asked.

"Since the last time you asked? Yesterday? No, nothing yet, Dad." Unless you counted the job offer she'd just had over breakfast. Which she wasn't counting, of course, because it was crazy. There was no way she was about to move to the middle of nowhere and work at a dog kennels.

"Have you spoken to Jack yet?" her mum asked. "Do you think you'll sort things out or should I make up the spare room?"

"Don't worry about the spare room." She picked up a

piece of cold toast and took a noisy bite. "I'll figure something out."

She really couldn't cope with moving back with her parents.

CHAPTER 4

"I can't believe you're married," Josie said to Lizzie as they sat on the beach and watched the waves rolling in. After a leisurely breakfast, they'd waved off the majority of the wedding guests and re-convened back at Lizzie and Max's house, then moseyed down to the beach to enjoy the lovely spring weather.

"Me neither," she said.

"And to think that not so long ago you were engaged to someone else!"

"I know. It's crazy how quickly things can change. Speaking of which, you should think about Annette's offer."

"You can't be serious," Josie said as Max wandered over and draped an arm around Lizzie's shoulder, kissing the side of her head.

"It's really not a bad idea," Max put in. "You need a job and Annette needs some help. And if you move in quick it would be good. Then we won't have to worry about her while we're away on honeymoon."

"Oh, I see."

"It'd be good for you too," Max said. "Free rent and food." He raised his eyebrows. "Sam right next door…"

"There's a good reason *not* to move then," Josie said lightly. "I'm completely embarrassed that you told him to keep an eye on me yesterday. I'm not some charity case."

"He wasn't supposed to tell you," Max said. "And he wasn't supposed to kiss you either…"

Lizzie's eyes widened. "You kissed Sam?"

"Shush!" Josie looked round and caught sight of Sam chatting to Max's nephew further along the beach. She looked back at Max. "I can't believe he told you that."

"I don't think he meant to, he was just excited."

"Sam's lovely." Lizzie cast a glance in his direction. "It's a bit soon after Jack, though, isn't it?"

"It was only a kiss," she said. "These things happen at weddings."

"Apparently so," Lizzie said. "Anyway, what about Annette's offer?"

"I'm not going to move in with Max's aunt. And I'm surprised you're okay with the idea. Has no one else noticed that I can't keep a job for more than five minutes? Why would you recommend me to Annette?"

"Better the devil you know," Max said deadpan, earning himself a shove from Lizzie. "Well it's true!" He laughed. "She's determined to employ someone, and she's basically a vulnerable little old lady living in an isolated farmhouse. I don't want someone we don't know up there. She'd be handing over her life savings before we know it. She's far too trusting."

"Thanks for the vote of confidence. Some brother you're turning out to be."

"Brother-in-law," he corrected. "As you keep reminding me."

escape to oakbrook farm

"Whatever. First day on the job and you're being mean to me!"

Putting an arm round her, he squeezed her affectionately. "You'd do a great job with the kennels. And I'm sure you and Annette would get on well. Just think about it."

She promised she would and went to mingle, chatting to one of Max's brothers and then an elderly neighbour, Dotty, who she'd met several times before. Eventually, she made her way round to Sam.

"I'm going to make an observation." His voice was suspiciously quiet. "And you can tell me what you think…"

"Okay." She tried not to focus on his proximity. "What?"

"Your sister's not drinking."

"So?"

"She wasn't drinking yesterday either."

"She was. For the toasts she definitely had champagne."

He shook his head. "She may have *held* a glass of champagne. She wasn't drinking it."

"What are you getting at?"

"Nothing." He shrugged. "Just an observation."

Josie looked over to Lizzie, sitting in the sand, cuddled up to Max. "You know when you said you live in a village full of gossips? I think it may have rubbed off!"

"I'm not gossiping," he said. "It's just an observation."

"An observation which leads you to believe Lizzie's pregnant?"

"Yes," he said firmly.

"No way."

"Okay."

"Do you know something I don't?" Josie asked.

"No. But I was visiting them a couple of weeks ago and I felt like there was something weird going on. Lizzie gave me a list of reasons why she couldn't have a drink with us in the pub. If she'd just said she didn't want a drink I wouldn't have thought anything of it. That's why I noticed yesterday. And today."

"She's not pregnant," Josie said. "No. Lizzie likes to plan everything perfectly. She wouldn't get pregnant before the wedding. It's not how she does things. She's very proper."

Sam's gaze stayed on an oblivious Lizzie for a moment. "I think she's pregnant."

"No. She's not."

He stuck his hand out for her to shake. "Fiver?"

She laughed. "I'm not betting on whether … oh go on then, a fiver." She shook his hand. "But if it turns out to be true and you already had inside information then the bet's off."

"I don't know anything," he insisted. "I'm just guessing."

"Hmm. If you say so. I know how you and Max like to tell each other everything."

He looked puzzled.

"You told him about last night … on the beach!"

"Oh, yeah." He grimaced. "Sorry. That just slipped out."

They both turned when Annette called out to Sam. She was standing at the top of the beach, waving to them. "I've got to play taxi," Sam said. "I think she's had enough. She doesn't like being away from the farm. I think this is the longest she's been away in years."

"I'll come and say goodbye," Josie said.

They walked up the beach to Annette. Sam was right; she was keen to get home.

"Why don't you come with us?" she said to Josie. "You could come and have a look around. See what you think about taking the job."

"Are you really serious about me working for you?"

Annette looked at her pleadingly. "Very serious. At least come and have a look around and then you can think about it properly."

26

"I should be getting home," she said.

Max appeared behind her. "You pretty much drive past Annette's place on the way to Oxford."

"Come on," Annette said. "Just have a look at the place. No pressure…"

Josie rolled her eyes. "Not much!"

CHAPTER 5

I t took forty minutes to drive from Hope Cove to Averton. The roads were winding, and when they reached the little village of Averton there really wasn't much to see: a pub and a small shop beside a village green. Houses stood back from the road, and it was all very quaint and peaceful. They drove out the other side of the village until they came to a driveway.

Beside the gate at the road was a large wooden sign engraved with *Oakbrook Farm: Boarding Home for Dogs.* Rhododendron bushes grew either side of the gate, splashed with gorgeous purple flowers.

The car crawled along the driveway, passing a barn before reaching the old farmhouse in the far corner of the property.

Following Sam's lead, Josie parked the car beside the house. Then she got out and took it all in. The property was dotted with beautiful big old trees and bordered by a wooden fence. Beyond, hills rolled away in every direction. It was stunning.

"Not a bad view, is it?" Annette said.

"It's beautiful," Josie agreed. She always considered herself a city girl at heart but it really was breathtaking.

"I've just got to fetch my dogs from the neighbour. Sam can show you around."

Sam raised an eyebrow. "Do you want me to drive round and get the dogs?"

"No." Annette was already walking away. "I feel like the exercise. Won't be long."

They watched her walk away and then Sam turned awkwardly to Josie. "So this is Oakbrook," he said. "Annette has lived here for nearly sixty years. My place is over that hill." He shifted his weight from foot to foot. "I can show you the barn. It's converted into kennels."

They set off together back down the drive and then ventured across a well-worn path through neatly mown grass. Josie marvelled at the wonderfully green scenery. "How long have you lived here?" she asked.

"Always," he said. "I grew up here. Moved away for a while and then, when my parents decided to move, I bought the house from them and moved back."

"That's…" She hesitated, wondering what to say. "Nice."

He laughed. "It's a quiet life. But I like it."

"What do you do for a living?"

"I work in construction."

"Wow," Josie said, nodding appreciatively. "That's a great job."

"Is it?" He gave her an odd look. "Most people aren't that impressed by it."

"I was expecting you to have a boring office job. Building work is so interesting. It's amazing that you can make something from nothing."

They stopped outside the barn and he looked thoroughly amused. "I think you might be confusing builders with magicians. If I could make something from nothing that would be impressive!"

She laughed and gave him a light shove. "You know what

I mean. You actually make stuff. At the end of the day you can say 'look I just built that house'…"

He smirked. "It generally takes longer than a day."

"Stop teasing," she said. "I just think it's great that you don't do some boring office job where no one even knows what you do. Like Max – he used to work in an office. What did he even do?"

"He was a lawyer," Sam said, opening the door to the barn. "He worked for a cosmetics company and he—"

"It was a rhetorical question!" Josie said.

They grinned at each other as the lights flickered on in the barn, and he held the door for her.

"The thing about Max's boring office job was they paid him loads of money," Sam said.

Recently, Max had given up his boring office job and now worked as a property manager in Hope Cove and the surrounding area. Josie found it much easier to understand what he did on a day-to-day basis.

"Yeah, but who needs money?" Josie's words were flippant as she walked slowly through the barn, looking around in awe.

Sam followed after her. "Is that another rhetorical question or am I allowed to answer? Because I have a lot to say about that…"

"Yeah, I know, everyone needs money." She waved a hand. "But you only need so much."

"That's true." He stopped and leaned casually against a red brick partition wall. "It was stables originally," he said as Josie opened one of the old stable doors and went into what was now a dog kennel.

"This place is amazing." She walked around the space and pushed open the dog door at the far end to peer out to an outdoor enclosure.

"It's pretty fancy," he agreed.

"No wonder Annette was upset about closing down."

"It was only supposed to be a temporary thing. Just while Wendy recovered from her operation…" He trailed off and his eyes glazed over briefly. Then he straightened up abruptly and moved to open the stable door for Josie. "It's too much for her to manage now, on her own."

Josie counted over twenty individual stalls in the barn. It was very impressive.

"There are infra-red heaters for the winter," Sam said, pointing overhead.

"It's a doggy paradise."

"It was very popular. People would book far in advance."

"I'm not surprised."

They ambled slowly back outside. "Are you seriously considering this?" Sam asked, when they made their way towards the house. "Moving here? Working for Annette?"

"I don't know." Gazing around again, she was struck by how still and tranquil the surroundings were. It almost didn't seem real, as though she were wandering through a painting. "I didn't think so. But now I'm here it's surprisingly tempting. I have to figure some things out first. It's complicated with my boyfriend."

"I thought he was your ex-boyfriend?" Sam squinted, puzzled.

"I'm not really sure."

Sam didn't reply and Josie felt a fleeting sense of guilt. She'd assumed that their kiss hadn't meant anything to him. Just an inevitable end to a day filled with champagne and romance. But the silence between them felt suddenly charged.

The golden retriever that barrelled up to them was a welcome distraction. Sam bent to ruffle his coat and the tension in the air dispersed. "This is Charlie," Sam said, dragging his attention away from the dog and grinning up at Josie. A small black terrier arrived next to vie for attention, throwing itself on the ground beside Sam and eagerly offering its belly to be rubbed. Sam happily obliged as the dog panted and wagged its tail. "This is Macy... And you know Tilly, I take it."

The gorgeous springer spaniel belonged to Lizzie and Max. She stood beside Josie, wagging her tail.

"Yes," she said, stroking Tilly affectionately. Tilly was staying with Annette while the newlyweds went on their honeymoon. "We know each other well."

Josie and Sam made a big fuss of the dogs while they waited for Annette to catch up.

"What do you think?" Annette said, puffing as she approached.

"The barn's fantastic."

"We fell in love with the stables when we moved in," she said. "So we tried to keep a lot of the original features when we refurbished. Once upon a time it was a working farm. We even thought about going into farming. The closest we got was our little vegetable patch, but we kept the name as Oakbrook Farm anyway. Have you seen inside the house?"

"Not yet."

"Come on then. You'll need to see where you'll be living!"

Josie chuckled. "Nothing's definite yet."

She was given a guided tour of the lovely old farmhouse. There certainly was plenty of room. The spare bedroom upstairs had a fantastic view out over the hills, and Josie could imagine sitting and gazing out. Of course, she'd prob-ably get bored of the views after five minutes. She was a city girl after all. She'd soon miss seeing buildings all around.

"Are you convinced yet?" Annette said as the three of them sat at the kitchen table cradling coffees.

Josie shook her head. "I don't know." She didn't even know Annette very well but already she was tempted to say yes just to please her. She felt so sorry for her all alone with nothing to keep her occupied. She couldn't make such a drastic change just to cheer up a little old lady, though. And she couldn't make any rushed decisions. She needed to think about it properly. And talk to Jack.

"I'm really flattered that you offered, and it is tempting. I'm going to think it through." She finished her coffee in one long gulp. "I really need to get home." It was about a four-hour drive back to Oxford and she was already tired.

"I thought you might stay for dinner," Annette said quickly. "Both of you. Maybe Sam could take you down to the local pub later so you get a feel for the village."

"I thought you were trying to tempt her." Sam stood when Josie did. "Taking her to the Bluebell Inn is a sure way to scare her off."

"Maybe another time," Josie said at the door. "Thanks for showing me round."

Annette picked up a business card from the windowsill and gave it to her. It had the address and phone number for the kennels. "Call me when you decide," she said. "Maybe you could give her your number too, Sam. Just in case she can't get hold of me."

"Oh my God," Sam muttered under his breath as they stepped outside.

"Bye, Annette!" Josie called, beaming.

At the car, she turned to Sam. "Do you think Annette offering me a job is just an elaborate ploy to get you a date?"

He frowned and then his lips twitched to a smirk. "It's a definite possibility."

CHAPTER 6

It was late by the time Josie arrived at Jack's place that evening. She should probably refer to it as home - she'd been living there for over a year. Somehow it had never really felt like home though. Moving in together had come about purely for convenience when Josie was unemployed and struggling with her rent. It was early in their relationship and was only supposed to be a temporary arrangement. That's probably why she'd never got beyond thinking of it as Jack's place.

Jack jumped up from the couch and greeted her enthusiastically with a big hug and a kiss.

"Get off me," she said, trying and failing to sound stern. "We split up, remember?"

"Nope," he said, with his charming boyish grin. "Don't remember that. You must have imagined it."

"Ha-ha!" She sat on the couch and scanned the living room. Items of clothing were scattered around, and takeaway boxes and beer bottles adorned the coffee table and surrounding area. "The place is a tip."

"I know." He went to the small kitchen and came back with a bin bag. "I missed you. You know what I get like when I'm upset. This is the result of a fog of self-pity." He threw rubbish in the bin bag and grinned sheepishly.

"It's the result of you being a lazy slob," she corrected.

"Maybe that too." Abandoning his half-hearted attempt at cleaning, he sat beside her. "Everything falls apart when you're not here. You're not really going to leave me, are you?"

"Will you stop looking at me like that?" she said, but couldn't help but laugh. "Put the puppy dog eyes away. They won't work on me any more." He pouted and she laughed some more. "I'm serious! Stop it!"

Leaning closer, he poked her playfully in the ribs before tickling her and pushing her back to lie on the couch. "I know you missed me really." He dotted kisses on her face as she squirmed to get away.

"Okay," she said. "I missed you. Just stop tickling me!" He eased off and she wriggled to get comfy under his weight.

"It's too late to move out tonight anyway," he said.

She ran her hands through his short blonde hair. "You're going to have to stop breaking up with me."

"It's you at least half the time," he said.

"I know. We need to stop it. It's childish."

"Aww, but I'm only twenty-six, I thought I had a few more years of being immature before I had to grow up."

She sighed. "We live in a tip and we have stupid fights far too often. I'm getting sick of it."

"Okay." He rested his weight on an elbow. "They're just small things we can easily fix. And you know what the great thing about fighting is?"

"Yeah," she said wearily. "Making up. It's getting less fun though…"

"Okay."

"I'm serious, Jack."

"I can hear that." He looked at her sadly. "I will try and keep the place tidier. And no more arguing, I promise."

"Go on, then," she said, pushing him off her.

He crashed purposefully onto the floor and gave a dramatic display of being injured. She laughed and he kept up a limp as he tidied up the living room. "Does this remind you of when we first met?" he asked.

A smile twitched at her lips as she thought back to the acting job. They were extras in a military soap opera. They only filmed the pilot and it wasn't commissioned for further episodes but it was her favourite job ever. It was such a buzz being on a TV set, and it was so much fun. Meeting Jack had been another perk. She thought again about her ambitions to have a career in acting and then her mind flicked to Annette and the job at the kennels. She brushed the thoughts aside and focussed on Jack. "Your wounded soldier act doesn't get any better. No wonder it all ended up on the cutting room floor."

"No, it was definitely your dodgy barmaid skills that let us down. Although, I suppose it was confusing for you, being on the wrong side of the bar." She threw a cushion at him and he threw it back. "I'm trying to tidy up, you know!"

"Good," she said. "This better not be a one-off event."

"By the way, I saw an advert in that Italian restaurant down the road. They're looking for a waitress. I didn't know if you might fancy doing that for a while…"

"You want some rent money?"

"Well, no stress," he said. "I can't support us both for long though. Not if we want any kind of social life anyway."

"I was going to call Michaela again," she mused. "Just in case she has any auditions for me."

"I thought you'd given up on the acting?"

"I had." That's what she'd said after the last audition a few weeks ago. It was always so disheartening being turned down. She'd sworn she was giving up a few times so far. But she always decided she'd just give it one more try, sure that her big break was just around the corner. The auditions had become few and far between, but she still spoke to Michaela at StarSearch acting agency now and again, just to see if there was anything interesting she could audition for.

"I'll just check in with Michaela." She tried to keep her voice light. "You never know, maybe she has something more exciting for me than a job in the local Italian restaurant."

"I'm amazed she hasn't blocked your number by now."

"Hey! She likes me."

"You're not exactly bringing much commission for her though, are you? You really think it's worth your time to keep calling her?"

"Probably not." She paused, wondering whether to mention her job offer or not. "I was actually offered a job this weekend. Max's aunt wants me to go and work for her."

Jack picked up the last of the beer bottles and then began collecting up dirty clothes. "Doing what?"

"She's got a dog kennels and she's looking for someone to manage it. Actually, I think she just needs someone to help out. She's old, like eighty or something, and can't do it all herself."

"That sounds all right."

"It's in a little village though – Averton. It's over towards Lizzie and Max's place. She offered for me to live there – rent free, food provided. She said she can pay pretty well too."

"So you could live there during the week and come back on the weekends?"

"I don't know really." That hadn't occurred to her as an option. Although if it was possible it would be much more appealing. "It was all a bit out of the blue so I didn't ask too much."

"You should find out. It sounds like a good gig."

"And you wouldn't miss me too much if I was away all week?"

"I'm sure our relationship could cope." He gave her a wink. "Absence makes the heart grow fonder and all that."

CHAPTER 7

On Monday morning Josie called Michaela at StarSearch. She didn't have any auditions to put Josie forward for, and there was a weariness to her voice, as though she thought Josie was wasting her time. Usually she was much more positive. Unless Josie had imagined that.

Next, she wandered down to the Italian restaurant, but the waitressing job had already gone. Then she continued the job search by skimming through the old familiar employment websites. All the while, Annette's business card sat beside the laptop, taunting her.

Eventually, she got out her phone and tapped the numbers in. As she suspected, Annette agreed to her spending the week at the farm and having two days off. She was slightly hesitant about those two days being at the weekends since that was often the busiest time but said she could definitely be flexible and she was sure they could work something out to suit them both.

Josie was fairly sure she'd agree to anything to get her there. When she ended the call, she stared into space for a while, trying to digest the conversation. She was fairly sure she'd agreed to start work the following week. It seemed like a pretty drastic career change, even for her.

Lizzie was at the airport when Josie called her to tell her the news.

"You're really going to work for Annette?" she said. "I'm very surprised. But it's great news. I bet you'll love it. Max looks happy."

"Very happy," she heard him shout down the phone.

"I start next week," Josie said. "I'm a bit nervous, though. I'm worried I'll be no good at it and it'll end up being awkward for everyone."

"Just give it a try. I'm sure you'll be great. If it doesn't work out, it doesn't work out."

Josie had a sinking feeling then. She'd not stopped to think too much about it not working out. Things could definitely end up very awkward. "I might be regretting it already," she said. "What if I don't like living in the countryside? You know I like the bright lights."

"You might find you like the gorgeous sunsets, and the starry skies and the—"

"Yeah, I get it. You've been converted. I'm just not sure it's my thing."

"I thought you'd already agreed to the job. Why does it sound like you want me to persuade you?"

"I'm having cold feet already."

Lizzie sighed. "We have to get on the plane soon. Hang on… Max wants to talk to you…"

"Hey!" Max said.

"I'm stressing out," Josie said. "Promise you won't hate me if it doesn't work out?"

"I won't. Honestly, I don't expect it *will* work out long term. But Annette is determined to employ someone and you'll at least buy me some time to find someone suitable for the job. I don't want her rushing into it and employing just anyone."

"I think that's exactly what's happened!"

"You know what I mean." There was a tannoy announcement in the background.

"Oh, no," she said drily. "Seems like you have to fly off to the Caribbean now. How awful for you!"

He laughed and passed the phone back to Lizzie. "Just try not to lose your new job before we get back."

"You're hilarious," Josie said. "Have a great time. See you in a couple of weeks."

She sat back in the chair. Now that she'd accepted the job with Annette she was keen to get started. A week was a long time to kill when you didn't have any money.

In the end it went fairly quickly. Jack took her out to dinner one night and the cinema another. He even lent her money so she could get the train into London and visit her best friend, Emily. She was keen to fill her in on the latest developments in her life, and it was fun to have a wander round London too. You couldn't beat a stroll around Greenwich Market, and it didn't matter at all that she had no money to spend; she just enjoyed the bustle.

"Won't you miss the city?" Emily asked as they sat on a bench eating sandwiches. She didn't have much time but was eager to meet Josie for lunch. "I can't imagine you living in the countryside."

"I'll give it a go," she said. "It might be fun."

"I suppose it might." Emily didn't sound at all convinced.

"You're not making me feel better." Josie rolled her eyes. "Tell me about the book…" Emily was a writer and had published her first book with a small press six months previously. It had been very exciting to start with, but the excitement seemed to be wearing off as she struggled to juggle a waitressing job and writing the next one.

"I'm officially a starving artist," Emily said with a humourless laugh. "And this next book is killing me. I can't seem to get it right."

"You said that about the last one and it came out brilliantly. I can have a look if you want. I reckon I'll have lots of time for reading in the back of beyond."

"I sent it to Lizzie actually. She's going to have a look over it while she's away."

"I see. Ask the pro!" Lizzie was an editor, and it had been helping Emily with her book that had inspired Lizzie to become a freelance fiction editor. She'd previously been a magazine editor. Now she worked from home, picking and choosing which projects to work on.

"How was the wedding?" Emily asked. "I can't believe I couldn't make it."

"It was amazing." Josie's smile was automatic and far too wide.

"I thought Jack had split up with you and you were upset about going alone?"

"It turned out to be fun going on my own."

Emily looked suspicious. "What happened?"

"Nothing. The best man was pretty cute, that's all."

"You're terrible," Emily said, laughing. "You don't waste any time."

"It wasn't like that," Josie insisted, trying not to let her thoughts drift back to that moment on the beach. "He's actually a really sweet guy." She grinned, remembering him telling her off for calling him sweet. "He's Max's best friend. And it was only a bit of flirting. He lives next door to the kennels so I guess I'll be seeing him again."

"This sounds like it's about to get complicated. Didn't you say you worked things out with Jack again?"

"Yeah. It's not complicated. Jack and I made up. The thing with Sam was just a momentary weakness. You know how it is at weddings… So much champagne and romance. It was nothing."

"I might have to come and visit then… if there's a hot guy going spare."

"You should!" Josie said. "Definitely. There's a pub in the village. We can go wild!"

CHAPTER 8

J osie arrived at Oakbrook Farm on Sunday afternoon and gave a quick knock at the door. She presumed it wasn't the sort of place where you had to wait to be invited in and opened the door herself.

"I'm here!"

"So you are!" Sam's eyes crinkled in amusement. He was making coffee, and a young woman stood beside him while a little boy held on to his leg. Josie was only expecting to find Annette, and the scene confused her.

"Sorry." Her smile faded to fixed and unnatural. She was glad that the dogs were jumping around her and she distracted herself stroking them in turn. "Where's Annette?"

"Upstairs," Sam said. "Checking your room's perfect!"

"Hi!" Josie said to the redheaded woman.

"Sorry," Sam said. "This is Amber."

"I've just been hearing about you," Amber said, smiling brightly.

"All good I hope?" Josie's brain was busy trying to figure things out. Who was the woman? Did Sam have a wife and kid that no one had mentioned? Surely not or they'd have been at the wedding – and he wouldn't have kissed Josie.

"Definitely all good," she said. "Do you want a coffee?"

"Yes, please. Who's this then?" she asked, smiling at the kid. Sam picked the little boy up and Josie walked over and tickled his cheek.

"This is my godson," Sam said. "Kieron."

"Sam and I went to school together," Amber explained. "I live at the other side of Averton. Kieron and I often call up here in the afternoons. I like to get him out for a walk and he usually falls asleep in his buggy. Wasn't interested today, though. Hopefully he'll sleep on the way home."

Sam threw him up in the air, making him giggle. "I'll take him outside for a run around. That'll wear him out."

Amber nodded her approval. "Thanks, Sam."

The dogs followed Sam outside and the room fell silent.

"My husband's away this week," Amber said, passing Josie a coffee and taking a seat at the table. "So I feel like a single parent. Sam takes pity on me and helps with Kieron."

"That's good." Josie picked up her coffee, feeling slightly uncomfortable. There was something about the way Amber looked at her that made her wonder what had been said about her. She wasn't sure she was going to like living in a village. What if Sam wasn't exaggerating when he said they were all a bunch of gossips?

"It's great that you're helping Annette out," Amber said. "We've all been a bit worried about her since Wendy died. Opening up the kennels again will be good for her." She stopped talking at the sound of footsteps on the stairs.

"There you are." Annette grinned at Josie. "And I see you've met Amber. How was the drive?"

"Long! But fine."

"We're a bit out of the way here," Amber said. "It sounds

like it's going to be a change for you, living out in the countryside?"

Josie blew on her coffee and took a sip. "Annette has promised to let me get back to civilisation from time to time. I'll be needing a fix of traffic and pollution... crowds... those sorts of things."

"We really are lacking in those aspects," Amber said lightly. "Though there's a chance you'll get stuck behind a tractor on our little country roads once in a while. Not quite the same as queuing traffic but not far off."

"That's something to look forward to then." Josie smiled. "Seriously, though, I don't know what to expect. I've always lived in cities. I visit Lizzie and Max in Hope Cove now and again, and that's always good fun, but it's only ever a short visit."

"You're going to love it," Annette said. "I bet you'll enjoy being part of a community."

"I won't have to get involved in things, will I? Fundraisers and committees and stuff? I'm not quite sure what I'm getting myself into!"

"Not yet," Amber said. "First, everyone will want to meet you, check you're a suitable addition to Averton. Then there'll be a swearing in ceremony before you're forced to join committees."

"Stop teasing," Annette said. "You'll scare her away before she's even unpacked."

"Speaking of unpacking," Josie said. "I'm going to unload the car."

"I can help," Amber said.

"Thanks. I haven't actually got much. Only one suitcase."

"I'll get off then, leave you to settle in. It was lovely to meet you." She gave Josie a hug, which took her by surprise. After being unsure at first, Josie thought she'd probably get on well with Amber. It would be nice to have a woman close to her age around the place.

Outside, Sam was kicking a ball to Kieron, who toddled around unsteadily. The dogs wandered freely and didn't seem at all bothered when Kieron pulled their tails or patted them roughly on the back. Macy bounced around Josie's feet, watching as she pulled her suitcase out of the boot.

"I'll help," Sam said, once he'd said goodbye to Amber and Kieron.

"This is all I've got," she said. "I travel light."

He flashed his cheeky grin. "So you can make a quick exit if you need to?"

Josie tried to ignore the way her stomach went all fluttery. She brushed aside thoughts of dancing with him, of kissing him. "I can't actually believe I'm doing this," she said. "Moving here and working in a kennels. Especially since I don't actually know anything about dogs."

"I'm sure you'll be great."

She wished he'd stop smiling; it made her feel funny. And for some reason, her mind just wanted to rewind to the evening on the beach at Hope Cove.

"I hope so," she said, looking quickly away from him and heading inside. She wondered how much he was going to be around. Was he there every day? She hoped not. Her brain seemed to go all foggy around him.

She was glad he only came inside for a few minutes and then left. It was unnerving, the way she felt so self-conscious around him. The looks he gave her were teasing and lingering and made her heart race in a way which would be exciting if she was single. She wasn't, though; she'd agreed to give things another go with Jack.

She tried calling him as she unpacked her clothes into the large chest of drawers in her new bedroom. The flowery wallpaper wasn't really to her taste, but the room was light and airy and Josie had never been too concerned by interior design. When Jack didn't answer she left a message saying she'd arrived safely and would talk to him soon.

It didn't take her long to unpack, and then she went down and ate dinner with Annette in the kitchen.

"I've been doing some research," Josie said, when they sat in the living room later that evening. "Into boarding kennels. I've been looking what other places are doing and I've got some great ideas. I thought I could start by revamping your website and updating all your social media accounts. We'll need to decide what services we're going to offer. I don't know what you were offering before but—"

Annette chuckled. "Slow down! I don't even know what all those words mean. What are you talking about social media for? That's the tweeting thing?"

Josie shook her head. "Twitter? Yes. But there's also Facebook, Instagram, Snapchat…"

"We did have a Facebook page," Annette said. "Max set it up. He said we needed it. I'm not really sure what it was for, though."

"People have different preferences when it comes to social media so we need to be available to interact on all of them."

"You've lost me." Annette stared at her blankly. "Who will we be interacting with? And why?"

"Customers," Josie said slowly.

"It's a boarding kennels. People bring their dogs, we look after them, then they pick them up again."

"I know that! But there's so much more you can offer. I can upload videos and photos so people can check in and see how the dogs are doing. They could even FaceTime with them if they wanted."

"You've lost me again."

"Video call…"

"With the dogs?"

"Yes!"

Annette started chuckling.

"Okay," Josie said, amused. "Maybe we'll build up to that stuff. I'll start with your website."

"Yes, I think we've got one of those."

Josie stared at her for a moment then slapped a hand to her forehead and dropped back dramatically onto the couch.

Reaching over, Annette patted her knee affectionately. "We might have a few generational differences."

"A few? How can you run a business and not know anything about your own website?"

"I have a telephone," Annette said proudly. "People call and book their dogs in. Then they bring them and we look after them until they pick them up again."

"Tell me it's a mobile at least?"

Annette shook her head. "It doesn't have a cord, though, and it works out on the patio too."

With her hands over her face, Josie whimpered a fake cry. "I guess I'm going to be busy."

CHAPTER 9

Josie opened up the big double doors to the barn the next morning. She wanted to take some photos for the website and was trying to let as much light in as possible. It was beautiful inside the barn with the neat red brick stalls and the quaint stable doors. Annette didn't know exactly how big each kennel was but they looked spacious to Josie, and she was keen to measure up so she could include the information on the website.

"What's wrong?" Annette asked when she wandered in. "I thought you were taking photos."

"I'm just thinking… what if I give the stable doors a lick of paint? Brighten them up."

"They're fine as they are," Annette said.

"But the kennels look a bit bare too. When I looked at other kennels online some of them were set up so that each kennel looked like a little living room. They had couches and carpets."

"I think you were looking at the luxury places," Annette said. "That's not what we do."

"But you could go a bit upmarket. Charge a bit more…"

"We've had the same customers for years. They'll all come back. We don't need to do a lot of refurbishing."

"Just the painting then," Josie said. "I could do the front gate by the road too."

"Okay," Annette said. "You can give them a lick of paint."

"And the big barn doors, of course."

"Of course," Annette said, rolling her eyes.

Josie hurried to catch up with Annette as she walked back outside. "And if I can find second-hand furniture – free or really cheap – would that be okay?"

"Fine," Annette said, shaking her head but smiling at the same time.

It was a half-hour drive to the nearest hardware shop, and Josie picked out terracotta paint very similar to what was already in the barn but a slightly lighter shade. It would be easy enough to slap a fresh coat on but should make a differ-ence. She was determined to do a good job for Annette.

It was a pleasant afternoon, especially painting the gates outside in the sunshine.

"It's amazing the difference a fresh coat of paint makes," Annette said, wandering over to check on the worker.

"I told you," Josie said, smiling. "By the way, I'll need a ladder for the barn doors. Have you got one?"

"No." She paused. "Call Sam, he'll lend you one."

"Okay," Josie said, following her towards the house. "What's his number?"

"I thought you two had swapped numbers already."

"Nope."

There was a look in Annette's eyes that Josie couldn't quite read.

ESCAPE TO OAKBROOK FARM

"I've got a boyfriend. I told you this. Don't start trying your hand at matchmaking."

"But surely this Jack fella isn't as good of a catch as Sam…"

"Annette!" Josie tried to sound stern but couldn't help but be amused. In Annette's eyes no one would be better than Sam. "Jack's great. I'm very happy. Please don't meddle."

"I'll try not to," she said as they reached the house. Annette opened a drawer under the microwave and pulled out a dog-eared red book. "Here you go."

"What's this?"

"An address book. Sam's number's in there."

"So you have people's numbers handwritten in a book? It's like I've moved to the dark ages."

"It's also number three on speed dial if you want to use the house phone."

"Speed dial on your cordless phone. Very high tech! I think I'll just send him a message." She flicked through the book and looked blankly up at Annette.

"His last name's Blake. Go to the tab with a 'B'." She tutted as she walked away, and Josie was amused as she flicked through the book and found Sam's number.

"Blake," she muttered as she walked back outside with her phone in her hand. "Samuel Blake." It was a nice name. "Josie Blake," she said without thinking and then cursed under her breath. Why was she trying out his last name? Was she going mad? Surely moving to the country hadn't made her crazy already.

She pressed call without meaning to and a sense of panic gripped her. She wasn't prepared to chat to him; she'd intended to send him a breezy text message.

When he answered, she panicked even more.

"Hi." Her voice sounded weird – too high-pitched. "It's Josie." There was a pause and she skipped the part where she should wait for him to reply. "Annette's new employee. Lizzie's sister…" Oh, God. She was an idiot.

"The bridesmaid with the quirky shoes?"

"Yes, that's me."

"Josie, my new neighbour who I saw yesterday?"

It was tempting to say no and hang up. If there were a rewind button for life, now was the time she needed it.

"I remember you," he said, his voice full of teasing. "I might seem pretty old to you, but I've actually got a decent memory. I think you'd have got away with just Josie."

"I wouldn't want any misunderstandings," she said confidently. You could usually minimise embarrassment by being confident.

"Of course not," he said. "What can I do for you?"

"Erm… I just wanted to say hi…" It was difficult to be confident when you forgot what you were calling for. Her mind whirred. "A ladder!" she blurted out. "I need to borrow a ladder, please. Annette said you have one."

"I have indeed," he said. "I'll bring it over after work."

She thanked him and hung up. Next time she'd definitely stick to breezy text messages.

Apart from the barn doors, she'd finished all the painting when Sam arrived. It had been a productive day and she was happy with the results.

Sam held up a red hand when he walked into the kitchen. "You could've warned me about wet paint."

"Sorry." Josie smirked at Annette while he went to the sink and began scrubbing.

"The ladder's in the barn," he said. "You don't waste any time, do you?"

"She's been a busy little bee," Annette said. "Do me a

favour and take Josie down to the pub for a celebratory drink. She deserves one after her first day on the job."

Josie opened her mouth to protest, but Sam agreed immediately and moved back to the door, beckoning for her to follow him with a flick of the head. "See you later, Annette!" he called over his shoulder.

Pushing her feet into her shoes, Josie followed after him. "I'm not sure what just happened," she said, pulling her hair up into a ponytail as she caught up with him.

"Annette likes to meddle," he said. "She's trying to set us up and it's probably easier to just go along with it…"

She slowed, then stopped halfway down the drive. "I can't go along with it."

"I didn't mean actually go along with it." He turned back, seeming to sense her unease. "I know you've got a boyfriend … and that thing at the wedding was just a … thing at a wedding! But Annette wants us to go for a drink together. I was planning on nipping to the pub anyway…" His confidence seemed to vanish and they stood locked in silence for a moment. "You don't have to come if you don't want to."

She supposed a quick drink couldn't do any harm.

CHAPTER 10

The Bluebell Inn was what Josie considered a stereotypical country pub. The furniture was wooden and dated, and the decor was old-fashioned. There was nothing remarkable about it but it was pleasant enough – and conveniently situated a ten-minute walk from Oakbrook Farm. Sam introduced her to the barman, Andy, who was chatty and welcoming. There were only a few other people in the pub.

Once Andy had poured their drinks, Josie followed Sam to a small table by the window.

"So you spent your first day painting the kennels?" Sam said, sitting on a stool while Josie took the chair opposite him. "What else have you got planned?"

"I didn't plan on painting," she said. "I only went out to take some photos for the website. I thought the photos would look better if I spruced the place up a bit."

"Don't tell me you managed to do the painting *and* set up a website all in one day?"

"No." She smiled. "The website is on my list for tomorrow. Along with setting up social media accounts."

"Lots of change at Oakbrook then. Annette won't know what's hit her."

"I spent a long time yesterday evening trying to explain social media to her and why we need a website. She thinks it's unnecessary. How can you run a business without a website?"

"You don't need to convince me," Sam said. "Max and I had this conversation with her and Wendy so many times. The trouble is, they did run a very successful business without any technology, so it's hard to argue."

"Well I'm giving the place a shake-up anyway."

He smiled kindly and took a swig of his beer. "Annette said you're going to stay here during the week and go back to your boyfriend on the weekends?"

"That's the plan," Josie said. "I hope it works out okay. It's about a four-hour drive back to Oxford so it's not really ideal."

"That'll be tough on your relationship." He shifted his gaze to the door as it opened and nodded at the older guy who walked in.

"Jack and I will be fine. We always are."

Sam bit his lower lip and his eyebrows twitched at odd angles. Clearly he was dying to say something.

"What?" Josie asked.

"Nothing." He paused. "Long-distance relationships are difficult, that's all."

"What are you, an expert on the subject?"

"Yes, actually." His grin was teasing. "And I happen to know that only one percent of long-distance relationships work out."

"Where did you get one percent from?"

"I made it up. But I guess it's fairly accurate."

"What makes you think Jack and I wouldn't be in the one percent?"

He chuckled. "Is that a serious question?"

The smile fell from Josie's face. The conversation, which had seemed casual, suddenly made her uncomfortable.

"Oh, come on," he said. "You kissed me a week ago."

She glared at him. "I'd drunk a lot of champagne. And I was upset about Jack."

"Okay," he said without inflection.

Josie reached for her glass and hastily swigged her drink. She needed to escape. "You don't know anything about Jack and me, and I really don't want to discuss it with you." For a moment she stared at her half-empty glass. "I think I'm just going to head back. I had a long day and I could do with an early night."

He stood when she did and caught hold of her arm. "I'm sorry." He paused, then sighed. "You're right; I have no right to comment on your relationship."

"Don't worry about it." She shrugged his hand away. "I just feel like an early night."

"Stay and finish your drink at least." He looked at her in earnest and it set her insides fluttering again. "We're probably going to be seeing a lot of each other, and I don't want it to be weird. Are we allowed to be friends? Even though you've got a boyfriend?"

She should probably have said no, they couldn't be friends. Not because she had a boyfriend, but because of the effect Sam had on her. When she was with him, she forgot all about Jack and tended to think mainly about the night she kissed him on the beach. It was completely inappropriate. She should definitely stay away from him.

"I guess we can be friends," she agreed. "And I'll stay and finish my drink if you promise not to comment on things you have no idea about."

"I promise," he said. "Although it's going to seriously limit the conversation!"

She relaxed again, smiling at his joke. They stuck to more neutral topics while they finished their drinks. Sam told her a little more about his job and filled her in on what there was to do in the area – not very much, apparently.

When they stepped outside, dusk was setting in and the air had turned cool. Josie pulled her jumper on and they walked slowly through the village. A couple of cars drove past but otherwise there wasn't much sign of life. There was a little shop beside the pub, and Josie peered at the opening times: Mon-Sat, 10 a.m. until 6 p.m. Not exactly extensive opening hours.

As they walked quietly across the small village green, Josie took in the neat rows of houses bordering it. There were probably twenty at most, though there were more on the streets that branched away from the village.

They moved away from the houses. Their side of the road was bordered by a privet hedge while woodland stretched out on the other side of the road. Lonely birdsong floated from somewhere nearby.

"Not quite what you're used to?" Sam seemed to read her mind.

"Not at all," she said happily. "But I'm sure I'll get used to it."

CHAPTER 11

Josie groaned when she woke, then pulled the pillow over her head. Birds could be really loud. In Oxford she had no problem sleeping through the hum of traffic, or a muffled argument between the neighbours in the apartment above. Even sirens and the odd car horn blasting wouldn't usually interrupt her sleep.

The birds at Oakbrook Farm were far more intrusive. It was almost as though they'd flown in the window and were sitting around the bedroom calling to each other. And as if the birds weren't determined enough to wake her, the sun was getting involved too. The thin material at the window was a poor excuse for curtains.

She padded into the kitchen and grunted a good morning to Annette. When Annette offered to make her scrambled eggs, she accepted gratefully. Coffee arrived in front of her too. It was slightly different to living with Jack.

"I could get used to this," she said as the first sips of coffee hit the spot and the fog of sleep lifted. "I just hope I get used to the birds. They're so loud."

"I don't even notice them," Annette said, popping bread into the toaster.

"There's hope then!"

"How was your evening with Sam?" she asked. "You were back very early."

She had come back early, but Annette had been in bed already. "It was good. The Bluebell Inn isn't quite what I'm used to for a night out but it's pleasant enough."

Annette beat the eggs and poured them into the pan. "Sam's good company, isn't he?"

"Yes," Josie said with a frown. "But I have a boyfriend. You're going to have to stop matchmaking."

Annette quietly dished up two plates of eggs on toast and then joined Josie at the table. "I just think it's such a shame. Have you got a friend we could set him up with?"

"No!" Josie said, chuckling. "Leave the poor guy alone. Maybe he's happy being single."

"I don't think so. He's the sort of person who likes being in a relationship."

"Why isn't he then?" Josie asked thoughtfully. "I can't imagine he has any trouble attracting women."

"He was with someone," Annette said. "But …"

"But what?"

Annette shook her head. "Never mind. Just eat up. Your eggs will get cold."

Reluctantly, Josie tucked into her breakfast. It was annoying that Annette hadn't finished the conversation. She'd have quite liked to have heard about Sam's past relationships.

After breakfast, she dressed and got to work painting the barn doors. The dogs wandered around outside with her and she enjoyed being in the fresh air. The birdsong was much more pleasant when it wasn't dragging her from sleep. It was a gorgeous spring day, and Annette came out to water the rose bed along the side of the house and the flowerbeds around the patio.

When the barn doors were painted, Josie went back to her original task of taking photos. She found a bunch of dog toys and a few dog beds in a cupboard and set up one of the kennels as well as she could to take some snaps. She also took photos of the sign at the front gate and the house and the surrounding area. Macy, Charlie and Tilly dutifully modelled in a few of the shots, and Josie was reasonably satisfied with what she achieved. It would do, anyway; at least until they were up and running and she could get some better ones.

The rest of the day was spent setting up the website, and when Annette nodded her approval, Josie set it to live. Now she just needed bookings. Annette kept telling her there was no rush and it would just take time for word to spread that they were open again, but Josie was impatient. She set up accounts on all social media platforms that week and got new business cards printed, along with a load of flyers. Then she trawled the surrounding area, calling at every pet shop and vet's practice, asking them to display the flyers. It turned out to be a good way to get to know the area, and she ended up chatting away to the staff, who would surely be good contacts to have.

Whenever she drove through Averton village, she found herself keeping an eye out for Sam. After their evening in the pub at the beginning of the week, she hadn't seen anything of him. Somehow she'd had the impression that he popped in to see Annette most days, so she was surprised not to see him.

On Friday, Annette told her to leave early so she might miss some of the rush hour traffic. The drive back to Oxford was gruelling nonetheless, and arriving back at Jack's apartment was no relief at all. The place was a mess, and she cursed Jack, who was nowhere to be seen.

His phone rang for ages and she was about to give up when he finally answered.

"Where are you?" She wondered whether he'd be able to hear her over all the background noise.

"In the Fox and Greyhound."

"Great. I just got home, the place is a mess and you're in the pub. Can't you ever clean up?"

"I thought you were coming back tomorrow. I was going to clean up in the morning."

"No, I'm back now. And you'd have known exactly when I'd be back if you'd bothered to call me sometime this week."

He ignored the barb. "Just don't look at the mess, I'll sort it out later. Come down to the pub."

"I don't want to. I've just spent four hours sitting in the car. I want to relax."

"Shall I come home then?"

She sighed. She was too annoyed with him to want to spend time with him now. "No. I'm going to visit Mum and Dad. I'll stay with them and see you tomorrow."

"Okay. Whatever you want. I'm working tomorrow morning though …"

"So when exactly were you planning on cleaning up?" He started to talk but she'd had enough of the conversation. "Whatever, Jack, I'll see you tomorrow afternoon." She was fuming when she ended the call. It was so typical of Jack; he was laid-back to the point of being horizontal, and while his chilled-out attitude was one of the things she loved, it often made her feel like she was always nagging. Was it really too much to ask that he thought ahead and made a plan for the weekend? One which might involve his girlfriend. Why had she even bothered driving all the way back? And if he was expecting her to clean up his mess he was sorely mistaken.

She got straight back in the car and drove to her parents' place on the outskirts of Oxford. It was wonderfully clean and tidy as always. Her mum was a neat freak, and Dad knew well enough not to leave anything in a mess. After a glass of wine and a good whinge to her mum, Josie felt marginally better. She filled her parents in on her new job and her surprisingly enjoyable week with Annette.

When she walked back into Jack's apartment the following afternoon, it had been transformed. In fact, she didn't remember it ever being so clean and tidy. Jack was sprawled on the couch, fast asleep. He looked so peaceful she didn't have the heart to wake him and went and made a drink instead. This was the trouble with Jack: he could drive her mad and she'd be furious with him, then he'd buck his ideas up and be sweet and adorable.

He stirred when she sat beside him, then blinked up at her. "What do you think? Does it meet your standards?"

"It does," she said.

"So I'm forgiven?"

"I suppose so."

He sat up and wrapped his arms around her, squeezing until she laughed. "What's wrong with you?"

"Nothing. I'm just tired."

"What do you want to do this afternoon?" he asked. "The weather's nice – I thought we could go for a walk along the river. We could go to that cafe that does the huge ice cream sundaes. What do you think?"

She agreed, glad the atmosphere between them had gone.

Oxford was beautiful in the spring. The rich greens of the grassy riverbank were interspersed with delicate yellow and white wildflowers. Weeping willows swayed in the breeze, gently tickling the surface of the water.

Josie filled Jack in on her new job as they ambled along,

and told him all about village life and the little country pub. He enthusiastically asked lots of questions and even had his own ideas for the kennels, most of which were ridiculous, like installing a swimming pool for the dogs. Jack could always make her laugh.

They spent the evening on the couch watching a film, and it was late when Josie woke the next morning. Jack was still snoring and she left him in bed while she got herself some toast.

"What do you want to do today?" she asked when he finally emerged. "I can drive back late tonight. I don't think Annette cares when I get back."

Jack frowned and ran a hand through his hair. "I said I'd help Clive this afternoon." He glanced at his watch. "I need to leave soon."

She frowned. Jack often helped his uncle at his café on the weekends but she'd assumed he'd have said he couldn't this week in favour of spending time with her. Obviously not. "Can't you tell him you're busy today?"

"It's too late now. He won't have time to find someone else. Why don't you come with me and hang out? The weather's supposed to be great today."

She used to do that a lot. The café was right by the river. A beautiful spot. When she and Jack first got together she spent most Sundays down there while he worked. She'd lie on a picnic blanket on the grassy area by the café, soaking up the sun and watching the world go by. It had always seemed so idyllic. Of course Emily used to come and keep her company too. The novelty soon wore off when Emily got her book deal and ditched her to move to London.

"I'll just be bored," she said sulkily. "I thought you'd have made time for me this weekend."

"I skipped football this morning," he said.

"Wow!" Her voice was full of sarcasm and she could feel

her anger levels rising. "That was good of you. I can't believe you would sacrifice a morning of kicking a ball around a field to spend time with me."

He shook his head and gave her a look that said she was being unreasonable.

"Come on, Josie. You know I work at the weekends. I can't rearrange my whole life because you've decided to take a job in the middle of nowhere."

He went to get a cup of coffee and she stayed on the couch taking calming breaths. Of course she didn't expect him to rearrange his whole life, but was it really so unreasonable to think he might reorganise his weekend to spend time with her? He didn't actually need to work at the weekend. He already had a full-time job. Clive could definitely arrange someone else to work at the café.

"Jack," she said calmly, pulling her legs under her on the couch. "Did you know that only one percent of long-distance relationships work?"

He sat beside her and blew on his coffee. "Where did you get that rubbish from?"

"I just heard it somewhere." She brushed aside thoughts of Sam. "But it made me think. We need to put some effort in if we want this to work."

"Right," he said wearily. "And that means I should stop going to the pub on Fridays, give up playing football, stop working weekends and make sure the place is spotless for when Your Highness gets home?"

"You don't need to be like that about it," she snapped. "Of course I don't like coming back to a complete mess."

"But you're seriously asking me to give up football, and tell Clive I can't help him out anymore?"

"No." She wasn't quite sure what she was getting at, or what she expected him to say. "I'm just not sure how a long-distance relationship is going to work."

"Are you splitting up with me again? Because it was you who said we should stop doing that."

"I'm not breaking up with you." Her voice was confident, but for a moment she wondered where her relationship with Jack was headed. They never discussed the future. "Don't you think it's weird that we don't talk all week? Neither of us thinks about calling or sending a message. Do you even think about me when I'm not here?"

"Of course I do. You're worrying about nothing. We'll be fine. It might just take a bit of time to adjust to you working away, that's all. I'll make sure I'm not in the pub next Friday when you get home, and I'll talk to Clive about taking the odd weekend off. Okay?"

"Okay." She leaned into him when he put an arm around her.

He kissed her cheek quickly. "I've gotta get showered. Are you sure you won't come down to the café? Clive always likes to see you… "

She shook her head. "I'll probably just head back to Averton."

CHAPTER 12

The drive back to Averton was quiet and went much faster than Friday's journey. Josie was about half an hour away from the farm when she passed through a village and spotted a couple of older gentlemen struggling out of a house carrying a couch. She slowed, watching the scene, and then stopped behind the skip they were heading for and jumped out quick.

"Excuse me." She darted in front of them, blocking the way to the skip. "Are you getting rid of that?"

"Yes, love," the grey-haired man said. "Can you get out of the way? It's heavy. In fact, you couldn't give us a hand, could you?"

"Can I have it?" she said eagerly.

They stopped and eased it down to the ground. "You want the couch?"

"Yeah, please. I mean, if it's just going to go in the skip?"

"It's not in the best shape," the second man said, resting on it as he caught his breath.

"That's fine," she said. "It doesn't matter."

They glanced at each other and nodded. "You're welcome to it," the grey-haired man said.

Josie looked from the couch to her car.

"It'll never fit in that little car," one of the men said.

"Hmm." Josie looked between the car and the couch as though a solution might magically come to her.

"You'd need a van," the man said.

"Can you leave it next to the skip? I'll see if I can figure something out and come back later."

"The skip's being removed tomorrow morning. We can leave it until then."

She shouted her thanks as she got back in the car. The idea of getting furniture for the kennels had been niggling at her, and she'd been meaning to search online and see if she could find anyone giving old stuff away. Apparently all she needed to do was spend her Sunday afternoons driving around looking for people getting rid of things.

Now she just needed to find herself a van.

"Hi!" she called to Annette as she dumped her bag in the kitchen and greeted the excited dogs who circled her legs. Nudging them gently out of the way, she followed Annette's voice to the living room. She bent down to her in the armchair and gave her a quick kiss on the cheek. "Don't let me disturb your book. I've got to go out again. I need to ask Sam for a favour."

"You never stop!" Annette said. "How was your weekend?"

"It was okay," Josie said unenthusiastically. She headed back to the kitchen. "I'll tell you about it later. I shouldn't be too long."

She set off, walking briskly down past the barn in the direction Sam had pointed out to her the other day. Soon, she slowed her pace. It was so quiet and peaceful. An old oak tree stood regally just beyond the fence behind the barn, and the grass grew haphazardly under it with wildflowers mixed in. At the crest of the hill, she gazed at the blanket of bluebells which spread down the hillside to a small stream in the valley. It was an incredible sight. She caught a glimpse of a house between the trees, down in the valley. She upped her pace again, then circled round the house to reach the front door.

It took Sam a couple of minutes to answer, and Josie found herself getting nervous as she waited. His hair was dishevelled when he opened the door a crack, and his eyes were only half open.

"Sorry," Josie said, biting her lower lip. "Were you asleep?" He hadn't opened the door all the way and it made her uncomfortable, like he had something to hide. Maybe he had a woman in there. "I'm really sorry," she said. "I'll go ..."

"It's fine." He blinked slowly as he opened the door wider. "Come in. I must have fallen asleep on the couch."

She apologised again as she stepped inside. He was wearing jogging bottoms and a scruffy old T-shirt, and she felt like she was interrupting his lazy Sunday. When he gestured, she moved into the living room, where the muted TV flashed up adverts. The living room was homely with a worn leather couch and matching armchair. The place was neat and tidy. It seemed like he was going for the minimalist look.

"Need to borrow something?" he asked with a smile.

"Yeah," she said, slowly. "Kind of."

"Give me a clue ..."

"I need to collect a couch for the kennels. This guy said I

could have it for free but I need to pick it up today and it won't fit in my car."

He frowned. "This is going to involve me getting dressed today, isn't it?"

"Would you mind?"

"Okay." He pushed a hand through his hair. "Make yourself at home. I'll just be a minute."

He disappeared upstairs, and when she sat on the couch, it was still warm from where he'd been lying. Josie leaned back and looked around the room. It was a nice place, if a little bare. She got up and wandered through to the kitchen. There was a decent-sized garden out the back and rolling hills stretching beyond that. The kitchen was lovely – more modern than the living room, like it had only recently been fitted. It was all very neat. Apparently Sam didn't like clutter.

At the sound of footsteps on the stairs, she went back to the living room and sat in the armchair. "Do you know what you need in here?" she said.

"No. But I'm sure you're going to tell me."

"Cushions or a throw blanket. Something to soften the place up a bit."

"I'll bear that in mind. Thanks for the tip."

"You're welcome!" She smiled cheekily as she stood up. Sam had put a pair of jeans on and a long sleeved T-shirt. The sleeves were pushed up and showed off his toned forearms. His hair was still ruffled but slightly more styled.

"Lead the way then," he said.

Once they were in the van, he looked questioningly at her.

"If you drive as though you're going to Oxford … it's in a little village somewhere between here and there …"

He stared at her. "You don't know where we're going?"

"I was on my way back and I saw these guys getting rid of a couch so I just stopped and asked if I could have it …

But now you mention it, I didn't really pay much attention to where it was. I think it was about half an hour from here."

"So you disturb my nap to take me on a wild goose chase."

"No," she said confidently as she switched the radio on. "It's more like a treasure hunt!"

∽

"Just admit you're lost!"

It was well over half an hour later, and Sam's eyes twinkled with amusement.

"I'm not lost," Josie insisted. "I know exactly where we are. I just don't know where the couch is."

"You know you can take the A38 to Averton instead of driving through all the little villages?"

"I know but the main road's full of roadworks. Besides, it's much more interesting going the back way. You can even find free furniture!"

"And lose it again! Can I turn round yet?"

"I guess so," she said. "I'm sure it wasn't this far away."

"I can't believe you didn't check the name of the village."

She gave his arm a gentle shove. "All right, Mr Perfect! You don't need to go on about it."

"Sorry," he said. "It's quite funny, though."

She pouted as she scanned the streets trying to recognise something. "I really wanted that couch."

"We'll find you another couch," he said gently.

"I need about twenty."

"Twenty couches?" he said, laughing again.

"I can't just have a couch in one of the kennels. I want it to be standard."

"You're going to get twenty couches?"

"Or armchairs." She looked gloomily out of the window. "I can't believe I lost the couch."

He gazed at her intently for a moment before concentrating on the road again. After about ten minutes of driving in silence, he slowed right down and pointed.

"Is that it?"

"Yes!" She squealed excitedly.

"You know we must have driven past it once already?"

"You were probably talking and distracting me."

He pulled up in front of the skip and opened his door. "I might've known it'd be my fault."

"You take that end," Josie said brightly, surveying the maroon couch. It'd match her paint job nicely, and it didn't look to be in too bad condition.

"He definitely said you could take it?" Sam glanced around. "It feels like stealing."

"They said it was fine. It was only going in the skip otherwise."

Sam lifted his end and eyed her sceptically. "No way you can lift that."

"Hang on." She struggled to get a grip on it, and then managed to get it about a centimetre off the ground before she admitted defeat and put it down again.

"Just come here and help me drag it …"

She walked over to Sam, shaking her head. "You're going to ruin my couch dragging it down the street."

His mouth twitched to a smirk. "You're worried I'm going to ruin the couch that you're saving from a skip to give to the dogs? That's a genuine concern?"

She couldn't help but laugh.

"Just get over here and help me before someone comes and asks why we're stealing a couch."

She did as she was told but got the giggles and couldn't stop. Sam bumped shoulders with her and grinned.

"Do you need some help?"

Josie stopped laughing and looked up at the two burly-looking guys. They both had the same build – short and stocky – and were both covered in tattoos. On one of them, the tattoos crept all the way up his neck and onto his cheek.

"Yes, please," Josie said keenly. She let go of the couch and moved out of the way. "We just need to get it in the van, but it weighs a ton."

"You're not nicking it, are you?"

"No. The guy was getting rid of it and he said I could have it." When the tattooed man looked puzzled, she felt she should elaborate. "It's just for my dogs. I work at a kennels and I'm looking for old furniture."

He smiled at her and then he and his friend picked up the end of the couch and helped Sam load it into the van. Sam shook hands with them as he thanked them, and then the one with the tattoos on his face turned back to Josie.

"If you're doing a pickup service I've got an old couch in my garage you can have."

"Really?" She couldn't believe her luck.

"My sister filled up my garage with a load of her things and then went off for Australia for a year. She's marrying some Aussie fella now and I'm stuck with a garage full of her stuff. You'd be doing me a favour taking it away."

"That'd be amazing."

"It's not far away. Do you wanna come now?"

"Yes, please!" She glanced at Sam, who looked at her with wide eyes before fixing a smile and shrugging.

"Give me your phone and I'll put the address in …"

She handed him her phone and peered over as he opened maps and typed his address in the search bar. "Go right at the next traffic lights, then drive for five minutes, then turn right again. See you there in ten minutes."

"Thanks!" She slid back into the van with Sam. "How lucky was that?"

"Lucky he didn't steal your phone? Very lucky!"

"What?" she said, puzzled.

"You just handed your phone over to some thug as though it was the most normal thing in the world."

"Just because they've got tattoos doesn't mean they're thugs."

"He's got love and hate tattooed on his knuckles!"

She clicked her seat belt into place. "I only saw love."

"Well, what do you think the other might say?"

"It could say anything! And they're nice guys. They helped with the couch. And he's giving me another couch."

"Right, so we're really going to his place now? This is actually happening?"

"Why not?"

"Oh, Josie." He reached and stroked her hair condescendingly. "Sweet little Josie!"

"Get off me." She swatted him away, beaming. "Just drive, will you?"

He turned the engine on. "I was having a lovely nap. Now I've no idea what's about to happen."

She gave him a quick shove. "Don't be ridiculous! I didn't realise you were so judgemental."

"I'm not judgemental. But you're too trusting. If he'd said he had puppies in his car I bet you'd have gone with him for a look."

"Ooh! I love puppies!"

He shook his head. "Your parents must have had a nightmare. How have you survived this long?"

"Shut up and drive, will you!"

CHAPTER 13

Their tattooed friends were standing at the front gate of the semi-detached house when they arrived.

"I can't believe I'm getting two couches in one day," Josie said, beaming at Sam.

"Not sure I believe it yet either …"

"Oh, don't be such a grump." She opened the door and jumped out. "Thanks so much for this," she said as she approached the house. "I'm Josie, by the way."

"I'm Brendan," the one with the face tattoo said. "This is Ryan."

"That's Sam," Josie said, nodding in his direction.

"Come and have a look then," Brendan said. They followed him to the garage attached to his house and her eyes widened when he opened the door. It really was packed full.

Brendan raised an eyebrow. "You see what I mean when I say you'd be doing me a favour?"

"Are you sure your sister won't mind?"

"She's staying in Australia. She'll be happy I'm getting some space back."

The couch was in the middle of the garage with boxes stacked on top of it and all sorts of other pieces of furniture and junk around it. Josie scanned the items as the men began to dig it out.

"Would it be helpful if I took this chair off your hands too?" She looked at Brendan with big eyes as she ran a hand over the back of the tatty leather armchair.

"You're welcome to it," he said, smiling as he lifted boxes from the couch.

Josie watched as Sam took a box from the couch and placed it on a table. He stood for a moment, his brow furrowed. Then he rubbed at the wood of the table and bent to inspect the legs. He looked so serious. Josie tilted her head, wondering what he was doing.

"I'll give you twenty quid for the table," Sam said, looking to Brendan.

"Deal!"

Sam pulled out his wallet and Josie sighed. "You're making me look bad. You're paying for stuff and I'm taking things for free. I've not even got any cash."

"Don't worry about it." Brendan grinned at Josie and then looked over her shoulder at Sam. "Take the drawers too if you want." It was a nice wooden set of drawers in the corner, and he was looking them over just as he'd done the table.

"Better not," Sam said, pushing his wallet into his back pocket. "My garage will end up looking like yours at this rate. And I think we'll struggle to fit stuff in the van as it is."

It was a bit of a squeeze getting it all in, but they managed it.

She said goodbye to Ryan and when she reached to shake Brendan's hand, she couldn't help but take a better look at his tattoos. "I like your ink," she said.

He held his arms out for her to inspect.

"Notice he's got his name halfway up his arm," Ryan said merrily. "That's in case he forgets!"

Brendan smiled bashfully. "Some of them I got when I was young. I still don't regret them, though – they're part of me."

She held his hands, turning them and gazing over all the intricate patterns and pictures. "I like how you've got love written on both knuckles." She managed to keep a straight face and didn't dare glance at Sam.

"My mum would've killed me if I got love and hate."

She grinned at him. "I think you're a big softie underneath all the ink and muscles."

"Shh!" He winked. "Don't tell anyone."

She thanked them again and shouted goodbye as she hopped into the van beside Sam. "That was interesting."

"All right," he said as he drove away. "I think you made your point. They're good guys."

"They're lovely," she said, relaxing into the seat.

It had been a long day, and she was almost asleep by the time they got back to Oakbrook. She rallied to help Sam unload the couches. There was a lot of laughter as they struggled to get the furniture through the stable doors into the kennels.

Josie's cheeks were aching by the time everything was in place, and she flopped onto the blue couch which had once belonged to Brendan's sister. "This is actually a decent couch," she said, looking up at Sam.

He picked her feet up to sit at the end of the couch and his thumb brushed her bare ankle. He cocked an eyebrow. "Are these the same shoes you wore at the wedding?"

"Yes." In the silence, she was aware of their proximity and swung her feet away from him. "Why are you looking at me like that's weird?"

"I'm not," he said, chuckling. "But I think you're going to

have to invest in something a bit more sturdy if you're going to be out walking the dogs in all weather."

"I've got a pair of these in grey and another in navy. They don't show the dirt."

"You'll be tramping around here in wellies before you know it."

"No chance," she said.

"We'll see."

"Stop going on about my shoes," she said lightly. "It's a weird obsession you've got."

"I'm not obsessed," he insisted.

They sat in silence for a moment.

"Thanks for helping me with the couches," Josie finally said.

"You're welcome. It was surprisingly fun."

"It was also surprising that we didn't get beaten up by the men with tattoos!"

"Are you going to remind me about that forever?" He looked slightly embarrassed. "I'll admit I might have mis-judged them."

"You might have?"

"I did!" He leaned back and stared at the ceiling. "Leave me alone."

"Two couches and an armchair," Josie said, wistfully. "That was a good day."

"Three down, seventeen to go."

"I think it's going to come in very handy being friends with a man with a van!"

"Are you planning on ruining all my Sundays?"

She gave him a playful shove. "I didn't ruin your Sunday!"

"I'm kidding." He reached for the lock of hair that fell from her ponytail and pushed it behind her ear. It made her heart thunder in her chest, and she had to remind herself to breathe. "Sorry," he said, quietly.

Footsteps in the barn interrupted them and Sam stood abruptly.

"Oh, my goodness!" Annette stared at the large red couch in the first kennel. "You've been busy again, Josie!"

CHAPTER 14

"You never told me what was wrong with your weekend?" Annette remarked over breakfast on Monday.

Josie was puzzled. "There was nothing wrong with my weekend."

"You didn't seem so enthusiastic when you came back yesterday. I thought you might have fallen out with Jack or something?"

"Oh!" The weekend with Jack seemed a long time ago. After the fun collecting couches, she'd forgotten all about it. "Yeah. Jack was pretty busy so I didn't really see much of him. It's hard figuring out how to have a long-distance relationship. I'm sure it'll be fine when we get used to it."

"I'm sure it will."

"I'm going to walk the dogs," Josie said. "Then I'm going to figure out how to get us some customers. Maybe I should start approaching dog-walkers and offering them flyers with a ten percent discount or something."

"Stop worrying. Before you know it, the kennels will all

be full and you'll be wishing for the day you only had our dogs to walk."

"I just feel bad that we haven't had any bookings yet."

"I forgot to tell you – Graham asked us to have his two dogs next weekend while he's away."

"That's good." Her smile faded and she looked at Annette questioningly. "Is this a paid booking or a favour for a friend?"

"A favour," Annette said. "But it's good. Like a trial run for you. Except it's over the weekend so you'll be at home, won't you? Never mind."

"Maybe I can stay," Josie mused.

"Don't be silly. I can manage a couple of dogs on my own."

"Let's pretend it's a proper booking anyway and put it in the calendar."

"I already did," Annette said.

"Really? I thought I'd have to show you how to use the calendar."

"I've been taking bookings for fifty-odd years. I think I know how to write them in the diary." They stared at each other for a moment. "Don't tell me – you've got some new-fangled thing you want me to use."

"The online bookings go straight to the calendar on the computer, so we'll just have to add phone bookings to that."

"That doesn't make sense. What happens when you go home on the weekends and take your laptop with you?"

"I set it up on your computer too," Josie said. "It's all linked."

"We never really used that computer. It's another thing Max insisted on, but I never saw the point."

"I'll show you how to use it," Josie said. "You'll soon get the hang of it."

"Maybe we can just put my diary next to the computer

and you can transfer the online bookings into that. Things don't go wrong when you write them down."

"That'll just be confusing," Josie argued.

"It must be your system that doesn't work then, because I've been writing the bookings in the diary for fifty years and there's never been any confusion."

With a deep breath, Josie smiled tightly. It didn't seem like she was going to win this battle today, and since they didn't have any proper bookings yet, it didn't seem worth the headache.

"I'll write them in the diary until you get the hang of the online calendar."

Annette looked dubious but set about tidying the breakfast things away and didn't comment further.

"It rained in the night," she said, as Josie slipped her shoes on. "Take my wellies. Your feet will end up soaking wet otherwise."

"I'm fine," she said brightly, remembering Sam's comment.

Annette tutted and Josie called for the dogs and set off to walk them. She ambled over the hills for a couple of hours, and when the damp seeped from the grass through her trainers, an image of Sam came to mind again. She still wasn't about to start wearing wellies.

Back at the house, she wrote a few posts on the social media accounts for the kennels. She really thought they'd start getting bookings immediately and was disappointed by the silence. In the afternoon, she took the dogs out for another walk and was down by the barn when she saw a familiar face at the gate. Amber, the woman with the little boy she'd met when she first arrived. He was fast asleep in the buggy.

"Thought I'd call in for a cuppa while he sleeps." Amber gave Josie a warm hug. "How are you settling in?"

"Good," Josie said. "Come and see what I got for the kennels."

She proudly showed off her reclaimed furniture. Amber was suitably impressed. They had a good giggle when Josie explained how she'd come to get them.

"Sam's such a good guy," Amber said, as they wandered back out into the sunshine. "It's nice that he helped you out."

"It cheered me up after a crappy weekend anyway."

"What was wrong with your weekend?"

"Oh, nothing," Josie said. She had a tendency to talk too much and would generally tell her life story to anyone who asked. But there was something about Amber as well; she was very easy to chat to. "My boyfriend was driving me up the wall, but it's not really anything new."

"I didn't realise you had a boyfriend." Amber stopped, then opened her mouth to say something a couple of times before she finally spoke. "I thought you liked Sam."

Josie frowned. "He told you I kissed him?"

She shook her head before she started laughing. "No. He didn't tell me that!"

"Oh, God!" Josie headed to the house. "It never happened! I'll make coffee and we'll pretend I didn't say anything."

"Or you could make coffee and then tell me everything," Amber suggested.

After Annette said a quick hello, she left them alone and they sat out on the patio.

"So what happened with you and Sam?" Amber said, glancing inside to check Annette wasn't around.

"Not much. I kissed him at Lizzie's wedding. I'd split up with my boyfriend. Sam and I were dancing together for most of the evening … And then we ended up kissing on the beach. It was just a kiss." Albeit a kiss she couldn't think about without her stomach going into a sudden gymnastics routine.

"What happened with your boyfriend then?"

"We decided to give it another go. Sam and I are just friends."

"That's a shame," Amber said. "I thought you and Sam seemed perfect for each other. He didn't say anything about the kiss, but when he was telling me about you ..."

"What?"

"I don't know. He just seemed quite taken with you. Somehow I presumed it would be mutual."

Josie forced herself not to dwell on the comment. "We're definitely just friends." She paused, wondering if she and Jack really could survive the long distance. "I told Jack we'd give things another try. Although, I think long-distance will be hard. The drive back to Oxford is long when I just go for a weekend." She'd already been toying with the idea of going back every fortnight instead of every week.

The thing that was really niggling her regarding her relationship with Jack was that instead of absence making the heart grow fonder, she had the feeling that for them it was more a case of out of sight, out of mind. Making an effort for their relationship really shouldn't be so much work, should it? They should want to see each other. And shouldn't they be on the phone every day? She could go days without even thinking of him, and she was sure it was the same for him.

"I'm sure it will work if you really want it to," Amber said positively. "And the drive will probably seem shorter once you've done it a few times."

"Maybe." Josie was unconvinced. Part of her thought that when they broke up last time, they should have stayed that way. She pushed the thoughts aside.

Kieron's eyes flickered open and he immediately demanded to be taken out of the buggy. He spent a few minutes groggily cuddled up to Amber before he caught sight of the dogs. Tilly and Charlie lay sprawled under the patio table and barely moved when Kieron reached down to pat them. Macy darted around him, wanting to play, and Kieron happily toddled around the garden with her.

It was half an hour later when Amber made a move to leave.

"If you're ever around on the weekend, give me a shout. I'm usually in the pub on Friday evenings with my friend, Tara. You should come with us."

"I might be here this weekend," Josie said. Even though they only had the neighbour's dogs staying, Josie felt she should stay around and help Annette.

"Great." Amber reached for her phone and they swapped numbers. "You should definitely come out with us."

CHAPTER 15

On Wednesday morning, Josie took a call for a last-minute booking: two Bernese Mountain dogs to stay for the weekend. That cemented her decision to stay around. She was excited about her first customers.

Max came to collect Tilly on Thursday morning. Annette had gone off to do some shopping and Josie was sitting on the patio enjoying the sunshine. Tilly bounded over to him as soon as he got out of the car, and he made a big fuss of her before Josie got any attention.

She stood to greet him. "We weren't expecting you until later."

"I thought I'd come early and get some jobs done while I'm here." He kissed her cheek and then his gaze roamed over the flagstones on the patio. "I was going to jet-wash the patio but it looks like someone beat me to it."

"I did it yesterday," Josie said happily.

He glanced over towards the gate. "And you cut the rhododendrons back?"

"We've got our first customers arriving tomorrow so I wanted to make sure everything looked perfect. I jet-washed the sign at the front gate too. And I painted the gate and stable doors when I got here."

"All the jobs I've been meaning to get to. Do the dogs need a walk?"

"No." She sat down again. "All done."

"Did you leave me anything to do?"

She shrugged. "I wouldn't say no to a coffee!"

"Is Annette around?"

"Gone shopping," Josie called as he disappeared into the kitchen.

He returned a few minutes later with coffee for them both.

"Are you okay?" Josie asked when he stared blankly into the distance.

"Yeah." He stretched his tanned legs out and leaned back in his seat. "It's weird being here and having nothing to do. I don't really know the last time I just sat and enjoyed the view."

"It must've been hard when Wendy was ill." Josie had heard from Lizzie how torn Max had been, trying to juggle a new job and be around for Annette and Wendy too.

"I always seemed to be running around the place. There was always something that needed to be done. I didn't mind," he added quickly.

"Of course not." They sat in silence for a few minutes. "So how was the honeymoon?"

"Great." His face relaxed. "Really great."

He pulled out his phone and showed her a photo of him and Lizzie on a pristine beach. "Swipe through," he said, handing her the phone.

"It looks amazing." She flicked through pictures of the wonderful scenery and the two of them looking so happy. "Is Lizzie okay?"

"Yeah. She was going to come today but she's struggling with the jet lag."

"I'll catch up with her soon."

"Why don't you come over on Saturday? Sam was talking about driving over. You could come together. We can have a barbecue."

"Okay." It sounded lovely. Josie always enjoyed her visits to Hope Cove. That's why she felt so excited by the idea, she assured herself. Not the thought of spending time with Sam. Or maybe it was a bit of both.

Annette arrived home half an hour later, and Max stayed to catch up with her for a while before packing Tilly into the car and heading back to Hope Cove.

It was lunchtime on Friday when their first customers arrived. Josie had been waiting for them, full of nervous excitement.

"They're here!" She stood on the patio and waved as the car crawled up the driveway. Charlie and Macy were inside, out of the way.

"Hi!" Josie greeted the couple warmly as they stepped out of the car. Sarah and Ben Jones were middle-aged and both smiled warmly as they greeted Josie.

"I'm so happy you could take them," Sarah said. "We're going to Rome for the weekend. I found a last-minute deal that was too good to pass up but our usual kennels were full. My neighbour had seen one of your flyers in the local pet shop."

"That's perfect," Josie said. "We've just reopened after a little break. I'm so glad you found us."

"It's gorgeous here." Sarah looked around, smiling at the view.

"They can be a bit boisterous." Ben opened the car boot to get the dogs out. He took a firm hold of the leads as they jumped out excitedly.

"Oh, they're gorgeous," Josie said. They were huge dogs with wonderfully big droopy eyes.

Ben passed the leads to Josie and she cooed and fussed over them as though they were children. Very quickly, they rushed around her and she moved to avoid getting caught in the leads as they went in opposite directions.

She made a strange whimpering noise and tried not to panic as the leads tightened around her legs. If she fell over, she'd die of embarrassment. Sarah tried to help untangle her, but they just got into more of a mess.

Annette had been hanging back until that point. She took hold of the dogs by the collars, unclipping their leads and telling Josie to step out of the tangled mess she'd created.

Holding out a finger, Annette let go of the dogs and told them to sit, her voice taking on a strange tone as though she were suddenly possessed. Amazingly, the dogs did as they were told, and Josie watched in shock as Annette told them to stay. They did exactly what she said.

"That's amazing," Ben said. "I've tried to train them so many times. They don't listen to us."

"It takes some practice." Annette picked up the leads and clipped them back onto the collars. "We'll show you where they'll be staying."

Josie felt utterly useless as they walked towards the barn. She was used to Charlie and Macy, and it hadn't occurred to her that she could make a fool of herself so quickly. She'd looked utterly incompetent and hoped that Annette wouldn't be annoyed with her. She listened intently as Annette chatted with the couple and gently put them at ease about leaving their dogs with them. It was amazing to see her so confident and professional.

When they walked back up to the house, leaving the dogs safely locked in their kennel, everyone chatted easily, and Josie made small talk with Sarah about her weekend away.

Josie turned to Annette when they stood waving the couple away. "I'm sorry. That was so embarrassing."

"Don't be silly," Annette said. "It's your first day on the job. You'll get used to handling the dogs."

"I hope so. I thought I was going to fall on my bum!"

"Me too." Annette chuckled. "Perhaps when you walk them, you should take them out one at a time. Just while we're quiet, and until you get a bit more confident."

"Sounds like a good idea to me. What do I need to do? Should I take them for a walk now? Or feed them?"

"No." Annette looked thoroughly amused. "Let's go inside and have a cuppa. We can go through the routine."

Annette patiently explained everything to Josie over the course of the afternoon. They walked the dogs together, and Annette showed Josie a few tips for keeping the dogs under control. She had a sing-song voice that she used for the dogs, and somehow they did exactly as they were told. When Josie tried it, it didn't work quite so well. In fact, the dogs kept jumping up at her, and they were so powerful, they almost knocked her off her feet a few times.

"Why don't they listen to me?" Josie complained as they stood outside the barn with the dogs. She'd spent ten minutes trying to get them to sit, but it was like they were completely deaf to her instructions.

"It takes time, that's all. You'll get the hang of things. Let's get them back inside. Graham should be here soon with Pixie and Skittle."

"Those are very weird names for dogs!" Josie said.

Annette nodded. "I know. But you'll no doubt hear far worse soon enough. You have to learn to bite your tongue."

"Great," Josie said. "Another new skill to learn!"

When Graham arrived half an hour later, Josie was relieved to see that Pixie and Skittle were far smaller dogs than their other guests. They seemed much more docile, and

Josie was sure she could handle them. Graham had a quick chat with Annette and then promptly left them to it.

Late in the afternoon, Annette took Josie out to the barn to explain the feeding routine.

"I'll get used to this smell eventually, won't I?" she asked Annette as she scraped the dog food from the tins. It was an effort not to gag.

"What smell?" Annette asked.

"This!" Josie mushed the food in the bowl.

"You'll get used to it. I don't even smell it any more."

Josie turned her nose up and decided Annette's sense of smell must have just given up and died at some point. She almost wished hers would do the same.

"I might go up to the pub later," Josie said, trying to distract herself from the stench. "If you don't need me."

"That's a good idea," Annette said. "Why don't you give Sam a call? He'd go with you."

"Amber said she'd be there so I thought I might join her. She said she always meets her friend there on Friday nights."

"Tara?" Annette said. "Yes, you'll get on well with those two. Tara can be a bit wild. You'll have fun, I'm sure."

CHAPTER 16

It was a funny feeling, walking into the pub on her own. In Oxford or London, she wouldn't think twice about going into a bar alone. Village pubs were different. Everyone turned to look when she walked in. She plastered on a smile and scanned the room for Amber. She'd messaged to make sure she'd definitely be there, but she couldn't see her. Feeling self-conscious, she headed for the bar.

"Hello!" a familiar voice said. It was Sam, sitting on a stool at the bar. She was relieved to see someone she knew. "Annette let you out to play, did she?"

"She did," Josie said with a grin.

"I'll get you a drink. What you having?"

"No. I'll get you one. I owe you for helping me with the couches."

"It was nothing. I actually quite enjoyed it."

"Me too." She registered his almost-empty pint on the bar. "Beer?"

He picked it up and sighed. "I was just about to go home."

A wave of disappointment swept through her. "One more?"

"Go on then."

She slipped onto the stool beside him and said hello to Andy, the barman, before ordering their drinks. He poured the beers and moved on to serve someone else.

"So do you know everyone in here?" Josie asked.

Sam swivelled to scan the room. "Not everyone. Most people."

"I can't imagine living in the village where you grew up."

"It's kind of nice," he said. "Most of the time. Have you met many of the locals yet? Has Annette been introducing you around?"

"So far I've just met Amber. Actually, I'm supposed to be meeting her and her friend."

"Tara? They're around here somewhere," Sam said. "I saw them come in. They're a good laugh those two."

Josie scanned the room again until she caught sight of Amber and another woman in the corner. "There they are." She gave them a quick wave. Amber immediately stood up and came towards them.

"Sorry," she said, giving Josie a quick hug. "I didn't see you come in."

"It's fine. I only just got here."

"Come and sit with us. You gonna join us, Sam?"

He slid off his seat. "Why not?"

"Sam!" a tall, lanky guy shouted from the other end of the bar. "I need you on my darts team!"

"I'm just finishing this." He raised his glass. "Then I'm going home."

There was a groan and some shouts of encouragement from the small crowd around the dartboard.

"All right, all right!" He held his hands up in defeat.

"Looks like I'm playing darts," he said to Josie and Amber. "I'll catch up with you later."

Josie smiled at him before following Amber across the pub.

"We saw you come in really," Amber said after she'd introduced her to Tara. "But when your face lit up at the sight of Sam, we thought we'd keep out of the way for a bit!"

Josie opened her mouth to protest but just laughed instead. The pair of them looked so cheeky, grinning at her.

"It's not like that," she insisted, glancing across the pub at Sam.

"Don't worry," Tara said. "He looked just as pleased to see you."

"Annette will try and set you up with him," Amber warned. "She and Wendy were always fond of Sam, and she's been on a mission to set him up with someone recently."

"Does he date much?" Josie was suddenly curious about his love life.

The girls shook their heads in unison.

"He was in a relationship," Amber said. "That was a few years back. They were living together in Bristol."

"What happened?" Josie asked.

Amber shrugged. "He moved back here and turned all moody for a while. He never really talked about it."

"He dated Belinda a while back." Tara's face gleamed with amusement. "She works in the chemist's over in Newton Abbot."

"One date," Amber clarified.

Tara leaned in to whisper. "She reckoned he was so shy he didn't speak a word the whole evening." She let out a sharp cackle. "But we think he probably just couldn't get a word in."

Josie was amused by Tara. She wasn't quite what she was expecting in a friend of Amber. They seemed to be completely different personalities. So far, Tara seemed bold and brash whereas Amber was soft and gentle. Tara was stunning, with rich brown hair that fell in soft curls down her back and matching dark eyes and skin. There was a touch of the exotic about her.

"So are you going to ask him out?" Tara asked.

"Sam? No. I've got a boyfriend."

"Oh, yeah. I knew that. That's a shame.'

"Yeah," Josie agreed. It took her a moment to catch the girls staring at her curiously. "I mean …" What did she mean? It was a shame she had a boyfriend?

"What's the deal with the boyfriend?" Tara asked, narrowing her eyes. "Sounds like there's an issue …"

Josie took a sip of her drink. "You're very direct. We only just met."

"Oh, but we're going to be great friends!" Tara said with a teasing grin. "Besides, Amber already told me all about you so I feel like I know you already. Come on, tell me about the boyfriend."

"You may as well just talk," Amber said. "Tara's like a dog with a bone once she thinks she's on to a bit of gossip!"

"Not true," Tara said. "I'm just a concerned friend."

"Okay," Josie said. She actually felt like telling someone what was going on in her head. "I haven't heard from Jack all week, and I guess he's expecting me to come home over the weekend. I was going to call him today and tell him I'm staying here for the weekend, but then I thought I'd just wait and see if he even notices I'm not there … That's a bit pathetic, isn't it?"

Amber and Tara glanced at each other, then looked sympathetically at Josie.

"It doesn't sound like the strongest of relationships," Amber said.

"Even by my standards that sounds pretty casual," Tara put in.

"We've been together quite a while – over a year. I don't think it should still be so casual after so long."

"Do you love him?"

Josie thought for a moment.

"You shouldn't really have to think about it," Tara said. "Especially not for that long."

"I kind of do love him, though," she argued. "In a way."

"Okay," Amber said. "I'll rephrase. Are you in love with him?"

Josie screwed her nose up.

Tara's laugh came out as a cackle. "Looks like Sam might have a chance after all!"

Josie shook her head and concentrated on the drink in front of her. "I can't believe I told you all that when I hardly know you."

"I told you we'd be good friends," Tara said with a wicked grin.

"Don't worry," Amber said. "You'll know all our secrets soon enough."

"What's the plan then?" Tara asked. "Split up with Jack and ask Sam out?"

"No!" Josie said firmly, then sighed. She'd never been good at hiding her feelings, and she really wasn't managing to keep anything from Amber and Tara. "I don't know." Her gaze landed on Sam across the pub. If you compared the amount of time she spent thinking about him to the time she thought about Jack, there did seem to be an obvious conclusion.

The girls were looking at her expectantly.

"I'm thinking that maybe it's time things came to an end with Jack," she said honestly. "But I can't just ask Sam out." Could she?

"I don't see why not," Tara said. "Maybe try and stop staring at him."

Josie dragged her gaze away. "I wasn't," she said unconvincingly

"How is it up at the farm?" Tara asked. "You're getting on well with Annette, I hear?"

Josie was thankful for the subject change. "Yeah, really well."

"She loves having you around," Amber said. "And it's great that you're reopening the kennels."

Once they got Josie talking about the kennels, she got carried away, telling them what she'd been doing with the website and how many bookings they'd had so far.

"Sorry." She finally took a breath. "I swear I didn't used to be so boring."

"Don't worry," Amber said. "We usually just sit and complain about the same old stuff, so it's a nice change."

"We only complain until the third drink," Tara said. "Then conversations get far more lively."

Amber grinned. "By drink five, Tara's usually dancing on the bar."

"I'm young, free and single," Tara said. "And I need to let my hair down after a week at work!"

Josie caught Sam's eye, and he held his empty glass up and flashed her a questioning look. She nodded and he moved to the bar.

"Aww," Tara said. "Sam's got a crush."

Josie's cheeks burned. "Shut up!"

"He usually has two pints and leaves by nine," Amber said. "He's definitely hanging around longer than usual tonight."

Josie shushed them when he walked their way. The laughter had subsided by the time he handed her another beer.

"Thanks."

"Come and sit with us," Tara said, pushing a stool out from under the table.

"Sam!" an elderly man called from the bar. "Come here, I need to ask you something."

He smiled at Josie and sighed before walking away again.

"He's just too popular," Tara said. "Everyone loves Sam."

"You should definitely ask him out," Amber said. "When you've ditched your current boyfriend, of course!"

"I don't need romantic drama," Josie said weakly. "I thought I was getting a quiet life in the country."

"You will certainly get that!" Tara stood. "Who's up for a shot?"

"No!" Amber and Josie said at once.

"I'll have a toddler jumping on me at sunrise," Amber said.

"And I'll have dogs jumping on me," Josie added.

"You're so boring!" Tara laughed as she carried on to the bar. When she arrived back, she launched into a story about her boss, who she was sure had a crush on her. She worked at a bookshop in one of the nearby towns. Josie was quite surprised; somehow Tara seemed too loud and brash to work in a bookshop. Apparently she enjoyed it, even with the slightly creepy boss. The conversations got louder and sillier the more Tara had to drink, and Josie thoroughly enjoyed the evening with her new friends. She caught Sam's eye a couple of times, but he always seemed to get roped into other people's conversations.

Finally, she saw him in the doorway, pulling his jacket on. He flashed her a smile and waved before disappearing outside.

"I think I might head home," Josie said, leaning closer to Amber. They'd joined a conversation with the people on the next table and it was all fairly raucous. She didn't think she'd be missed.

"Ask Andy, the barman. He'll give you a lift if you don't want to walk back on your own, or he'll find someone else to." It was the same advice Annette had given her about getting home.

"Sam just left," she said. "I'll catch up with him."

Amber smiled coyly.

"He lives right next door," Josie said innocently.

"I'll message you soon," Amber said as Josie grabbed her bag and called a quick goodbye to the group.

CHAPTER 17

The cool air hit her as she stepped outside, and she shivered in the pub doorway. She could just see Sam under the streetlights down the road. Hurrying after him, she called out to him.

"Are you walking home?" she said, catching up to him.

"Yeah. I need to abandon my van, thanks to you."

"How is it my fault?"

"Buying me another drink when I was about to leave two hours ago."

"You didn't take much persuading!" They fell into an awkward silence for a moment. "Can I walk with you?"

He flashed her his boyish smile. "I suppose so."

"It's pretty creepy," she said, as they walked away from the village. Last time she'd walked home from the pub with him it had been early, and still light. Today, it was dark and eerie. They were still under the streetlights, but the moon hung over them, almost full and casting shadows in the cloudy sky.

"There are streetlights for about half the way and then

you need a torch. Although with the full moon, it's probably bright enough without."

"You've got a torch?"

"On my phone," he said, slowly, like he might be talking to an idiot. She looked away quickly as she blushed, glad there wasn't much light.

"I don't generally take a torch to the pub," he said. "Do people even have torches that are just torches these days?"

She bit her lip and stayed quiet, the smile making her cheeks ache.

"Sorry," he said. "I didn't mean to tease."

"I think I asked for that," she said. "Sometimes my brain doesn't operate quite as quickly as I'd like it to."

"I'd just blame the beer," he said. "Seems like you're usually pretty switched on. All your plans for the kennels sound very impressive to me."

"We're starting to get more bookings," she said. "And it looks like the summer will be busy. I just want it to do well so I don't feel like a charity case."

"Why a charity case?" he asked, confused. "I thought it was the other way around: you being there to make sure Annette is okay?"

"Well, I also didn't have a job or any money, so it felt like she was doing me the favour." She'd said too much. Why was she trying to convince him she was a charity case? She could've made out she was a brilliant entrepreneur, stepping in to build up the kennel business. Annette's knight in shining armour. Though she shouldn't really care what Sam thought.

"It sounds like it benefits you both," he said.

Josie nodded and he changed the subject, discussing what time they would go over to Hope Cove the following day. Max had already messaged him to say that Josie would be joining too for the barbecue.

Sam was right about the moon: it was so bright they

barely even noticed they'd left the streetlights. There was no need for torches.

They reached the gate at Oakbrook Farm in no time. "Need me to walk you to your door?" he asked.

"I'll manage," she said, slipping through the gate.

One of the dogs howled in the barn, and the noise sent a shiver through her. It was such a calm and pretty place during daylight hours, but very creepy after dark. She lingered at the end of the drive. "Thanks for walking me home."

"You're welcome." He seemed to be waiting for her to walk away, but her legs stayed rooted to the spot. Her mouth, on the other hand, worked at its usual speedy rate.

"I wasn't sure what kind of night to expect with Amber but I really enjoyed myself."

"Fridays in the pub are usually pretty lively," he said.

"It was busier than I thought. And you're right – Tara and Amber are good fun."

Sam leaned on the other side of the gate, a foot resting on the bottom rung. "Can I ask you a personal question?"

Her heart quickened, and there was something about the way he looked at her that made her light-headed. She nodded.

"Are you scared of the dark?"

"What?" She spluttered out a laugh and stood up straighter. Her gaze went to the house, then back to Sam, who had a silly smirk on his face. "You think I'm standing here wittering about nothing just to avoid walking up there on my own?"

"Or you really like my company?"

She shifted her weight and hoped her cheeks weren't quite as red as they felt. She was fairly certain they could be seen from space.

Without a word, he climbed the gate and they set off up the drive together.

"Just to be clear," she said, "I'm only scared of the dark in certain circumstances."

"Really?" he said, amused.

"I sleep in the dark," she said with mock pride. "In the house, I'm fine. But …" She turned, looking across the field. "When it's dark here … and the dogs howl. It's really creepy."

"I can understand that," he said. "It is pretty spooky."

The security light clicked on as they neared the house, and Macy barked twice. "I think you were only being brave because you had me with you," Josie said. "I'll bet you'll run home from here!"

He pulled his phone from his pocket. "That's why I always carry a torch with me."

She smiled at him, and there was an awkward moment when he looked at her for just a millisecond too long. He was standing too close too.

Macy barked again, drawing Josie's attention to the house. When she looked back, Sam was already walking away.

"See you tomorrow," he said, throwing up an arm to wave.

"Bye," she called after him. "Thanks!"

It was strange slipping quietly into the house. The dogs circled around her while she took her shoes and jacket off. She ruffled the fur on their heads before she sent them back to their beds in the utility room.

The house was still, and she half expected Annette to be waiting up for her, as her mum used to do sometimes when she was a teenager. There was no sign, though, and she crept upstairs and slipped in to bed with a smile on her face. For once, she was feeling very hopeful about her future. She had a feeling she was going to enjoy life in Averton.

In fact, moving to the country might just have been the best thing she'd done in a long time.

CHAPTER 18

On Saturday, Josie woke up thinking about Sam. She ate a quick breakfast with Annette as usual and then set off to the barn. Annette shouted something after her, but she didn't register it. Her brain seemed to be stuck on Sam. On the way to the barn, it occurred to her that she still hadn't heard from Jack.

Part of her was actually quite happy about it. The longer they went without speaking, the more certain she was that she needed to end things. Her mind wouldn't focus on Jack for long, and her thoughts jumped quickly back to Sam. It had been a fun evening in the pub, but she couldn't help but think that her favourite part of the night was the walk home. There was something about standing outside the house with Sam in the moonlight that reminded her of the night they'd kissed on the beach.

And that was exactly what she was thinking about when she opened the door to little Pixie's kennel and slipped inside. The only problem was that as she stepped quickly inside, Pixie – who'd previously seemed like a docile little dog – ran out.

"Woah!" Josie shouted. She hadn't closed the barn door behind her when she'd come in, and she quickly panicked about whether or not the gate to the road was open too. She was sure it wasn't. "Stop," she called as she raced after the speedy little dog. Outside, she glanced at the main gate and breathed a sigh of relief. At least Pixie was fenced in and couldn't get out …

"No, no, no!" Josie said quietly as Pixie jumped the fence. It didn't even seem possible for such a small dog to make such a jump, but she made it look easy. Josie stopped for a moment, glancing at the house to make sure Annette hadn't seen. Then she ordered Macy and Charlie to stay put and took off at a run after Pixie. There was no way in the world she'd catch her at the speed she was going. Josie felt like she was about to have a heart attack after two minutes, and she was sure she was about to lose the dog from sight.

In the valley, she hopped the stepping-stones over the little stream but lost her footing and ending up with soaking wet feet. She carried on regardless. At the top of the next hill, she had to stop to catch her breath.

Pixie was nowhere to be seen. Had she really lost a dog? It was only her first day of looking after dogs and she'd lost one. She straightened up and scanned the area. There were fields stretched out to one side, and she could just about make out the village in the distance. Trees were dotted around the place and one direction led to a wooded area. She hoped Pixie hadn't gone that way.

Cupping her hands around her mouth, she called out to Pixie, although she wasn't really expecting it to have any effect. She had to do something. The last place she'd seen Pixie was at the stream, so she walked quickly back there and then jogged beside the water, calling out and scanning the area as she went.

Before long, she came to Sam's house and contemplated

asking him for help. He knew the area, and he probably knew the dog too; he might know where to look. It would be embarrassing, though, admitting to him that she'd lost a dog. Plus she looked a complete state. Her hair had come loose from her ponytail and she had mud splatters up her legs. She was still struggling to catch her breath too. It didn't really matter, though – it was just Sam, and who cares what he thought? She did, she admitted to herself reluctantly.

Josie was about to turn around and go back the way she'd come when she saw movement by the garage at the back of the house. Sam stepped out. He had the Road Runner of dogs in his arms. Josie wasn't sure whether to laugh or cry. She was so relieved.

"Did you lose something?" Sam called.

She headed over to him, pulling her hair into a fresh ponytail as she went. "She's so fast," Josie said. "I opened the door to the kennel and she took off. And you should've seen her jump the fence!"

"Pixie's a little rascal. Didn't Annette warn you?"

Josie thought back to when she was leaving the house. Annette definitely shouted something to her. "She might have done." She stroked the little dog in Sam's arms and quickly became aware of her proximity to him. She was a sweaty mess after her spontaneous run.

"You okay?" he asked when she took a step back. "You look a bit red."

She inhaled deeply. "It's more exercise than I was expecting this morning."

"Come in and have a drink," he said.

"I probably shouldn't ..." she stammered as Sam wandered to the back door. "I think I'll just take Pixie home. Don't take the dog inside anyway, she'll be all wet and dirty ..."

"It's fine," he said, then turned and caught the panic in her eyes. "What's wrong?"

"Nothing. But I can sit out here for a drink." She gestured at the patio table.

"Why don't you want to come inside?" he asked with a raised eyebrow.

Her shoulders drooped as she sighed. "If I tell you, you'll tease me."

"I promise not to tease." He managed to keep a straight face but his eyes sparkled.

Josie's gaze dropped to her shoes. "The blue ones don't show the dirt … but they're not really waterproof." She lifted up onto her toes and then squelched back down again.

"Nope," Sam said, barely suppressing a smirk. "They're definitely not waterproof. I'll bring you a glass of water out!" First, he went into the garage and found some string to tie Pixie up.

Josie baulked when he went to secure her to the table leg. "I've seen how that dog moves. You should attach her to something fixed down or you might lose your table!"

Sam dipped his eyebrows and chuckled before tying the dog to the outside tap. "Better?"

"Hope so." Josie took a seat. "Or she takes out the whole wall. We'll see!"

Pixie lay down and closed her eyes, apparently worn out after her little adventure. Sam fetched two glasses of water and sat down with Josie.

"I'm curious as to how you think I'd tease you," he said, smirking. "Did you think I'd remind you how I suggested you'd need waterproof boots around here?"

"I didn't know I was going to be chasing a dog through a stream!"

"It's probably something you should always assume," he said.

"Hey!" Josie straightened a leg to kick him, and he tapped her soggy foot away with his. "I'm not going to lose a dog again. This was just a drill. Practising what to do if I lose a dog."

Sam broke into a full laugh. "Really?" he said. "Well at least now you know what to do … Run through the stream to Sam's house to ask for help!"

"I wasn't coming to ask for help," she said. "I followed Pixie straight here."

"You were quite a way behind her!"

She grumbled. "I knew you'd tease me."

"Sometimes it's really hard not to. What is this, your first official day of work? And you lost a dog?"

"No!" she said. "I haven't lost a dog. The dog's right there. We had a morning run, that's all. And technically it's my second day of work since the dogs arrived yesterday."

Sam didn't comment further, just sat looking quietly amused.

"Fine," Josie said after a moment. "I lost a dog already. I can't believe I did that. Don't tell Annette, will you?"

"Annette wouldn't care," he said. "And like you said, the dog isn't lost. She's right there. No harm done."

Josie sighed, embarrassed. Was this going to be another job she couldn't manage to keep? Surely she wouldn't last long if she kept losing dogs. It was a depressing thought. She was enjoying life at Oakbrook much more than she'd expected.

She stood abruptly. "I better get back, I suppose."

"Are you sure? I can get you a coffee if you want …"

"No, thanks." She wriggled her feet in her squelchy shoes. "I need to go and dry off. I've got to walk the other dogs too. Wish me luck with that. Hopefully I won't lose any more dogs today." She meant to sound bright and breezy, but somehow it came out quite the opposite.

She felt Sam's eyes on her as she untied Pixie and nudged her awake.

"It's a new job," he said. "Any new job takes time to get used to everything."

"I know." Again, she didn't manage the breezy tone she aimed for.

"Don't worry about today. Pixie's always full of mischief."

"Thanks for catching her," she said quietly as she led Pixie down the garden.

"You know, I had bacon for breakfast," Sam called after her. "I bet Pixie smelled it. It's probably all my fault she ran away."

Josie smiled, but her eyes involuntarily filled with tears, and she focussed on Pixie so Sam wouldn't see. "I'll see you later," she called over her shoulder.

Her feet squelched in her shoes as she marched wearily back to Oakbrook. She really wanted to be good at this job, and she felt like she was failing already. It was embarrassing that Sam had been witness to her incompetence. And then he was so sweet to try and reassure her.

It was a fairly stark contrast to Jack, who hadn't called her all week and apparently hadn't even noticed that she hadn't come home for the weekend.

CHAPTER 19

I t was late afternoon when Sam arrived to collect Josie. The drive over to Hope Cove was pleasant. He didn't mention the lost dog incident and Josie was grateful. Conversation was easy and came in waves. Josie spent much of the journey lost in thought. She'd intended to call Jack in the afternoon, tell him that things were over – and for good this time. The day had got away from her, though, and she knew it wasn't going to be a quick five-minute conversation. She'd nipped to the shops to get a few things for Annette and then walked the dogs and fed them.

She'd spent far too much time deciding what to wear for the visit to Lizzie and Max. In the end, she'd pulled on a pair of denim shorts and an old favourite T-shirt. Who was she trying to impress anyway? Well, Sam, obviously, but she shouldn't be. Waiting for him to collect her had felt like waiting to go on a first date. She was excited and nervous, but then felt guilty for her feelings. She really should have found the time to call Jack.

"I love this place." Sam broke her thoughts as they pulled up outside Seaside Cottage.

She hopped out of his van and took a deep breath. The sea air was wonderful. "Me too," she said.

Lizzie opened the door when they were halfway up the front path. She greeted them happily and gave them both a big hug before ushering them through the cramped hallway and into the kitchen.

"Beer?" She opened the fridge and handed them a bottle each without waiting for an answer.

"Max showed me photos of the honeymoon," Josie said. "It looked amazing."

Lizzie pulled salad items from the fridge with her back to them. When Josie caught Sam's eye, he looked pointedly at his beer, then nodded at Lizzie with raised eyebrows. Josie couldn't help but be amused by his little mime act. He was still convinced Lizzie was pregnant. When Lizzie turned around, Sam smiled sweetly, revealing a dimple that Josie had never noticed before.

"I wanted to show you the photos myself," Lizzie said. "I bet Max just let you skim through them with no explanation."

"They seemed fairly self-explanatory," Josie said. "Gorgeous beaches, wonderful sunsets, great food, happy couple, the usual honeymoon stuff ..."

Lizzie whipped a tea towel in Josie's direction, and she giggled as she jumped out of the way, almost crashing into Sam.

He reached a hand to steady her. "Where *is* Max?"

"He bought a new barbecue." Lizzie nodded in the direction of the back door. "The honeymoon is officially over and he has a new love in his life. He's been playing around with it for ages."

"I better go and check out his new toy." Sam wandered out into the back garden, and they heard him and Max exchange greetings.

Josie slumped into a chair and rested her head on the kitchen table.

"What's wrong?" Lizzie asked.

She lifted her head. "It feels like a date."

Lizzie frowned and shook her head in confusion.

"Me and Sam coming over here to hang out with you guys. It feels like a double date. Which would be fine if I didn't have a boyfriend."

Lizzie sat opposite her. "I'm confused. You're going to have to get me up to speed. Last I heard, you and Jack were giving it another go and you were pretending the kiss with Sam never happened …"

"Except I can't stop thinking about kissing Sam." Josie let out a fake sob and buried her head in her arms. Her head shot quickly back up. "I can't get Sam out of my head. I haven't spoken to Jack all week. The only time I think about Jack is when I'm feeling guilty for all the time I spend thinking about Sam—" She stopped abruptly as Sam appeared in the doorway.

"The cook needs a beer." He crossed the kitchen and grabbed a bottle from the fridge. If he'd heard the conversation, he did a good job of pretending he hadn't. Josie was bright red when he smiled at them and went back outside.

"Oh my God," Josie mouthed at Lizzie.

Lizzie pressed her lips together in an attempt not to laugh. Crossing the kitchen, she closed the window above the sink.

"Did he hear?" Josie whispered.

Lizzie made a poor attempt at hiding her amusement. "They're sitting right outside the window."

With a groan, Josie buried her head again.

"I was going to ask if Sam knows how you feel, but I guess if he didn't before, he does now!" Lizzie moved back to the sink and started washing the salad. "Are you going to split up with Jack then?"

"Yes." Josie went to help Lizzie, reaching for a knife to chop vegetables. "I shouldn't have got back together with him after the wedding. It just seemed easier to keep plodding along as we were. I think we fell into just being friends and flatmates at some point, and neither of us wanted to admit it was really over."

"It's probably for the best."

Josie stopped chopping the cucumber and glared at Lizzie. "Don't start Jack-bashing."

"I'm not! I don't have a problem with Jack. I'm not sure why he always thought I didn't like him."

"Probably because you looked down your nose at him." Josie resumed chopping. "And he never noticed you do that to everyone."

"I do not," Lizzie insisted. "I don't mean to, anyway!"

Josie pretended her declaration of feelings for Sam hadn't happened and soon got over her embarrassment. The four of them sat together on the patio, eating, drinking and chatting. It was all very relaxed.

"We should go down to the beach to watch the sunset," Lizzie suggested as the sky became streaked with orange. When they began to move in that direction, Lizzie muttered something about tidying away the dinner things. She glared at Max as she said she'd catch them up. Max dutifully hung back to help. They weren't particularly subtle about leaving Sam and Josie alone.

The trouble was, Josie didn't want to be alone with him. At least not before she'd sorted things out with Jack. It was a stunning view, though. At the end of the garden there was an old wooden door through the high hedge. It led out onto the coastal path, and beyond that to a beautiful sandy cove. They stopped together on the dusty path. The grass lining it was dotted with purple wildflowers and was a beautiful sight in itself. It was slightly overshadowed by the craggy coastline, which stretched out in either direction. Then there was the little sandy beach which led the way to the sea. The sun sat on the horizon, gloriously throwing out reds and oranges across the sky and spilling down to sparkle on the surface of the water.

"Wow," Josie whispered.

She followed Sam halfway down the lonely beach, all the while resisting the urge to slip her hand into his. When they sat side by side in the sand, she tried to focus on the breathtaking view and the wonderful smell of seaweed and salt, but her senses seemed to be only interested in Sam.

She wanted to lean closer and inhale the scent of him, feel his body against hers, gaze into his eyes and taste his lips on hers …

"Are you okay?" His voice snapped her from her trance, and he looked at her with concern.

"Yes." She swallowed hard. "I was just thinking I should get back soon and check on Annette."

What she really needed was to get back and call Jack.

CHAPTER 20

The drive back to Oakbrook was uncomfortable. All Josie could think about was taking Sam's hand or running a hand through his hair. The desire to touch him was becoming overwhelming, and being in such close proximity was torturous.

Annette was already in bed when she crept into the house. After lavishing some attention on the dogs, Josie retrieved her phone from the bottom of her bag. There were two missed calls from Jack from earlier in the evening. Her phone had been on silent and she hadn't checked it. Jack finally missed her then.

It was late, but she knew he'd still be up. She just hoped he wasn't in the pub. He answered after the first ring and sounded cheerful as he greeted her.

"I thought you'd be back on Friday," he said lightly. "You could've called me."

"And you could've called me," she snapped, suddenly angry. "You didn't bother calling me all week!"

"So I take it you're not coming back this weekend?" He ignored her irritation.

"No. I'm working."

"That's fine. It would just have been useful to know. How's everything there then? Getting busier, I take it?"

She sighed. "Does it bother you at all, not seeing me? Do you even care when I'll be coming back to Oxford?"

"Of course I do," he said. "I was just about to ask …"

"I really don't think this is working any more, Jack. Us, I mean."

"Oh, come on. We'll be fine. We always are."

"Do you even love me?"

"Are you serious? Of course I do!"

Josie bit her bottom lip. She loved him too. In a way. "Are you in love with me?"

He wasn't so quick to answer that one.

"I'm going to take that as a no."

"We should talk in person," Jack said.

"I'm not sure when I'll be back next. And I don't think we need to talk in person. It's been over for a while, really, hasn't it?"

She heard his sigh, imagined him shaking his head as he searched for the right thing to say.

"Neither of us makes any effort," she said gently. "I don't want to keep going like this."

"I can make more effort," he said quickly. "Why don't you let me know when you have some time off and we can talk in person …"

"I don't think I have much more to say."

"Do you remember that time I tried to break up with you on the phone and you said only face-to-face break-ups count?"

She couldn't help but smile at his cheeky tone and of the memory of him calling her to say he was going to have to break up with her because she'd left dirty pots in the sink. Since she spent so much time telling him off for not tidying up after himself, he thought it was hysterical to turn the tables.

"That wasn't a real break-up," she said. "You were just messing around."

"Yeah, but still, it's a good rule."

"Jack!"

"You made the rule," he said lightly. "Don't get mad at me."

She paused and exhaled loudly.

"Please," he said seriously. "Can we at least talk about it in person?"

"It won't make any difference."

"Please."

She'd never been very good at saying no to Jack, but she really couldn't carry on the way things were. "I'm going to call you back in a minute." Before he could object, she ended the call.

She paced the kitchen, stopping at the window. All she could see was darkness and her own reflection. An image of Sam came to mind, wishing her goodnight as she hopped out of his van. She hadn't wanted to leave him.

She reached for her phone again. Jack looked weary when he answered.

"A video call doesn't count as face-to-face," he said.

"I thought it was me who made the rules," she said, forcing lightness to her voice.

"I'm going to hang up."

"Don't," she said quickly as tears dampened her eyes. "I'm breaking up with you. I'm not in love with you. And you're not in love with me. This relationship makes no sense."

He sighed and sank back on the couch. "You're one of my favourite people in the world. Top three I reckon."

Her chest tightened. He really could be so sweet. What

was really heart-wrenching was she knew he meant it. "We can still be friends," she said softly. "That's all we really are anyway: flatmates and friends."

"I can't imagine not having you in my life."

"Me too," she insisted. "But we can still be in touch. I promise." She also couldn't imagine cutting all contact with him.

A few minutes later, she ended the call. Relief washed through her, followed closely by a twinge of excitement. She was single and free of the guilt that had been niggling at her since she met Sam.

Over breakfast the next day, Josie briefly told Annette about breaking up with Jack. She brushed over it. There wasn't much to say, really. Perhaps she should have been upset, but if anything there was a spring in her step as she set off to walk the dogs that morning. She was careful not to let Pixie escape again, but it occurred to her as she walked beside the sea of bluebells that it would be a good excuse to visit Sam if Pixie ran in that direction again.

It was tempting to go and knock on his door. She was desperate to see him. What would she do, though? Just wrap her arms around him and kiss him? Ask him on a date? It made her nervous thinking of it, and she decided to leave things until she next saw him and see what happened.

By Monday morning, she was dying to chat to someone. It occurred to her to visit Lizzie and chat everything through with her, but on a whim she messaged Amber instead, asking if she had time for a coffee. Amber messaged back quickly, saying she was going over to the bookshop to visit Tara, but she invited Josie to come along and added the address in the message.

The small town of Newton Abbot, where Tara worked, was a twenty-minute drive from Averton. Josie arrived mid-morning. The Reading Room was easy to find, in the heart of the town. The shopfront stretched across two wide windows and the displays in them were artfully laid out. The window to the left of the door was decorated like a forest, with books dotted between trees, some balancing in branches.

To the right of the door, children's books were spread out amongst a variety of toy vehicles: some loaded in the carriages of a toy train, some flying in aeroplanes, some on horseback and some in open-top cars. It was fascinating, and Josie stood gazing at it until Tara's grinning face appeared in the display, making her jump.

The bell tinkled as she walked inside. "This place is gorgeous," she said to Tara as she embraced her in a hug.

"I'm so glad you're here! We should have Monday morning coffee every week!"

Josie followed her to the back of the deserted shop, where Amber sat in the cosy children's corner with Kieron. The colourful carpet was adorned with bright beanbags and cushions and a few cuddly toys.

Josie scanned the area. "This is so cute."

"The lower shelves in the kids' corner are full of second-hand books," Tara told her. "Because kids are brutal! The nice ones are high up, out of reach."

"The kids' corner was Tara's idea," Amber said proudly. "And she does the window displays."

Josie was impressed. "I love the windows!"

"She's given the place a makeover since she started," Amber said. "It used to be very dreary here."

"The things I have to do to make it acceptable for my friends to visit me at work! The complimentary coffee was my idea too." She grinned as she headed to a small table with a coffee urn.

"So your creepy boss isn't here today?" Josie asked.

Tara glanced around. "He's in the back," she said quietly.

Amber shook her head. "He's not creepy."

"You should see the way he looks at me!" Tara said. "And he asks me out for a drink every weekend. It's basically harassment."

"He sounds annoying," Josie agreed.

"James is lovely," Amber insisted, passing a board book to Kieron.

"You don't have to work with him …" Tara fell silent as a tall blond guy walked over to them.

He winked at Tara. "Talking about me?"

"Nope," she replied. "Never."

His eyebrows twitched. "Hard at work, I see."

"I'm having a coffee break," she said.

"You're not supposed to take your coffee break in the middle of the shop."

Tara rolled her eyes. "We've not got any customers."

When his eyes landed on Josie, she held out her hand and introduced herself.

"You're James?" she said, unable to hide her surprise. "You're not quite how I pictured you."

His gaze shifted to Tara. "So you *have* been talking about me."

"Sometimes I mention my slave driver of a boss!" She waved a hand as though shooing him away. "Everything's under control out here. Why don't you get back in your office?"

His eyes sparkled with amusement. "I can't join you for a coffee?"

"No," Tara said tersely.

"Because you want to talk about me?" he said, backing away.

"Just go!" Tara snapped.

He wandered casually behind the counter of the shop and disappeared from view.

"Tara thinks that's harassment," Amber said.

"It is!"

"He's gorgeous," Josie said.

"That doesn't excuse the constant flirting! If he was fat and balding you'd agree that his behaviour was unacceptable."

Josie ignored the remark, though Tara had a good point. "And he's asked you out?"

"Every week."

Josie grinned. "How can you resist?"

"He's my boss," Tara said. "And he's kind of annoying. Did you notice his cocky eyebrow movements? It drives me crazy."

"But the hair," Josie said with a sigh. "It looks so soft and silky. I'd just want to stroke it all the time."

"Urgh! Maybe you should ask him out."

"No way," Josie said.

"Oh yeah," Tara said wearily. "You've got a boyfriend hidden away somewhere!"

There was a short pause before Josie spoke. "I haven't actually."

"What?" Amber said. "What happened?"

"We broke up at the weekend."

"Oh my God!" Tara squealed. "Did you ask Sam out yet?"

Josie set her coffee down as she laughed. "No."

"Does Sam know you're single?" Tara asked.

"No. Although I'm fairly sure he overheard me telling my sister that I can't stop thinking about him."

Amber reached to pick Kieron up as he stumbled over a cushion. "It's so exciting. You and Sam will make such a cute couple."

"Let's not get too excited," Josie said. "I don't know if anything's going to happen with Sam."

There was a loaded silence before Amber and Tara started laughing. The more Josie protested, the more they laughed. She was trying not to get her hopes up too much, though, worried that she'd misread things and Sam wasn't interested.

The girls reassured her that he was interested, but she was impatient to find out for definite.

CHAPTER 21

The week dragged on without any sign of Sam. Josie was hoping she might bump into him, but she had no such luck. Jack called twice, just for a chat. That was more than he'd called her when they were together. He seemed genuinely concerned about their friendship, and Josie was glad they could stay in touch.

By Friday, she was desperate to see Sam. Spending time with him without feeling guilty about her feelings for him was a thrilling prospect.

She didn't see him when she first walked into the pub, but when she sat with Amber and Tara, she scanned the room again and saw him by the pool table. He flashed his lovely smile in her direction.

"Did you just get butterflies?" Amber said. Apparently Amber had caught her looking at Sam, though she'd been deep in conversation with Tara.

"What?" Josie said, innocently.

"You did, didn't you? When he smiled at you, you got butterflies?"

Josie didn't answer but felt the heat rise to her cheeks.

She turned her attention back to the girls. "So James said what?" she asked Tara, hoping to redirect the conversation back to her.

Tara shook her head. "Let's talk about Sam. Have you got a plan?"

Josie shook her head.

"It's simple," Amber said. "Walk home with him again tonight. Tell him you split up with Jack. And then kiss him."

"It's a great plan!" Tara agreed.

Josie's face lit up at the thought of it. "Maybe." She searched him out once again, then looked away quickly. He was playing pool and laughing. Her stomach really did go all fluttery every time she saw him. In the last few weeks, Sam had taken over her every thought, and now she could hardly keep her eyes off him.

She steered the conversation away from herself and then tried very hard to focus on conversations with Tara and Amber, but the glances she and Sam exchanged across the crowded room became more frequent and more meaningful.

She'd moved to the bar to get more drinks when he sidled up beside her with a silly grin on his face.

Her face twitched into a similar expression. "Hello."

"Having fun?"

"Always," she said, her eyes flirting with him.

Andy appeared and broke the tension between them. "What can I get you, Josie?"

She ordered drinks for herself and the girls, and with a glance at Sam's empty glass, ordered him a pint too.

"I'll get them," he said, when she reached for her purse.

"Thank you." She turned and smiled at him. "How was your week?"

"Okay," he said. "Nothing special." He leaned an elbow on the bar but the casual gesture was somehow awkward. His

Adam's apple bobbed. "I had a drink with Max on Wednesday. He told me you'd split up with Jack?"

So he already knew. "Yeah."

"Sorry."

She shrugged. "It's not really a big deal." Her smile was forced. "Apparently most long-distance relationships don't work out so it wasn't a big surprise …" She'd meant to sound jokey but her tone missed its mark. She was nervous and uncomfortable.

Sam shifted his weight, standing up straighter. "I wasn't going to say I told you so or anything."

"I know," she said gently.

"And you're okay about it?"

"Yes." She brightened and he smiled warmly. "And I still disagree with your view on long-distance relationships …"

"Really?" he said, amused. "Even though you just proved me right?!"

"All I proved is that you have to be really committed. But I definitely think that if you're really committed, you can make it work. I even think it can be quite romantic."

He shook his head. "It never works."

Over his shoulder, she noticed the guys glaring at them from beside the pool table. "I think they're waiting for you."

"I said I'd play another game of pool …"

"Try not to lose this one." She'd been watching when he lost the last game.

"Hey! I was distracted."

"Really?" She relaxed as he smiled cheekily. "By what?"

He picked up his drink, his eyes sparkling. "I don't know." At the pool table, someone grew impatient and called his name. He took a step away from her, then turned back and lifted his glass. "I'll probably go after this."

She nodded. "I'll walk with you if that's okay?"

The dimple appeared in his cheek again. "How else would you find your way home?"

It was half an hour later when they stepped out of the pub together. Josie was surprised by the rain. It had been drizzling when she arrived, but now it was coming down heavily. The disappointment she felt was out of proportion. They'd have to get a lift home with Andy, and she'd miss out on spending time alone with Sam. She'd been hoping for a goodnight kiss.

"Should we ask Andy to drive us?" she said, hovering in the doorway.

Sam zipped his jacket up and looked at her blankly. "Why?"

She laughed as he stepped out into the street. "The rain."

"Is it raining?" Walking backwards, he flashed a grin. "Come on …"

He held his hand out and she hurried to catch up with him. She was completely drenched in no time, but she was more aware of Sam's hand in hers than the torrential rain.

She laughed loudly, and when he turned to her, she nudged him into a puddle. In return he kicked water up at her.

"Have you noticed it's raining?" he said.

"I wondered why my feet were soaking wet!"

"It's your inappropriate footwear."

"I do spend a lot of time with cold wet feet recently."

"Time to admit you're a country girl and get some wellies?"

"No chance!"

They were completely drenched when they arrived at the house. Josie turned to Sam as he lingered in the doorway. All she wanted to do was reach up and kiss him. They gazed at each other, the sound of the rain on the covered patio drowning everything out. The air was charged between them, but she hesitated too long. Why didn't she just kiss him?

"I better go and get dry," he said, shaking his head and sending drips flying from his hair. After a couple of steps away from her, he stopped and turned back uncertainly. Moving quickly, she closed the gap between them. His arms snaked around her and pulled her closer still.

Her hands on his face drew his lips to hers. Not that he needed any encouragement. He kissed her greedily. The first time they'd kissed it was gentle and tender. This time it was full of urgency. Their bodies pressed forcefully together.

She didn't want to stop, but the rain had soaked through to her skin, and Sam's body heat wasn't quite enough to keep her warm.

"You should get in and get dry." He pulled back, brushing the wet hair from her face. "You're shivering."

"I'm fine." But her teeth chattered until she clamped her jaw shut.

Sam kissed her once more before she hurried inside, grinning.

CHAPTER 22

The birdsong had never sounded so sweet when she woke the next morning. She practically floated down to breakfast.

"Someone's cheerful this morning." Annette poured them both coffee. "Had a good night did you?"

"Very good."

Annette waited, a sly smile on her face. Josie didn't elaborate, just sipped her coffee and beamed.

"Sam's coming over later." Annette popped bread in the toaster but kept a close eye on Josie's reaction. "I've got some jobs for him."

Josie pursed her lips together in an attempt to stop grinning, but it didn't help much. She couldn't wait to see him again and was happy she wouldn't have to search him out or spend time wondering when she'd see him again.

"Lizzie called last night too." Annette put toast on the table and sat opposite Josie. "She and Max are going to come over later. They want to take us out to the pub for dinner. I think I'll stay here though and let you young 'uns go alone."

"Don't be daft," Josie said. "We'll all go. It'll be fun."

After breakfast, Josie went through the usual routine with the dogs. They had two beagles staying – cute dogs and well behaved. It was a glorious day in late May. The weather was unusually warm. Josie spent a pleasant morning walking the dogs and playing with them. In the afternoon, she put on a pair of shorts and vest top to work on her tan. Although, after spending so much time outdoors she already had a lovely bronze glow. After applying a layer of sunscreen, she lay with her face to the sun. The noisy birds sang sweetly, making her smile. They'd annoyed her so much when she'd first arrived, but now she found the sound soothing.

It was utterly relaxing, and sleep had just begun to creep over her when the sound of an engine rumbling disturbed her peace. Sam was down at the barn on a ride-on lawnmower. He drove it up to the house and then killed the motor.

"You're going to tell me to move, aren't you?" she said, her face lighting up.

"'Fraid so," he replied.

"Well there's no need to look so happy about disturbing my peace!"

"It won't take long." He looked slightly apologetic. "Then you can have your spot back."

She gathered up the blanket. They exchanged a look before she left him to it and went inside.

"I could mow the lawn," she said to Annette in the living room. "Don't we look a bit pathetic getting a man to cut the grass? I'm quite capable of driving the mower around."

"Sam always does it," Annette said, looking amused. "If that makes me pathetic, so be it! And I wanted him to do it today before this job in Brighton starts. I thought you'd be happy to see him."

"I was enjoying the peace until he showed up," she said,

but her face gave away how happy she was to see him. "He's working in Brighton?"

"Hmm. Didn't he mention it?"

"No. I haven't really had chance to talk to him properly."

"You told him about Jack, though?"

She nodded. "Yeah."

"And what did he have to say about that?"

Josie laughed. "You're very nosey today!" Annette just smiled and looked at her expectantly. "He didn't say a lot ... but he seemed quite happy about it." The memory of kissing him the previous evening jumped into her head. He'd definitely seemed happy.

Annette didn't comment further, and Josie grabbed a cold drink and wandered back outside. She spread her blanket out again and sat down, inhaling the wonderful aroma of freshly cut grass. Sam was working his way from the house towards the barn. For a few minutes, Josie watched him, taking in the look of concentration on his face. When he glanced over, she was embarrassed at being caught and lay down to enjoy the sunshine once again.

The noise of the lawnmower finally died out half an hour later. A few minutes after that, Josie was aware of a shadow falling across her and opened her eyes as Sam flopped down beside her.

"I'm hot," he said wearily.

She passed him her bottle of water and he gulped at it before lying down on the blanket and closing his eyes. Josie stared at his face, then watched the steady rise and fall of his chest. He looked so relaxed. Her heart was beating fast and she averted her gaze, worried that he'd catch her staring again.

"I told Annette I could mow the grass," she said. "Seems daft for you to do it when I'm quite capable."

Lazily, he opened his eyes. "Don't ever cut this grass," he said flatly.

Her mouth twitched to a confused smile. "Why not?"

"It's *my* job," he muttered.

"What?" She couldn't tell if he was being serious or not.

His eyes opened fully and he sat up, his gaze roaming over the freshly cut lawn. "I've been cutting this grass since I was ten years old. So that's like …" He winced slightly and sucked in a breath. "Twenty-five years. For twenty-five years no one but me has mowed this lawn. Even when I was living in Bristol I used to come back and mow the grass. Don't start stealing my jobs."

"Okay," she said, beaming. "Since you have so much experience!"

He lay down again. "Annette will still offer to pay me. I think the last time I accepted money I was about sixteen, but she still offers. I don't know what the rate would be now. Do you reckon she'd give me more than the 50p she used to give me when I was a teenager?"

Josie laughed and lay beside him. She concentrated on the fluffy clouds above, hoping that might help bring her heart rate back to a more normal tempo.

"Don't laugh at me," she said, after a few minutes, "but I've been reading all these books about dogs. About training dogs and different dog breeds and stuff … and now all the clouds look dog-shaped. Is that just me?"

"Yes," he said. "It's just you."

"Seriously, though …" She raised an arm to point. "German shepherd … beagle ... bulldog … Airedale."

"I think you know your dogs better than your clouds …" He moved her arm. "Cumulus … stratus … cirrus …"

She batted him away, laughing. "Okay, know-it-all, you're ruining my fun!"

"Well I don't see dogs," he said. "But I see a dinosaur."

"It's actually a golden retriever standing on its back legs, begging."

When she put her arm back down it landed alongside Sam's. The feel of his skin against hers made her light-headed. She was glad she was lying down.

"I think you need to get away from here more often," Sam said. "You've got dogs on the brain."

"You might be right." She paused, conscious of his hand so close to hers. She moved her little finger and it grazed the back of his hand. In return he gently stroked the back of her hand with his thumb. "I quite like it here, though."

"Do you?" He propped himself up on his elbow.

"Yes. Why?"

"I don't know. I just always had the impression that you wouldn't stay around long."

She looked into his green eyes, then quickly shifted her gaze to the clouds again. "Who knows. I'm surprised by how much I like it here. Everything is turning out way better than I expected."

His fingers continued trailing over her hand. "Did Annette tell you I'll be working in Brighton for a few weeks?"

"She mentioned something."

"I leave tomorrow."

Josie felt a ridiculous sense of panic, which she hoped didn't show. "So you stay down there and come back at the weekends?"

"We only get Sunday off and it's too far to come back for a day."

"Oh." Josie's voice was barely a squeak. "What is it you're doing there?"

"It's a new build. Some big six-bedroom house. It's already underway but they keep hitting problems, and now the company's so far behind schedule that they're bringing in a load of guys to get it finished as quickly as possible."

"How long will that take then?"

"I don't really know. They're saying three to four weeks but that could change."

Josie stared at the changing shapes of the clouds, trying to think of something casual to say. Nothing sprang to mind. She actually wanted to laugh. Finally, she'd split up with Jack and could spend time with Sam without feeling guilty, but he wasn't going to be around.

"I know what you're thinking," Sam said, hooking his hands behind his head.

She flashed him a puzzled smile.

"You're wondering how you're going to get home from the pub on Friday nights without me to escort you."

She spluttered out a laugh. Although, now that he mentioned it, she realised he had a point. She loved her evening walk with Sam after a night in the Bluebell Inn. "I don't know how I'll manage!"

"I'll have a word with Andy. He'll be happy to drive you home. Obviously he's not as charming and quick-witted as I am, but he'll get you safely home."

Their eyes locked, and after a moment Josie's smile faltered. "I'll miss you," she blurted out quietly.

"I'll miss you too." He leaned closer, his lips gently brushing hers. Her heart hammered on her ribcage, and she hooked an arm around his neck, greedily pulling him closer.

After a few minutes they broke apart, grinning at each other.

"I was going to ask you to have dinner with me tonight," Sam said. "But Max called me earlier and said we're all going to the pub. It'll just have to be another double date, I'm afraid."

Josie closed her eyes in embarrassment as she remembered her conversation with Lizzie the previous week. "You heard me talking to Lizzie, didn't you?"

"It was hard not to. The window was wide open."

Josie felt her cheeks turning pink.

"It's all right," Sam said. "I can't stop thinking about you either."

She reached up and lightly kissed his lips. "That's okay then."

"As soon as I get back from Brighton I'll take you on a proper date."

"I can't wait."

"I think I better go home and shower now."

She wrinkled her nose as she pretended to sniff him. "Good idea."

Max and Lizzie arrived late in the afternoon, just as Sam was arriving back, fresh from his shower. Between the four of them, they convinced Annette to have dinner at the pub too. She jokily told Andy that she'd been bullied into it when they arrived but seemed to enjoy herself regardless.

It was yet another evening when Lizzie didn't drink. She used driving as an excuse, but Josie didn't quite buy it. There was something different about Lizzie too. She looked exhausted and yawned frequently throughout their meal in the pub. With a laugh, she blamed it on jet lag, but that was surely dragging on a bit now. For the first time, Josie had an inkling that Sam might be right. Maybe Lizzie *was* pregnant. If she was, she obviously didn't want anyone to know yet.

It was a lovely evening. The atmosphere was relaxed and conversation was light and cheerful as always. As much as Josie enjoyed it, she looked forward to a date with just her and Sam. It was an effort to keep her hands off him. She hoped the next few weeks without him around would go quickly. She expected the opposite, and on the walk home she felt suddenly melancholy. Lizzie dropped back to walk with her.

"I take it something's going on with you and Sam," she said quietly. "Judging from the way you gazed at each other all evening!"

"Is it that obvious?"

"Yes!"

Josie managed a half-smile and shook her head. "I can't believe I finally split up with Jack and Sam's going away. Talk about bad timing."

"Maybe it's a good thing," Lizzie mused. "You don't want to jump straight into another relationship. A bit of breathing space will probably be good." It was a typical response from Lizzie; she was always so sensible and level-headed.

"Maybe," Josie said, though really she disagreed. She didn't need breathing space. Her feelings for Sam were nothing like what she'd felt for Jack. And it wasn't just the excitement of a new relationship; it was more than that. "But I hate the thought of not seeing him for three weeks. I'll miss him so much."

"Aww! You love him!"

Josie blushed bright red and bumped her shoulder against Lizzie's.

"Seriously, though," Lizzie said. "You never spoke about Jack like that. I've never heard you talk about any guy like that."

Josie stared ahead at Sam and butterflies took flight around her whole body.

"He'll be back before you know it," Lizzie said, then went quiet when they caught up to the others at the gate.

She hoped so.

CHAPTER 23

S am promised he'd see Josie the next day before he left, and she was pleasantly surprised to find him in the barn the next morning when she went out to the dogs. He was sitting on Brendan's sister's couch, playing around with the two beagles.

"These guys are cute," he said, as Josie leaned on the stable door. Then he walked over and kissed her like it was the most natural thing in the world. "I'd have come up to the house, but I was hoping to get some time alone with you."

She opened the door and bent to stroke the dogs. "I'm afraid I have to work this morning."

"You call this work?" He bent to ruffle the fur of the excited dog. "This is too much fun to be work."

"I suppose I can't complain," she agreed. "When do you have to leave?"

"Not until this afternoon. I thought we could walk the dogs and then have a quick lunch at my place?"

She agreed happily, glad to have some time with him before he left. They spent a wonderful couple of hours wandering the countryside. Sam was so easy to be around and conversation flowed seamlessly.

At lunchtime they sat out on Sam's patio eating sandwiches. Josie had taken the dogs back home and told Annette her lunch plans. It was a nice little garden at the back of Sam's house, and they enjoyed the peaceful surroundings as the sun came and went between fluffy white clouds. They sat opposite each other, bare legs touching beneath the table.

"How did you get into the building work?" Josie asked, polishing off her sandwich. "Have you always done it?"

"Yep. My mum sent me to a woodwork class one summer when I was a kid and I got really into it. I started making furniture when I was a teenager and did carpentry at college. When I figured out it was hard to make a living from making furniture, I got a job with a construction company." He pushed his plate away and leaned back in his chair. "It's not glamorous but I like it."

"What kind of furniture did you make?"

"All sorts of stuff." He glanced around. "I made this table. And the chairs. Pretty much anything around here made from wood I made myself."

"Really?" She examined the patio furniture in a new light. "That's amazing."

"I still do some custom orders for furniture in my spare time. Mainly for people who know me. And I do the odd bits just for fun. My garage has been turned into a workshop over the years."

"I can't believe I didn't know that about you. Annette is always singing your praises, but she never mentioned that."

"Half the furniture in her house is my stuff," he said casually.

Josie beamed excitedly. "Can I see your workshop?"

He nodded and stood up. "It's not very exciting, though. It's a bit of a mess."

The smell hit her as soon as he opened the garage door: all woody and fresh. Wood shavings crunched underfoot as she walked around the furniture in various stages of assembly and repair.

Sam leaned on the doorframe, watching intently as she explored his space.

"This is beautiful." She gazed at an antique-looking dresser.

"It's mahogany," he said, moving beside her. "I'm just restoring it. Some of the wood's damaged here ..." He ran a hand along the scratches in the front. "I'm thinking about taking out these panels and putting glass in to make a display case ... Then there are some chips in the wood on this corner ..." He kept talking, mesmerising Josie with his passion for the project.

He'd just moved around the side of the dresser, pointing out some other imperfection, when he stopped abruptly. "Sorry. I'm going on. It's boring."

"It's not," she said, trying her best to look serious.

"Why are you laughing, then?" His mouth twitched to a smile.

"I'm not laughing." She was, though; she couldn't help it. "Sorry." She took his hand. "I wasn't laughing at you. I just remembered something Tara and Amber told me."

"What?"

"They were telling me about you going on a date with whatshername ... the woman from the pharmacy ..."

His eyebrows shot up. "Belinda?"

"Yes. Apparently she said you were so shy you barely spoke ..." She grinned. "It seems quite hard to believe now ..."

"Have you met Belinda?" He raised his hand to make a talking motion with his thumb and fingers. "I couldn't get a word in!"

"You don't seem to have a problem with your conversational skills."

He looked serious. "Get me talking about furniture and it's hard to shut me up. I realise it's pretty boring."

"It's not." She walked around some more, taking it all in. "It's fascinating, actually. That you have something you love so much. I always wanted that. I never really found anything."

"Seems like you do a great job at the kennels."

"I don't know about that but I enjoy it. It's not my life's dream, though."

"What is then?"

"I don't know. That's always been my problem – I'm constantly looking for something but maybe there just isn't anything. For a while I was sure I wanted to get into acting. I was working on a TV show for a while but it never took off. It was so much fun."

"I can imagine you as an actress," he said, smiling.

"It's a hard business to get into. I gave it a try, anyway." She laughed. "You wouldn't believe how many auditions I went to!"

"It sounds frustrating."

She bit her lip, remembering how many times she'd got her hopes up after an audition only to be rejected. "I guess it wasn't meant to be."

Sam frowned. "Annette thinks you're doing an amazing job for her. She says you have a head for business and a knack with people."

Josie registered the fact that there was no mention of how she handled the dogs. "It's definitely one of the more enjoyable jobs I've had." She paused, looking at a vaguely familiar table. "Is this the one you got from Brendan?"

He nodded beside her. "I sanded it down and gave it a good polish and a coat of varnish."

"It looks great. Will you sell it?"

"Yeah. I take stuff to car boot sales now and then. I don't make a lot of money from it – it's more of a self-sustaining hobby. At some point this place gets rammed with stuff and I just need to make space."

"I think it's a nice hobby." They drifted back outside just as the sun reappeared from behind a cloud.

"I can't believe the girls told you about Belinda." Sam's arms snaked around her waist, drawing her close. "What else have they been saying about me?"

"Not much … they said you lived in Bristol for a while with your girlfriend, but it didn't work out."

"I'm not sure I like you hanging around with those two. They're telling all my secrets."

"What happened? With the girlfriend in Bristol?"

He shrugged. "We wanted different things."

"It must have been pretty serious, though, if you were living together?"

"Not serious enough to last," he said.

Clearly he didn't want to talk about it, which made Josie curious. "How long were you together?"

"Why are we talking about my ex?"

"Because I'm nosey," she said. "Also because that's what people do on dates. Talk about their lives to get to know each other better."

"Who said this was a date?" He gave her a cheeky grin.

"Feels like a date to me," she said, her arms lightly hooking around his neck.

"You must have very low standards. The bread for the sandwiches wasn't even fresh."

"I did notice that."

"As soon as I get back we'll have a proper date."

"Great. Then I can quiz you about your ex-girlfriends!"

"I'm sure we can find more interesting topics of conversation."

"We'll see. Do you think on a proper date you can try not to look at your watch so often? It's off-putting."

"Sorry." He automatically glanced at his wrist again.

"You need to go?"

"I do, unfortunately." His arms tightened around her as he leaned down to kiss her. Josie savoured the kisses. It was hard to pull away from him. When she finally left, it was with an ache in her chest she was sure would remain until she saw him again.

CHAPTER 24

On Monday morning, Josie sat on a bright orange beanbag in the children's corner of the Reading Room, telling Tara and Amber all about her weekend. There was a lot to fill them in on since she'd seen them on Friday. They happily indulged her in all her talk of Sam and reassured her that he'd be back before she knew it.

She was thankful to have the two of them as friends; they brought balance to her quiet days with Annette. They met another couple of times that week, and it was always relaxed and fun. She also had a trip out to Hope Cove for an afternoon on the beach with Lizzie. It was good to be close enough to call in on her sister without it being a major event.

The week didn't drag quite as much as she expected, and she spoke to Sam on the phone a couple of times.

It was Friday when she really missed him. The evening in the Bluebell Inn wasn't the same without him around. Josie spent a lot of time glancing around looking for him. It was automatic. Every time she looked up, she expected him to be there, grinning at her across the room. It was earlier than usual when she slipped away from the pub.

When Amber had told her to ask Andy for a lift home, she'd waved the suggestion away, insisting on walking. It was such a short distance, it seemed silly to trouble someone for a lift. Except it seemed longer than usual that evening, and everything was so creepy in the dark.

When her phone rang, she pulled it from her pocket and grinned when she saw Sam's name on the display.

"Hi," she said, excited by the call.

"Hi," he said quickly. "Sorry. I know you'll be in the pub, but I just had a really quick question …"

"It's fine." She hugged the phone closer to her ear, as though that made her somehow closer to him. "I already left the pub. I'm just walking home."

"Boring night, was it?"

"It was okay," she said. "What did you want to ask me?"

"Oh, yeah! Small breed of dog … nine letters … Any ideas? Fourth letter's an 'h'. I'm stumped."

She blurted out a laugh. "Sam, are you doing a crossword?"

"Are you going to tease me now? You don't know the answer either, do you? As someone who works at a dog kennels I'd have thought—"

"Chihuahua!" she said, grinning widely.

An owl screeched nearby and chills ran down the back of her neck. Her smile slipped and she quickened her pace. What was it about the sound of wildlife in the dark? It always freaked her out.

"Are you still under the street lights?" Sam asked casually.

"No. I just left them."

"Almost home then," he said. "Put me on speaker and turn the torch on your phone on …"

She did as he said, pressing the buttons carefully so she didn't accidentally cut him off.

"That's better," she said, as the light from her phone illuminated the road in front of her.

"Thank goodness you always carry a torch with you," Sam said cheekily.

"I wouldn't leave the house without one! Anyway, where exactly are you? What kind of place has less going on than Averton on a Friday night? I can't believe you're stuck in doing crosswords!"

"I decided I'd just have a quiet night in. And I'm not really doing a crossword. I was just testing your knowledge. You passed the test!"

She laughed. "And how's the job going?"

"It's pretty good. I wave my magic wand and a house appears from nothing. You'd be impressed!"

"I'm very impressed," she said.

"And how are things there?" Sam asked. "Lost any dogs recently?"

"No!"

"You're doing well."

"I am actually. We've been a bit busier this week. It's tiring."

"I know. When I was younger I spent my summers working for Wendy and Annette. It's hard work."

"I can't imagine how it is when the kennels are full."

"You'll find out, no doubt. Then you'll be wishing you didn't plaster the entire area in flyers and posters."

She couldn't help but laugh. Somehow she'd reached the gate at Oakbrook. She'd barely noticed the last part of the walk. "I just wanted to drum up business," she said.

"I think you managed it."

"I suppose I did." She thought of the bookings that had been coming in over the past week. It was a relief that all her advertising was paying off.

At the kitchen door she took the phone off speaker and

moved it back to her ear. Macy and Charlie came to greet her, and she stroked them affectionately before ushering them back to their beds.

"You've gone quiet?" Sam said.

"Have I?" she said in a loud whisper. She didn't want to wake Annette.

"Are you home already?"

She lowered herself into a chair at the kitchen table. "Yeah."

"And you've brought me inside?!"

"Yes." She beamed into the phone. "Is that a problem?"

"Not at all," he said lightly, before launching into another anecdote about the project he was working on in Brighton. It was so lovely chatting to him, and she stayed in the kitchen whispering into the phone for almost an hour before she finally said goodnight.

The next week followed in much the same way as the previous. They had eight dogs staying in the kennels so her days were busy trekking over the countryside and trying her hand at obedience training. Unfortunately, the dogs still ran rings around her, and the obedience training seemed to make the dogs naughtier rather than obedient.

She was amused and suspicious on Friday night when she stepped out of the Bluebell Inn and her phone rang immediately.

"How did you do that?"

"What?" Sam asked innocently.

"I just left the pub," she said. "I literally just stepped outside."

"Good timing then."

"Is it?" she asked, glancing behind her into the pub

window. Did he have a spy? "Because you did the same thing last week. It seems like more than good timing."

"Great timing?" he suggested. "Perfect timing?"

She laughed and set off through the village.

"How was the pub?"

"Hmm." Her mouth twitched into a half-smile. "There was a bit of an incident."

"Have I missed some excitement?"

"We were playing darts …"

"*You* were playing darts?" he asked, his surprise evident.

"Yeah. The tall guy with the flat cap asked me to join his team."

"Martin? He's replacing me already?"

"Yes," she said, amused.

"Can you even play darts?"

"He was teaching me. And it was going well." She paused and smiled at the memory. "What's the name of the short guy with the curly hair?"

"Dean?"

"Yeah. So it was my turn, and Dean was standing just to the side …"

"Oh my God. Does this story involve paramedics? Tell me Dean survived the evening?"

"Yes!" she said, laughing lightly. "But the dart somehow hit the edge of the board and bounced off. It flew sideways and smacked Dean on the head."

"Ouch."

"It didn't stab him or anything!"

"Hmm. Did anyone tease you about this?"

"Everyone! Martin marched me away from the dartboard and sat me back with Amber and Tara. He said I'm banned from going anywhere near it! And then he loudly announced that if anyone ever sees me with a dart in my hand they should tackle me to the ground! Stop laughing! It was really embarrassing."

"At least I still have my spot on the darts team."

"You definitely do!" Josie sighed, wishing he was beside her instead of on the other end of the phone. "Are you coming home anytime soon?"

"Looks like it'll be next weekend."

"Try and make it for the pub on Friday night. It's weird without you there."

"I guess I won't make it back until Sunday."

She beamed into the phone. Sunday was okay too. Just knowing he'd be back soon was good enough. "I can't wait."

CHAPTER 25

Josie didn't even bother messaging Amber on Monday morning, just set off for the Reading Room after she'd walked the dogs. It had become a regular meet-up.

"Sam called me again on Friday night," she said as she plonked herself down on a beanbag. She ruffled Kieron's hair when he toddled past her.

"That's sweet," Amber said.

"Right after I left the pub," Josie added, carefully monitoring Amber's reaction. "Literally as I stepped outside."

"That's good timing." Amber reached to wipe Kieron's nose, and Josie wasn't sure if it was just a ploy to avoid eye contact.

"That's exactly what he said!"

Tara gasped dramatically and glared at Amber. "Did you message him?"

"I was wondering the same," Josie said. "How did he know exactly when I was leaving?"

"Anyone could've messaged him," Amber insisted. "Why do you assume it was me?"

Josie shrugged. "Seems like something you would do."

"I was sitting right next to Tara. She'd have seen if I messaged Sam …"

"I don't watch you that closely," Tara said. "It was definitely you, wasn't it?"

"No." Amber laughed, and Josie couldn't tell if she was lying or not. "It's so cute that he calls you, though. Does he know when he'll be back yet?"

"He said it should be next weekend."

"Has he asked you on a date?" Tara asked.

"We haven't arranged anything yet. He's not sure when he'll be back." Josie assumed they'd have a proper date as soon as he got back, like he'd promised before he left.

"Only another week," Amber said. "It'll fly by."

It didn't, though. The week seemed to drag on and on. The closer it got to the weekend, the slower time seemed to go.

In the Bluebell on Friday night, she was subject to more teasing about the darts incident. It was actually quite comforting to be teased by the locals. She felt like part of the community.

"I'm going home," she said after a fun evening chatting with the girls and the other locals, who were becoming more familiar to her. "Keep an eye on Amber," she said to Tara. "Let me know if she's Sam's spy!"

"I'm not messaging him," Amber said adamantly. She laid her phone on the table and held up her hands. "I did speak to him earlier, though. He'll definitely be back this weekend. I invited him over for a drink tomorrow night, but he said he already has plans."

"What plans?" Tara said eagerly.

"I don't know," Amber said. "He was being a bit coy but I presume he's planning on taking Josie on a date!"

"That's a bit presumptuous," Josie said. "I might be busy."

Tara smirked. "Busy sitting in front of the TV with Annette?"

Josie couldn't help but laugh as she reached for her bag. Her evenings were pretty quiet these days, not that she minded. She said her goodbyes and headed for the door.

When she was outside, she peered in the window at Amber. The phone was still on the table, and she held her hands up again when she saw Josie checking up on her.

When Josie set off towards Oakbrook, she had her phone in her hand, waiting for it to ring. It didn't, though, and eventually she scrolled to Sam's number and pressed call.

"Your timing's not so good today," she said when he answered. It sounded like he was moving around, and he didn't say anything for a moment.

"Sorry," he said, finally. "Are you walking home already?"

"Yeah. I thought you'd know that!"

"I told you it was just good timing." She could imagine him smiling as he spoke, and she remembered what the girls had said about him taking her out the next day. She hoped that was his plan.

"How's work?" she asked.

"Job's all finished."

She grinned. "So you'll be home soon?"

"Mmhmm."

She was annoyed by his vague grunting. Couldn't he tell her exactly when he'd be back? She wanted to know to the nearest second. She'd just moved away from the streetlights when she saw movement ahead.

"You okay?" Sam said.

"Yeah." She slowed her pace and peered into the moonlit street. "There's someone on the road."

He laughed. "How rude. Someone else is walking on your stretch of road?"

"I never see anyone at this time of night. It's making me nervous."

"Don't worry. You live in a village now. You probably know him."

"How do you know it's a him?" she asked suspiciously. The figure was getting nearer and she smiled as she recognised his profile.

"Just a guess. Is he on the phone by any chance?"

She laughed and moved her phone aside as Sam neared her. She quickened her pace until she was in his arms, kissing him.

"When did you get home?" she asked when she finally pulled back.

He narrowed his eyes as though contemplating the question. "About three minutes ago. Maybe four. When did you call me?"

She grinned and squeezed him tightly. It was so good to have him back.

"I thought I'd come and walk you home. I hear there are some creepy characters roaming the streets this evening."

She gave him a quick nudge as they fell into step together. Their hands entwined automatically. "You scared me. It's creepy enough round here without you skulking around in the dark."

"I wasn't skulking around," he said, laughing. "I was coming to walk you home."

"I suppose I'll forgive you then."

He glanced at her and smiled warmly. "I don't really like working away."

"Try not to do it again anytime soon then."

"I won't," he said as they reached the gate at Oakbrook.

At the front door she couldn't bear the thought of saying goodnight to him so soon. "Do you want to come in for a beer or a cuppa?" she asked hesitantly. "Annette will be in bed."

He followed her confidently into the kitchen. "I was actually wondering if I could raid the fridge. I've got no food at home and I've barely eaten since breakfast."

"Be my guest," she said, bending to ruffle Macy's fur.

Sam scanned the contents of the fridge.

"There are frozen pizzas," she suggested.

"Perfect." He turned the oven on and then grabbed two beers from the fridge. "I like the changes you've made around here. Annette would never have had pizzas in the freezer before you came along. And there were only beers in the fridge on special occasions!"

She sat beside him at the table and they clinked their bottles together before falling into easy conversation. They stayed like that for an hour, chatting and laughing and fighting over pizza slices.

"You look exhausted," she said eventually. He'd stretched his legs out and leaned back in the chair, looking as though he might fall asleep like that.

"It's been a long day," he said through a yawn. "I should probably go and get some sleep."

Josie wondered when she'd see him again. He hadn't mentioned doing anything the next evening. Maybe the plans he'd mentioned to Amber were something else entirely. He kissed her when he stood up and then made a fuss of the dogs before moving to the door. "I'll see you soon," he said vaguely.

"Yeah." *But when?* "I thought maybe we could do something tomorrow, but Amber said you already had plans …"

He shook his head in amusement. "I told you this place was full of gossips. You can't have any secrets."

She forced a smile. He was doing quite a good job of keeping his plans secret. "So I'll just see you another time, if you already have plans for tomorrow?"

He hovered in the doorway. "I made the plans ages ago. I don't really want to change them …"

"No, of course not," she said quickly. "Don't worry about it."

"I can give you a call over the weekend, see what you're up to?"

"Yeah, whatever." Somehow the casual tone she was going for came out slightly manic. After spending three weeks desperate to see him, she was left feeling somewhat deflated.

CHAPTER 26

A t lunchtime on Saturday, Josie sat nursing a cup of tea on Amber's couch. "He said he was busy tonight but he'd call me." It wasn't the first time she'd relayed the information. The conversation was being well and truly rehashed and dissected.

"What would he be doing tonight?" Amber mused. "It's weird that he doesn't just say."

Her husband, Paul, lumbered in the front door laden down with shopping bags. He shouted hello as he passed the living room.

"What are you talking about?" he asked when he joined them ten minutes later.

"Sam," Amber said bluntly.

"I just saw him in Tesco," Paul said.

"Really?" Amber patted the chair beside her for him to sit down. "What was he doing?"

Paul's eyes narrowed. "Shopping," he said slowly.

"What was he buying?"

"Food, of course. It's Tesco! And I was too busy trying to

decipher your writing on the list to worry about what anyone else was buying."

"You're useless," Amber scolded playfully.

"Why do you want to know what Sam was buying?"

"Because he's got plans tonight and he won't tell us what he's doing."

"How dare he!"

The front door burst open and Tara barrelled in. "There you are," she said. "Did you see my message?"

Josie had started a group chat with the girls that morning to fill them in about Sam, but she'd not checked her phone since she'd arrived at Amber's place. Both her and Amber looked blankly at Tara.

"I saw his van in Newton Abbot as I was coming out of work." Tara dropped her handbag and flopped onto the couch.

"Well I hope you followed him," Paul said mockingly.

Tara sat up straighter. "He went in the chemist's, so I went in after he'd left."

"Ooh. What did he buy?" Paul said, his voice dripping with false intrigue. "Please tell us before I die of suspense."

Tara swatted at his leg. "This is serious business!"

"What did he buy?" Amber asked.

"Ibuprofen. But Belinda told me she was chatting to him …"

"Of course she was," Paul said. "It's Belinda. Going in that place is like being lined up for the Spanish inquisition. He should know better than to go in the chemist's at Newton Abbot."

Amber shushed him and looked at Tara. "Did Belinda know anything?"

"Nothing," Tara said dramatically. "Apparently he said he had no plans all weekend."

"Hmmm," Amber said. "Why's he lying?"

"He obviously doesn't want anyone to know what he's doing," Josie said. "Let's just stop talking about it."

"He must have a date," Paul said. "It's the only explanation."

"Of course he's not got a date," Amber said. "If he had, it would be with Josie."

"He can do whatever he wants." Josie stood abruptly. "I'm going home. This is crazy." She couldn't stand the suggestion that he was on a date with someone else. She was sure he wouldn't be, but just the thought made her want to go and curl up in bed and never come out.

"Wait here," Paul said, moving past Josie to the door. "I'll do some recon and see what I can find out." He glared at Amber. "I can't believe you've got me intrigued about this."

"Oh come on," Josie said. "Let's just drop the subject."

"I won't be long," Paul said, taking no notice of her.

Amber made more coffee, and Tara complained about James and her morning at work. Josie was happy at the change of subject.

They all looked to the door when Paul arrived back half an hour later. "He's definitely got a date."

"No!" Amber said. "He can't have."

Josie definitely wanted to go and hide away somewhere. Had she completely misread things between her and Sam? Surely not.

"I just had a stroll through the village," Paul said, "to make some casual enquiries. I went in the Bluebell to see if Andy knew anything, and Sam was in there having lunch." The women leaned in, hanging off Paul's every word. "So I got a pint and sat with him. Then casually asked about his plans for the weekend."

"And he said he had a date?" Tara asked.

"No! He said he had nothing on. So I said it's Saturday night, he should be out doing something fun. I may have made a remark about him not having a ball and chain or something …" He grimaced in Amber's direction. "But it was only to get him talking."

"And *did* you get him talking?" Amber said.

"He said he had a few things to do, but nothing exciting!" Paul looked outraged. "So he's lying to me now too!"

"So we don't know he's got a date?" Tara said.

"He's going on a date!" Paul said. "Otherwise he'd just say what he was doing. He wouldn't tell me he's got a date because he knows I'd tell Amber, Amber would tell Tara and everyone within a ten-mile radius would know within the hour!"

Josie laughed then and they all stared at her. "You know how crazy you all sound? You need to get a life! And me too. If he doesn't want to see me, he doesn't have to. And I'm not about to start throwing myself at him and demanding to know what he's doing all the time. You're a bunch of gossips!"

The three of them looked up at her like a group of naughty schoolkids. "I only wanted to talk to you about it because I thought you'd put my mind at ease and calm me down," she continued. "You've done the opposite."

"Sorry," they muttered. Kieron cried out, waking from his nap upstairs, and Paul jumped up to get him.

"I'm going home," Josie said calmly. "And I'm not going to worry about Sam. What will be, will be."

"Great attitude," Tara said as Josie made for the door.

"You're right," Amber said. "We should get a life!"

"I'll talk to you later," Josie called over her shoulder.

Her determination not to worry about Sam lasted about three minutes. She was walking home through the village when she remembered he'd been in the pub for lunch. It was too hard to resist a quick glance in the windows. There was no sign of him. His van was nowhere to be seen either. She ambled slowly home, hoping she might bump into him. When she got back to Oakbrook, Annette was in the kitchen, baking biscuits.

"Have you got plans this evening?" she asked as Josie kicked her shoes off.

"Nope."

"I thought you might be out with Sam …"

"No," Josie said. "He's got plans."

"Oh, really? What's he doing?"

Josie smiled. "No one knows!" She sighed and pushed her feet back into her shoes. "I'm going to check on the dogs." Rattling around the house wasn't going to do her any good, and she didn't want to get into speculation with Annette about what Sam was doing.

Eventually she gave up on trying not to think about him. She was out walking the dogs and stopped by the stream in the valley, sitting on a rock and staring into space. It was so frustrating: she'd spent three weeks missing him and counting the hours until he got back, and now she didn't even know when she'd see him next.

When her bum went numb against the rock, she called to the dogs and had a minor panic when only Macy and Charlie came to her. She'd got another lovely Labrador with her who was placid and obedient, or so Josie thought. She breathed a sigh of relief when the dog wandered out from behind a bush. Slowly, they set off for home.

She was settled on the couch watching TV that evening when Tara arrived, shouting hello as she let herself in.

"Well this is a sorry sight for a Saturday night," she said to Josie. "You and I need to have a proper night out some-time." She bent to greet Annette with a kiss on the cheek, then plonked herself on the couch beside Josie. "I just drove past Sam's house," she said. "His van's there and the lights are on."

"Right," Josie said flatly. "Well done on the detective work. Why exactly are you stalking Sam, though?"

"I'm not! I just don't like him being so secretive."

"He might have a friend over," Annette chimed in.

"Why would he be secretive about that?" Tara asked. "I think he's on a date."

"No!" Annette said. "He loves Josie. Why would he be on a date?"

"We don't know," Tara said, sinking back into the couch.

Josie let out an exasperated sigh. "Why don't you just go and knock on his door and find out what he's doing?"

"I can't do that," Tara said. "He's always telling us the village would be a better place if everyone minded their own business."

"Maybe he has a point," Josie said.

"Don't be daft!" Tara grinned cheekily as she stood up. "I've got to get to my mum's. We're having a takeaway. I'll leave you to it."

She was gone as quickly as she'd arrived, and Annette went back to her book. Josie tried very hard not to wonder what Sam was doing. It was five minutes later when Annette mumbled about not being able to hear the TV and reached for the remote.

"Since when are you interested in the TV?" Josie asked as Annette began banging the remote on the arm of the chair. "I thought you were reading your book."

Annette ignored her and frowned at the remote. "This thing's playing up again."

"Let me have a look," Josie said, reaching out for it.

"It used to do this a lot," Annette said, turning it over in her hand. "I need to take the back off and give things a wiggle around."

"Okay," Josie said, dipping her eyebrows. "Give it to me and I'll have a look."

"I know what to do," Annette said forcefully. "I need a little screwdriver, that's the only thing. We used to borrow a really tiny one from Sam. I don't have one small enough."

Josie's shoulders slouched and she raised her eyebrows at Annette. "Give me the remote!" she said firmly.

"Could you just nip round and ask Sam if we can borrow the screwdriver?"

"No!" Josie snapped. "I can't. Now pass me the remote!"

"Fine!" Annette said. She kept a firm hold of the remote and shuffled in her chair as though she might get up. "I'll just go myself if you can't do me one little favour. It would only take you five minutes to walk down and ask him for the screwdriver but if you can't manage that—"

"Oh, sit down!" Josie said. "I'll go. But what if he really is on a date?"

"Of course he's not on a date! Just go and ask for the screwdriver. Tell him it's for the TV remote. He knows the one."

Josie grumbled but reluctantly moved to the door. Walking quickly down the road, she was torn. If she was really honest, she was secretly pleased to have an excuse to go round to Sam's place. But at the same time she had the distinct feeling she was about to completely embarrass herself.

CHAPTER 27

Sam was wearing a crisp blue shirt. She noticed his clean shave about the same time the scent of his aftershave hit her. He looked and smelled delicious.

"I've been sent to borrow a screwdriver," she said bluntly.

"What kind?"

"A small one for the TV remote. Annette said you'd know."

A smirk hit his lips and Josie felt self-conscious. He opened the door wider and she stepped inside.

"It's in the kitchen."

She followed him through and stood in the doorway, scanning the room as he rifled through a drawer. Then he turned, holding up a screwdriver. "Do you want to stay for a drink?"

Her eyes flitted from him to the table. It was covered with a bright white cloth and two places were set, with a candle in the middle and a large bowl of salad to one side. "Are you expecting someone?"

The dimple appeared in his cheek when he smirked. "I arranged a date a few weeks ago but I think she might have

169

forgotten." He raised an eyebrow. "Shame because she was really hot too."

Josie bit her lip. "Annette didn't really need a screwdriver, did she?" He shook his head and crossed the room to her. She shoved him playfully. "You're so mean!"

"You're hanging out with the village gossips too much!"

"I'm not!" she insisted. "I asked you what you were doing tonight and you said you had plans."

"Plans I made with you three weeks ago! What else did you think I'd be doing?"

"I don't know."

"Tara was even following me in and out of shops today. She's not as stealth-like as she thinks."

"I didn't tell her to!"

"I know, they were like this well before you came along. Paul's just as bad."

"He's offended that you lied to him."

Sam grinned and moved to the fridge to pull out a bottle of wine. "So you're staying for a drink?"

Josie didn't reply as her gaze landed on the neatly set table again.

"Are you annoyed with me?" Concern wrinkled Sam's features. "I thought you'd see the funny side. If I'm in trouble I'd like to point out that I bought you flowers ..." He nodded to a bunch of red roses standing in an inch of water in the sink.

She moved to touch a petal, then automatically bent to sniff at them. "Thank you," she said quietly.

He eased the cork from the wine bottle. "You're annoyed, aren't you?"

"No." A slow smile crept across her face. "It's really lovely in here."

"Is it too much?" he asked.

"No," she said quickly. It wasn't too much; it was just

more than she was used to. Jack making an effort had generally been picking up his clothes from the floor and ordering a takeaway. "It's all perfect."

"It's my standard first date routine! Don't expect this treatment too often."

"I'll bear that in mind."

He put the wine bottle down when she went over and wrapped her arms around him. "What are you doing?"

"I was thinking about kissing you."

He frowned and shook his head. "You have to wait until the end of the evening, I'm afraid. It's a first date rule."

"Maybe you could bend the rules," she said, her lips grazing his.

"Maybe I could," he whispered.

His breath was fresh and minty, and she loved the feel of his soft lips on hers. Their kisses became more fervent and Sam groaned as Josie pushed her body closer to his and gently bit his lower lip.

"Do you know why kissing is generally saved for the end of the date?" he asked, pulling away.

She flashed a cheeky smile. "So you don't forget to eat dinner?"

"Exactly."

He didn't move away, though, but kept his arms firmly around her and gazed at her longingly.

She trailed a hand down his torso until it landed at his belt. "Any chance dinner can wait?"

A smile spread over his face. His lips found hers again. A moment later he tugged her T-shirt over her head.

"Dinner can definitely wait."

CHAPTER 28

That first date set the tone for the next two weeks. Life became a whirlwind filled with laughter and whispering and love-making. They spent every spare moment together, and Josie was as happy as she'd ever been.

When Sam mentioned doing a car boot sale one Sunday, Josie invited herself along. Her phone rang as Sam arrived to pick her up. Seeing it was Jack, she shoved the phone back in her pocket, feeling slightly guilty. He'd tried to call her a few times over the last few days, but he had a knack for calling at a bad time. She'd definitely call him back soon.

"Dinner will be ready at five," Annette called as Josie hurried out the door. They'd already had this conversation. Lizzie and Max were coming over and Annette had told Josie to invite Sam too.

"I know," she called over her shoulder. "See you later."

"Have fun!"

Sam greeted her with a kiss when she climbed into his van. "Ready for your first car boot sale?"

"I'm so excited."

"Don't be," he said, as they set off. "It's pretty boring."

"I don't believe you! By the way, Annette's cooking. We're supposed to be back by five for dinner. Lizzie and Max are coming over."

"I know. Max called me. Seems like they wanted to make sure they got us all together …"

"What's that look for?" she asked as he smirked.

"I just think there might be some sort of announcement, that's all."

"She's not pregnant!" Josie insisted, yet again. She looked out of the window as they drove through the village. "Lizzie would have told me already."

"People wait until they've had scans and stuff."

She shook her head. "I'm telling you I'd know about it."

"We'll see!"

It was only a twenty-minute drive to Exeter racecourse, and Josie was surprised at the number of cars and vans as they pulled into a spot beside the racetrack. There were rows and rows of vehicles and people unloading various items.

"It's not boring at all," she said to Sam. "It's exciting!"

"I promise you'll be bored after sitting here for three hours."

"I bet I won't." Her eyes were fixed out the window, taking in the bustle. "I didn't expect it to be so busy. This place is huge."

"There should be a good crowd since the weather's so nice. Hopefully I can get rid of everything. I hate taking stuff home again."

"I'm excited about bartering," Josie said, hopping out of the van. It was a glorious day with a bright blue sky and warmth in the air.

"I hate it," Sam said, walking round and heaving the side

door of the van open. "I'm usually thinking about the effort of reloading the van with anything that doesn't sell, so I mostly just take whatever people offer."

"That's not very good business."

He dragged a cardboard box out of the van and placed it on the ground before beginning to unload the furniture.

"I told you – it's a hobby not a business."

Josie opened the box and peered in. "Wow! Where did you get this stuff from?"

"People give me things," he said, setting Brendan's old table carefully down. "Everyone in the village knows I do car boot sales. Any time anyone has a clear out, they give me their junk!"

"This isn't junk." She held up a beautifully ornate teapot. "It's treasure! I'm tempted to keep it."

Sam chuckled and climbed into the back of the van. He passed things out to Josie, who thoroughly enjoyed setting everything up. "It's like playing shop."

"Yep." He jumped down from the van. "You made it look a bit more organised than when I do it."

"How much do you want for Brendan's table?" she asked, running a hand across the smooth surface. It was a good-sized sturdy table in perfect condition.

"I gave him twenty quid for it so if I get thirty I'll be happy."

"I'm sure you can get at least fifty."

"I think you might be slightly optimistic. Everyone here is after a bargain. They really like to haggle. I'll be surprised if I get thirty."

Josie glanced at a couple opposite, unloading their car. "Ooh, I like that vase," she said to no one in particular. She migrated over for a closer look and then strayed to the other sellers nearby to have a look what was on offer.

It was another half hour before customers began to arrive.

Sam was amused when Josie told him off for selling the tea set too cheaply – just a measly two pounds. Then he sold a nice little set of drawers for six pounds and a set of two stools for a tenner. Every time he sold something, she chastised him for letting it go too cheaply.

"It's a car boot sale!" He casually draped an arm around her shoulders as they watched the couple walk away with the stools. "People want cheap stuff."

"That's not true." She leaned into him, enjoying the weight of his arm around her. "They want a bargain. There's a big difference."

"You can go and have a wander around," Sam said when he caught her looking up and down the row. "You don't need to stay here."

She set off to explore with a smile on her face. "Just don't give everything away for free while I'm gone."

He shook his head in amusement and she turned her attention to the other sellers nearby. When she got a whiff of hotdogs she felt a pang of hunger. Then she thought of Annette cooking a roast dinner and decided she'd better wait.

She hadn't gone far when she glanced back in Sam's direction. He was leaning casually against the van. He had half an eye on the middle-aged couple who were having a good look at Brendan's table. Sam really was a terrible salesman, she thought to herself. She probably ought to go back and help him out.

It only took a moment to retrace her steps, and she stopped abruptly beside the couple, who were quietly discussing the table while Sam continued to hang back. They shuffled aside when Josie invaded their personal space. She acted as though she hadn't even noticed them.

"You are going to save this for me, aren't you?" she said sharply. She laid a protective hand on the table and glared at Sam.

He nodded dumbly.

"I just need to find my boyfriend to carry it, but I'm definitely coming back for it."

"Okay," he said, bemused.

"And you said fifty quid, didn't you? We agreed?"

He nodded again.

Josie lowered her voice as she finally acknowledged the couple. "I saw one identical in the shops the other day. Four hundred quid! I was gonna go back and buy it next week." She pointed at the table. "You can't beat a good bargain, can you?"

They shook their heads vaguely and Josie waltzed away again. "I'll be back soon," she shouted loudly.

It was a couple of minutes later when she finally glanced back. Sam was deep in conversation with the couple but looked up long enough to catch her eye. She shot him a quick wink. How on earth could he say it was boring?

Twenty minutes later she ambled slowly towards Sam again. Now and again she glanced over her shoulder at the portly, balding man following close behind her. She didn't really need to look to check she hadn't lost him – his breathing was loud enough. He'd waved her away when she'd offered to help carry the armchair. It was a quirky old thing with a high back and blue velvet cushioning. As soon as she'd seen it she knew she had to get it for the kennels. She hadn't realised quite how far she'd ventured when she asked him to carry it back for her.

He was huffing and puffing when she finally directed him to put it down beside Sam's van.

"Thanks so much." She hoped he wasn't about to have a heart attack.

He nodded and forced a toothy grin.

Josie took out her purse. "Four pounds," she said, handing over the cash. "Thanks!"

He nodded again, still unable to speak through his ragged breathing, and set off back the way they'd come.

Sam draped an arm over the back of the chair when she flopped into it. "You just paid the guy four quid for this and got him to carry it for you too?"

"Yep," she said proudly.

He beamed down at her. "It must be nice being so pretty!"

"I notice Brendan's table has gone," she said. "I hope you got a good price?"

He grinned. "They gave me fifty-five."

"It was a bit cheeky of them, really, when they knew how much I wanted it!"

"Excuse me," a guy cut in. He was a tall, well-dressed older gentleman. "I'll give you ten pounds for this nest of tables."

"No way!" Josie called before Sam could get a word in. She swung her legs over the arm of her new chair and shuffled to get comfy. "They're worth way more." She shook her head and looked pointedly at Sam, then nodded at the nest of three mahogany side tables. They had leaves carved down the legs and looked very fancy. "I told you not to bring them here. You'll never get anything close to what they're worth. I saw some very similar on the Antiques Roadshow last week and they valued them at six hundred pounds."

"I'll give you twenty," the man said.

"No, sorry," Josie said before her gaze drifted back to Sam. "Put them back in the van, darling. I'll take them to auction next week and get a decent price."

"Forty!" the gentleman said when Sam moved towards the tables.

Josie curled her lip. "Fifty."

He looked the tables over once more before taking out his wallet.

After the man had left with the tables, Sam went back over to Josie. "I feel like I'm hanging out with a con artist!"

"I'm not conning anyone," she said. "I'm just making sure people see what things are really worth. They still got a good deal."

"You know what I really can't understand?" Sam said, amused. "How your acting career didn't take off. I think your acting abilities are amazing."

She chuckled. "I think this chair helps too. I feel like the queen, sitting here giving out orders!"

"The queen of the car boot!" Sam teased.

"'Scuse me, love!" a burly-looking guy called out. "Are you selling that chair?"

"I wasn't planning on it. But feel free to make me an offer!" If she could make a quick profit she might just force herself to part with it.

"Twenty quid?"

She stroked the soft velvet as she mulled it over. Sixteen pounds profit with absolutely no effort sounded okay.

"Twenty-five?" he said, clearly taking the pause to be indecision.

"Go on then," she said, jumping up from her throne.

When the guy lumbered away with the chair, she caught Sam gazing at her intensely. She looped her arms around his neck. "What's that look for?"

His eyes never left hers. "I love you."

Her silly smirk fell away. "I love you too."

CHAPTER 29

They were still laughing about their afternoon adventure when they pulled onto Annette's driveway a couple of hours later.

"Is someone else coming for dinner?" Sam asked, looking at the car parked next to Max's in front of the house.

Josie's stomach lurched and Sam looked at her questioningly. She stared in confusion. "It's Jack's car."

In the kitchen, Jack looked about as awkward as Josie felt. He was sitting at the table with Max and Lizzie while Annette bustled around, setting yet more food on the already well-laden table.

"You're late," Annette said. "I told you dinner would be at five."

"Sorry," Josie said. She was fairly sure it was only five minutes past but being late for dinner was really the least of her problems.

"Jack's here," Lizzie said, glaring at Josie.

"I can see that!" Josie gave him a puzzled look and sat in the chair beside him. "What's going on?"

"I've been waiting for you for hours," he said pointedly.

"It's nice to put a face to the name," Annette said. "We've been getting to know each other."

"Josie told me you're a great cook," Jack said to Annette. "Smells like she was right."

Sam quietly took a seat at the end of the table, and Josie rubbed her sweaty hands on her jeans. What on earth was going on?

"It's lovely to see you, Jack," she said. "But why exactly are you here? You could've called first."

"I tried," he said with an undertone of annoyance "You weren't answering your phone." Of course. She'd completely forgotten about calling him back.

Annette joined them at the table. "Tuck in before it gets cold!" There was a roast chicken and all the trimmings. It was Josie's favourite meal, but her appetite had vanished. She looked at Jack, waiting for more of an explanation. If only she'd remembered to call him back.

"I thought it'd be good to finally see this place too after I've heard so much about it." He casually piled food onto his plate and then turned his attention to Sam. To be fair, Sam had been glaring at him fairly ferociously since they walked in and it was hard to ignore. "Sorry," Jack said. "We've not been introduced. I'm Jack. Josie's boyfriend."

For the briefest moment Josie closed her eyes with the vague hope that she might open them to find this had all just been a very weird dream. No such luck. "Ex-boyfriend," she said quickly. "Remember?"

"It's hard to keep track," he said with a boyish smile. She knew he was joking. It was Jack's sort of humour. She didn't really appreciate it at that moment.

Josie finally glanced at Sam. He looked blankly back at her, clearly not enjoying the joke either.

"How's work, Jack?" Max asked. Josie was grateful for the change of subject and dutifully put some food on her plate, even though she was fairly sure she couldn't eat a thing.

"Good thanks," Jack said through a mouthful of food. He pointed his fork at Josie. "I need to talk to you about work. Something happened …" He glanced around and shook his head. "I'll tell you later."

"Are you still at the mobile phone shop?" Lizzie asked.

He nodded. "Seems like I'm quite good at sales. The staff are all nice. It's a good place to work."

Lizzie nodded benignly before Max moved the conversation on once again, asking Sam about the car boot sale. Conversation floated around Josie and she nodded and smiled in what she hoped were appropriate places. It was hard to concentrate. How on earth had her lovely day with Sam ended with the world's most awkward meal with her boyfriend and her ex-boyfriend?

"Hurry up and eat, Jack," she said finally. "I've got to feed the dogs. I'll show you around the kennels."

"What on earth are you doing here?" she hissed as soon as she was alone with Jack.

"You weren't answering my calls. I was worried about you."

"Sorry," she said weakly. "I've been busy the last few days. I can't believe you just turned up here."

"It's great here," he said as they wandered towards the barn. "I can see why you like it."

She nodded and looked around; everything had become so familiar to her that she forgot how beautiful her surroundings were. So many shades of green. The grass was dotted with delicate daisies and buttercups.

"Annette's really sweet," he added. "And it seems like it didn't take you long to get over our break-up!"

"What's that supposed to mean?"

"The guy who looked like he might punch me when I said I was your boyfriend … I presume there's something going on with you two?"

She wasn't sure what to say and opened and closed her mouth like a goldfish. She couldn't lie to Jack. "It's early days."

"So you're all settled?"

"Yeah," she said as she opened the barn door. "I think I am."

Conversation was interrupted by barking dogs, and Josie told Jack all about her new job as she fed the dogs. It was good to catch up with him. She only wished she'd known he was coming. No doubt she'd have some explaining to do to Sam.

After they left the barn, they automatically migrated towards Jack's car. "I'm sorry you drove all the way here," Josie said. "I promise to keep in touch better in future."

"There was a reason I was trying to get hold of you," he said. "But now that I see how happy you are it seems a bit irrelevant."

"I don't want to get back together with you," she said instinctively. "I'm sorry but—"

"That's not what I wanted to talk to you about." He reached into his car. "I brought your mail."

Josie shook her head. Trust Jack to change the subject when things got awkward. "Thanks. But what did you want to talk about so urgently?" As soon as he passed the stack of post, she saw the familiar logo on the first envelope.

"What's this?" The logo was from the acting agency.

"I got one too," Jack said. "The TV show finally got

commissioned. Filming starts in a few weeks. They're offering all the extras their jobs again."

"Wow." She fingered the envelope, shocked. "Are you going to do it?"

"I don't think so. I like where I'm at now and this would probably only be a temporary gig. They need an answer soon, that's why I was trying to get hold of you. I thought you'd be interested and didn't want you to miss the chance. But now I've seen this place, I can't imagine you'd want to move to London."

She walked away, needing to move.

"You're not interested in it, are you?" he asked, following her. She walked until she reached the fence and climbed up to sit on it.

"I don't know. Is it for real? They're definitely doing it?"

"Twelve episodes for definite. Then they review again."

She frowned. It sounded good. A few months ago she'd have been over the moon and snapped it up. Now she felt completely confused.

"I couldn't leave Annette," she mused.

Jack sat beside her on the fence. "It seems like she relies on you."

"She does."

"So you're a country girl now?" he said with amusement. "I never thought this would end up being a permanent thing."

"Neither did I," she said.

"But you can imagine staying here long term?"

"I don't know." She shrugged and her eyes roamed her surroundings before landing back on the letters in her hand and the logo with the stars. "Why did this have to come now?" she said, irritated. "All those auditions I went to and all that time I spent on the phone to Michaela begging her to find me a job. And *now* I get this! I'd completely given up on it."

"Sorry," he said. "I feel like I shouldn't have brought it. You could just throw it in the bin …"

"I probably should." She inhaled deeply, taking in the wonderfully fresh air.

"I think I'll get going," Jack said. "We'll talk soon?"

"Yeah." She headed back to the car with him. "Thanks for coming. It was sweet of you."

"It would've been much easier if you'd just answered your phone."

"Sorry," she said sheepishly.

"There's still some of your stuff at my place," Jack said. "I should've brought it. I didn't even think."

"Don't worry. I'll pick it up next time I'm in Oxford."

"Okay. Tell everyone I said bye." He kissed her on the cheek before getting in his car. "And let me know what you decide about the job."

She watched him drive away and then headed back to the house, taking a deep breath before she walked in.

"What've you done with Jack?" Annette asked when she joined them in the living room.

"He had to get back."

"What's going on?" Lizzie said. "Why did he just turn up without warning you?"

Josie held up the envelopes in her hand, discreetly shifting the one from StarSearch to the middle of the pack before dumping them on the stairs. "He brought my post, that's all."

"A four-hour drive just to bring your mail?" Max said. "Surely he could've posted it to you?"

"He could," Josie said. "But he didn't. Anyone want a drink?"

Since everyone else had coffee, she went into the kitchen to get one for herself.

"Everything okay?" Sam asked, joining her.

"Yeah. Sorry. I had no idea he was going to turn up. It was slightly awkward."

"A little bit," he agreed, leaning on the work surface. "Was there a reason for his visit? Other than bringing your post."

"Not really." She busied herself making coffee and tried hard to ignore the guilt that crept in when she thought about why Jack had really come. No doubt he had expected Josie to be thrilled by the news about the TV show. He probably thought she'd have started packing as soon as she heard. She really couldn't leave Annette, though. Sam reached for her hand. She couldn't leave him either.

"Are you sure everything's okay?" he asked.

"Yes!" She gave him a hasty kiss before moving back towards the living room. "Come on."

"I've got something to show you," Lizzie said, when Josie sat beside her. She reached into her handbag and then casually held up an ultrasound picture.

The smile spread slowly across Josie's face, and she beamed at Lizzie, who looked like she was about to explode from excitement.

"What is it?" Annette asked, squinting to see.

"A scan picture of a baby!" Josie told her.

"That's not quite true," Lizzie said, handing the black and white picture to her for a better look.

Josie gasped and her hand shot to her mouth. "No?"

"Two babies!" Max said.

"Oh my goodness!" Annette's eyes filled with tears and she stood to hug Max and Lizzie.

"Twins?" Josie said, not quite believing it.

Lizzie's eyes filled with tears as she nodded. "I was terrified enough at the thought of one baby! Then we found out it's twins."

"Oh my God!" Josie squealed, wrapping her in a big hug. "Congratulations!"

"Are you crying?" Max asked when she hugged him.

She wiped at her eyes. "I'm just emotional. It's so exciting."

Sam looked almost as emotional as her, and she automatically hugged him too.

"You owe me a fiver!" he whispered in her ear. She gave him a friendly jab in the ribs then perched on the arm of the chair when he sat down. He ran a finger over the small of her back until she shuffled and swatted him away. She was far too ticklish.

"When are you due?" Annette asked.

"December," Lizzie told her happily. "It's been so hard not telling anyone."

"I can't believe you're having twins!" Josie said in complete shock. "That's crazy."

"I know. I'm terrified."

"I'm so happy for you," Josie said. At one time, Lizzie had been adamant she never wanted children. That had been when she was completely wrapped up in her career. Back before Max had come along and turned Lizzie's world upside down.

Lizzie seemed relieved to be able to talk about the pregnancy, and they chatted for almost an hour. She talked about morning sickness and how they were going to decorate the nursery, and what she'd do about work, and lots of little things that she'd obviously been dying to talk about but couldn't. The excitement was infectious. When she complained about how tired she'd been, Lizzie started yawning, making them all laugh. She couldn't seem to stop, and Max suggested they get home.

When Josie mumbled about checking on the dogs, Sam

offered to come with her. They waved Max and Lizzie off first.

Sam watched Josie intently as she walked around filling up water bowls and chatting to the dogs. "We could take a couple of them out for a walk," he suggested. "It's a nice evening."

She agreed. They'd all had long walks in the morning and Annette had said she'd had them out in the garden. None of them would complain about the extra exercise, though.

Sam leaned on an old stable door while she clipped the border collie on a lead. "You can leave her off," Sam said. "She's as good as gold."

"I'm still scared of losing dogs," she said. "Which others can I take without a lead?"

Sam glanced into the stalls. "Get Pippa and Jeanie." She looked at him and shrugged. "The Scottish terriers," he said, walking down the barn and letting them out himself.

"They only arrived yesterday," she said as the three dogs jumped around Sam. Usually she at least knew the names of the dogs. "And I don't usually take more than two at a time."

"These three are fine," he assured her.

"How do you know more than me?"

"They're old customers. And I've been helping Annette out since I was about six."

She sighed and followed the dogs outside.

"What's wrong?" Sam asked, hurrying to keep up with her.

"I've been here two months and I still don't really know what I'm doing."

"It doesn't seem that way to me," Sam said. "And Annette seems more than happy with you."

She opened the gate behind the barn and the dogs slipped through beside her legs. "I can manage the business side of things no problem. It's the dogs I'm not good with. That's a bit ridiculous, isn't it? Someone working in a kennels who's not good with dogs? I have no control over them."

"That's just experience."

"I'm not sure it is," she said. The letter from the acting agency popped into her head, and she wondered whether she would be better to go and do something she knew she was good at. But then Sam's hand slipped into hers and she remembered everything else she'd have to give up, not just a job she wasn't very good at.

He squeezed her hand. "You worry too much."

They walked in silence for a while, and Josie couldn't stop thinking about the acting job. It would be amazing to be back on the TV set. If only the offer had come earlier. Or not at all. That would've been better. Her mind whirred in overdrive. She shouldn't even be giving it a moment's consideration.

"Are you going to tell me what happened with Jack?" Sam asked as they reached the bottom of the hill and walked along the small stream in the valley.

"He brought my mail," she said. Suddenly, she wanted to get back and open the stupid letter and see for herself what they were offering.

"And wanted to get back together, presumably?"

She hesitated. That would be an obvious reason for his visit. "He just wanted to chat things through."

"But everything's fine? He understands it's definitely over?"

"Yes."

"Are you sure?"

She felt guilty. Jack's reappearance had obviously worried Sam. "I'm sure. You really don't need to worry about Jack."

"I just think it's weird that you were in a relationship which basically had an on/off switch."

"It wasn't like that." It was, though, in a way. "It's hard to explain."

"And he's not going to keep turning up to try and get you back?"

"No." She began to lose her patience with the conversation. "He's okay with it."

"Idiot," Sam said flatly, then turned and beamed at her.

She reached up for a kiss. "I guess I owe you a fiver, by the way."

"You do! Can you believe they're having twins?"

"No," Josie said, chuckling.

Sam glanced around, automatically checking on the dogs. Usually Josie would be obsessively looking around, but she felt more relaxed with Sam around. "Two kids at once," he remarked. "I'm scared for them!"

"Really?" She gazed at him intently. Even though it was very early days, she realised she had a spark of envy for Lizzie and could just imagine having a family with Sam one day. The thought didn't scare her at all, not like it did when she'd been with Jack. "I can imagine you having a few kids …" She hoped the comment didn't freak him out.

His arms tightened around her waist and he gazed lovingly at her. "I would be very happy with a few kids. I just think one at a time would be best."

"I think you're right," she said, beaming. "They're going to have their hands full."

He kissed her gently before they moved apart and set off back the way they'd come.

"I'll let you off with the five pounds," Sam said. "I never mentioned twins, after all."

"That makes me very suspicious. Max already told you Lizzie was pregnant, didn't he?"

"No," he said, laughing. "I'm just very perceptive."

CHAPTER 30

Josie had been staying over at Sam's house most nights and felt guilty when she brushed him off that evening. Keeping secrets from him didn't sit well with her, but she wanted some time to mull things over before she told him about the job offer.

She stared in disbelief at the letter from StarSearch when she was finally alone in her room. It hadn't quite seemed real before, but it was true: they were offering her the acting job again. The barmaid in the military soap opera. Even though it was a non-speaking part, she'd loved the buzz of being on a TV set. And it had been so exciting working in London. She'd always loved the city. She used to dream of living there, in the middle of so much action.

Her mind drifted as she lay in bed that night, unable to fall asleep. She imagined living in London, working at the TV studios. She could come back whenever she had time off; it wouldn't mean she couldn't be with Sam, just that she wouldn't see him so often. It was Annette who would be the real problem. Josie would feel terrible leaving her in the lurch.

For a moment, she imagined living with Emily while she got settled. That would be fun. Then she chastised herself for seriously considering it. Jack had been sure it would only end up being a temporary gig, and he was probably right. They'd film a few episodes and decide it wasn't working, and she'd be back to being unemployed.

She forced herself to think of Annette and Sam and the friends she'd made in Averton. The thoughts of leaving were absolutely crazy.

Unfortunately, they kept creeping back in.

Annette commented on how tired Josie looked the next morning. Josie brushed it aside but skipped breakfast and headed straight out to the barn. The dogs were barking furiously when she felt someone enter the barn behind her. Instinctively, she knew it was Sam, but she still jumped when his arms snaked around her waist.

"Are you trying to give me a heart attack?" she said loudly, as she turned to face him.

"Nope! Just wanted to say good morning."

His charming grin made her insides flutter, and she relaxed into him when he kissed her deeply.

"Good morning," she said lazily when he pulled back. "Next time don't sneak up on me." There was no conviction to her words, and a feeling of dread swept through her. There was no way she could leave Sam to go and work in London.

"I promise not to sneak up on you in future," he said, then moved to the Doberman, who was howling wildly. When Sam walked into the stall he calmed down immediately. "What's wrong?" he asked when he caught Josie staring at him, lost in a dream.

"Nothing," she said, snapping out of it. Sam made a fuss

of the oversized dog with big droopy eyes. Once he stopped howling, the rest of the dogs settled down too. "I'm just tired."

"Okay. I've got to get to work but do you want to do something this evening? Dinner or a drink or something?"

Shuffling her feet, she wondered why her automatic response was to make an excuse. She'd have to tell him about the job offer sooner or later, though. And it wasn't really a big deal since she wasn't going to take it. She smiled weakly. "Dinner sounds good."

Sam looked suddenly nervous. "Are you sure you're okay? You seem distracted. It's not to do with Jack's visit yesterday, is it?"

"No." Technically that was a lie. "I just had a headache last night and couldn't fall asleep. I'm tired. Stop worrying."

"Okay." He gave her a quick kiss before he dashed off to work.

"I need to tell you something before my head explodes," Josie said as she sat in the quiet children's corner in the Reading Room. She'd arrived later than usual due to a long phone conversation with Michaela at StarSearch.

"Sounds exciting," Tara said, wriggling to get comfy on a beanbag.

"You have to swear not to say anything to anyone, though." They both nodded and she looked at them sternly. "I mean it. If Sam hears about this from anyone but me there'll be a big problem." They frowned and nodded again.

"Just tell us," Amber said. "The suspense is killing me."

"Jack turned up yesterday …"

Amber and Tara looked surprised, and Josie shook her

head. "That's not the secret. Sam knows that part and it's fine. The problem is Jack brought my post—"

"Oh. My. God," Tara said dramatically. "The absolute cheek of him. Of course Sam can't hear about that!"

Josie extended a foot in an attempt to kick Tara. "Be serious for a minute! I had a job offer in the post."

"Really?" Amber said.

Josie nodded. "I told you I did a bit of acting before? They want me back for the same part."

"Wow!" Tara said. "You're going to leave us to be a TV star? Promise you'll remember us when you're rich and famous. I wouldn't mind going to some fancy red-carpet event if you ever need someone to go with you …"

"It's not like that," she replied, shaking her head. "It's only a non-speaking part. Although, I had a chat with my agent today and she said there's a good chance they'll develop the character later." Josie couldn't help but feel a twinge of excitement when Michaela had said that. She had to keep reminding herself that Michaela was prone to exaggeration and had good motives for wanting Josie to take the part – it was an easy commission for her.

"You have an agent?" Tara said. "I'm impressed."

"Everyone has an agent." Josie shrugged. "It's not glamorous."

"Sounds it, though," Tara said.

"So you're thinking of taking it?" Amber said seriously.

"No." Josie gave a quick wave of the hand. "It's bad timing." She screwed her face up. "Really bad timing. Before I moved here, I spent eighteen months auditioning for any part I could and had about a zillion rejections. Now I've stopped looking, they offer me a job."

"I'd jump at it!" Tara said. "In fact, do you reckon I could take it in your place? It sounds exciting."

"It *is* exciting," Josie agreed sadly. "That's what I loved about it."

"I thought you were happy here," Amber said. "And you and Sam are all loved up."

"I know. Of course I can't leave. It just got me thinking, that's all. My imagination runs away with me."

"I think you'd be crazy not to consider it," Tara said. "It sounds like a great opportunity, and you never know what else might develop from it. I'm really fond of Annette and I think it's amazing you're helping her out, but your job at the kennels is a dead-end career path if ever there was one."

"Tara!" Amber chastised, shooting her a look of contempt. "Working at the kennels might not be glamorous or ambitious, but Josie's happy there. Let's not forget that." Her eyes were full of sympathy when she looked at Josie. "And what about Sam?"

"Exactly," Josie said. "Of course I couldn't take the job."

"When do they need an answer by?" Tara asked.

"Friday," she replied with a grimace. "But I already know I'll turn it down."

Josie's thoughts were one big jumbled mess when she sat with Sam in Dolce Vita that evening. They'd been to the quaint little Italian restaurant in Newton Abbot once before and had enjoyed the fresh food and welcoming atmosphere. She wasn't feeling quite as relaxed as on their previous visit. Chatting everything through with the girls that morning was supposed to make things clearer for her, but instead she was even more confused.

She waited until they'd ordered the food and then blurted the news to Sam.

He listened quietly while she filled him in, and he looked concerned. "I thought there was something on your mind."

"It's the worst timing ever." She rested an elbow on the table and chewed a nail. "Six months ago I'd have been over the moon. Now I don't know what to think."

He sat up straighter and the concern in his features morphed into something else entirely. Confusion mixed with trepidation. "You're not thinking of taking it, though?"

"I don't know. My gut reaction was that I couldn't take it. I can't leave Annette to manage the kennels alone." She sighed and then rubbed at her temples. "But then I wonder if I should really pass up an opportunity just to be loyal to Annette."

"I thought you enjoyed working at the kennels?"

"I do," she said. "Kind of. I don't dislike it, but it's definitely not my dream job. And I can't help thinking it's not leading anywhere. It's not a career. Part of me feels like I'm a teenager doing a summer job."

"But if you enjoy it and you can make a living from it, what's the problem?"

There was a hint of defensiveness to his voice. She wished she was as content as he was with his job and his life. There was a spark of ambition in her that he didn't understand. "There was no problem, until they offered me my old job. Now I can't stop thinking about it. It's hard not to wonder." She wanted to be completely honest with Sam but he looked tense, as though he'd rather not discuss it.

"What about us?" he asked quietly.

She covered her hand with his. "I love you. That's not going to change."

Sam opened his mouth to speak but was interrupted by the waiter sliding their pizzas onto the table. They smiled and thanked him before he went away again. The conversation was set aside and they ate in silence. Josie was grateful when

Sam suggested they pay and leave as soon as they'd eaten. She wanted to talk things through more, but that would be easier back at Sam's place.

They held hands as they walked the short distance to Sam's van, and the tension radiated from him. Josie almost wished she hadn't mentioned it. Everything would be easier if she'd just ripped up the letter and put it in the bin. Sam was right; she had a pretty good thing going at the kennels. Why couldn't she just be content with it?

She was surprised when Sam stopped the van on the road by the sign for Oakbrook Farm. She'd expected to go back to his place, but he obviously had other ideas.

"Don't be angry with me." She unclipped her seatbelt and shifted in the seat to face him. Her fingers trailed over his hair and then stroked his neck. "I'm not saying I'm going to take the job. I need to consider my options properly, that's all."

He rubbed at his eyes. "I just don't understand what happens to us if you move to London."

"I'm probably not even going to take it." She hated how hurt he looked. "It's just made me think about things. I never really saw a future working for Annette, and I'd hate to pass up this job offer and then regret it later."

"You're saying you probably won't take it but it sounds like you want to. I'm amazed you'd even consider it."

"Of course I'd consider it," she said gently. "I spent so long wanting a career in TV. How can I not at least consider it?"

He nodded but didn't look at her and tensed when she pulled him in her direction.

"I don't even get a goodnight kiss now?" She was trying very hard to keep the atmosphere light but felt her eyes dampen.

Finally, he turned and ran a hand over her cheek. "Sorry,"

he whispered. "You caught me off guard. This wasn't quite what I was expecting for the evening."

"I know. It caught me off guard too. I just want to make sure I make the right decision. Let's sleep on it and talk again tomorrow."

He smiled sadly and kissed her goodnight.

CHAPTER 31

J osie hoped that Sam might call in and see her before work – he quite often appeared when she was out in the barn in the mornings. There was no sign of him, though, and she wasn't overly surprised. He hadn't taken the news of the job well, and she expected he needed some time for it to sink in. She messaged him later, hoping they could meet up that evening, but he said he had to work late. It was hard not to think that he was avoiding her. He called her on Wednesday for a quick chat but complained he was working late again.

Josie couldn't stop thinking about the job in London. It occupied her every waking thought and disturbed her sleep too. Her brain wouldn't switch off long enough for her to sleep. What was really bothering her was that the more she thought about it, the more she was tempted by the job offer.

On Thursday afternoon she set off to visit Lizzie. Her sister would give her sensible advice. She'd tell her to stop being such a dreamer. Lizzie had never thought much about Josie's acting dreams and a bit of level-headedness was exactly what Josie needed.

She blurted out the situation as soon as she was sitting with Lizzie and Max in their cosy living room. They exchanged a look but didn't seem overly surprised. For a moment, she wondered whether someone had already told them, but she didn't think so.

"Say something," Josie said, as they both sat silently.

It was Max who finally spoke. "Lizzie said you'd last six months at Oakbrook. I went with three."

"You had bets on how long I'd stay?"

"We just thought you'd get bored." Max looked sympathetic. "Averton is pretty quiet."

"I'm not bored," Josie insisted. "I love Averton. I'm just confused because of the job offer. It could be a great opportunity."

"When does the job start?" Lizzie asked. "We'd need to find someone to replace you."

Josie spat out a laugh. "Is this some sort of reverse psychology? Tell me I should go to get me to stay?"

"No." Lizzie gave her a puzzled look. "I know how much you wanted to work in TV. Of course you'd jump at it. We really never expected you to stay long with Annette. We just need to make sure we find someone to help with the kennels."

"I haven't decided for definite what I'm going to do," Josie said. She'd been so sure Lizzie would tell her to stay put. She shifted in her seat. "There's Sam to think about too."

Max and Lizzie exchanged a knowing look and it irritated Josie. It was like they had their own secret language. "What?" she asked, desperate to be let in on the silent conversation.

"It just seems like you're at different phases in your life," Max said gently. "Sam's ready to settle down, get married, have kids, all that stuff. And it seems like there are other things you want to do first."

She suspected what he really wanted to say was that she still needed to grow up, but he was diplomatic as always.

"So you think I should take the job? Move to London?"

"If that's what you want." Lizzie shrugged. "What does Sam think?"

"He wasn't very happy with the idea. I need to talk to him properly."

Josie really hadn't expected Lizzie to be so understanding, and when she left Hope Cove she was determined to discuss things properly with Sam. She was supposed to give Michaela an answer about the job the following day, and she had no idea what she would say.

It also felt strange that she hadn't seen Sam for two days. She missed him. Thankfully he sounded a bit more upbeat when she called him. He invited her over to his place after work.

"Have you really been working late, or were you avoiding me?" she asked when she arrived.

"I was really working late." He followed her into the living room and she glared at him, trying to gauge if it was the truth. His eyebrows dipped. "Maybe I was avoiding you a bit too."

"Thanks a lot!" She dropped onto the couch and he perched close beside her.

"I was just trying to get my head around things. Get my thoughts in order."

"And?"

He shrugged and reached for her hand. "And I don't want you to leave, of course."

"I have to decide by tomorrow," she said wearily.

"So soon?" He leaned forward, resting on his knees. "Did you speak to Annette about it?"

"No." The thought of discussing it with Annette made her feel like crying. How could she leave Annette? "I wanted to talk to you about it but you were avoiding me."

"Surely you know I'm not going to encourage you to go? It seems like something you have to decide for yourself."

"But I wanted to discuss what happens between us if I take the job. I know we'd be fine but—"

"Would we?" He glared at her in surprise. "How can we have a relationship if we live 200 miles apart? You know my thoughts on long-distance relationships."

"But—"

"I don't want a long-distance relationship," he said firmly. "I don't even want to try and figure out how that might work." He shook his head. "It wouldn't work."

"Don't say that." She sat up straighter, leaned her head on his shoulder and wrapped her arms around him. "I love you. It's not like I like the idea of us living so far apart, but I need to be level-headed and think about my future."

"Which apparently won't include me if you move to London."

"We'd make it work," she said quietly.

"So you've already decided?"

"No," she said miserably. "I still need to talk it through with Annette. I feel like I'm being torn in half. There are reasons to go and reasons to stay. I don't know how to decide."

When he didn't say anything, she tugged gently on his arm. "You realise you haven't kissed me in days."

His features softened when he turned to her. The distance she'd been feeling between them seemed to disappear when he kissed her.

"Can I stay here tonight?" she asked when they broke apart.

He gave her that look where he pretended to mull something over, then he grinned and pushed her back on the couch.

"I'll take that as a yes." She giggled as he positioned himself on top of her with a look of mischief.

CHAPTER 32

She thought she'd sleep better at Sam's place but instead she spent most of the night watching him sleep. He looked so peaceful in the glow of moonlight that filtered in the window. How many nights would she get to spend with him if she moved to London? It would become an exception rather than the norm. Maybe that would make their time together even sweeter. Maybe not.

She was exhausted when she walked into the barn on Friday morning and was thankful they only had three dogs staying. It was nice and quiet. Unfortunately one of them was the mischievous Pixie who belonged to Graham, the neighbour up the road. Since Josie had lost her on that first day, she'd always been vigilant with her. But with her head in the clouds when she opened the stable door, Pixie slipped right past her. The barn door was open and Pixie was off like a shot. Josie made it outside in time to see her scale the fence and disappear down into the valley.

It was hard to summon the energy for a chase, but Josie set off briskly in the direction Pixie had gone. Tears came to her eyes almost immediately. She was too tired and emotional to deal with a lost dog. There was no sign of her at Sam's house. That's where Josie looked first, hoping she'd done the same as last time. Sam had already left for work so she couldn't even ask him for help.

For almost an hour, she wandered the hills and fields, calling out to Pixie and feeling completely defeated. Finally, she headed for home to tell Annette she'd lost the dog. She kept her head down and only noticed Annette sitting on the patio when she was almost there. Pixie was sitting on her lap.

Josie attempted a smile but her eyes filled with tears and her chin twitched madly. She sat at the table and put her head in her hands. Sobs wracked her body.

She felt Annette's hand on her shoulder. "I'm sorry," Josie said, her chest heaving as she fought against the sobs.

"She came back," Annette said. "No harm done."

"It's not the first time I've lost her."

"I know. And I'm guessing that's not really what you're so upset about either. You've been in a funny mood for days."

"Did Sam tell you I lost her before?"

"No." Annette chuckled. "I saw out the window. That first day."

"Why didn't you say anything?"

"Pixie always comes back. And I thought it would be good for you to lose a dog on the first day. You'd be extra careful."

Josie sniffed. "I'm not very good at this job."

"Don't be silly." Annette seemed genuinely surprised by the remark. "You're great at it."

"The dogs don't listen to me. I nearly trip over them about twenty times a day. I thought I'd get better but I'm not. I'm just no good at it."

"Of course you're getting better with the dogs. You just don't notice because it's gradual. Is this what you're so upset about?"

She shook her head and brushed tears from her cheeks. "I've been offered a job. In London."

"Ah." Annette inhaled deeply and then shot Josie a sympathetic look. "You're leaving me?"

"I feel terrible." More tears appeared. "But it might be really good for me. I want the job. I don't want to leave you. Or Sam. I don't want to hurt Sam."

Annette patted her hand. "Sam loves you. He'll want whatever's best for you. Whatever makes you happy."

"You need me here, though …"

"I *like* having you here," Annette said. "But I'll survive. You don't have to worry about me."

"It's the acting job," Josie said. "The TV show I worked on before. I'm just so torn. It feels like whatever I decide will be wrong."

"Nope," Annette said brightly. "Whatever you decide will be right."

By the time Josie spoke to Michaela that afternoon, she was adamant there was no way she could leave Annette. When she'd transferred an online booking from the computer to Annette's old-fashioned diary earlier, and replied to comments on social media, she was reminded that Annette definitely couldn't manage the place on her own. She also wasn't physically fit enough to walk the dogs. It was almost always Josie who did that now. She couldn't stand the thought of a stranger coming in to help.

She slinked up to her bedroom when her phone rang and closed the door behind her.

"I thought you'd have called me by now," Michaela said quickly. "You suddenly think you're some big star who can keep me waiting?" Her words were jokey, but Josie detected a hint of annoyance in her tone too.

Josie stood in the window, gazing out over the fields. "I needed time to think about it."

"What's to think about? It's exactly what you want. I can't actually believe how lucky you are that they've requested you back. You know they specifically requested you, don't you?"

"I thought they were asking all the supporting artists to come back?"

"They're asking them all. But they specifically asked for the same barmaid. And they asked whether you'd be willing to develop the role."

"Did they?" Josie asked, sceptically.

"Do you think I'm making it up?" Michaela sounded indignant.

It had definitely crossed Josie's mind. "I don't know." She didn't know why she was hesitating. All she had to do was say no thanks and get off the phone. Why was she stalling? "Can I have more time to think about it?"

"I need an answer before you get off the phone," Michaela said. "And if you say no there's no changing your mind later. I can't believe you even have to think about this. It's an amazing opportunity. Do you know how many people would kill for this? I spend half my time on the phone to people like you, begging me to find them a job. You were one of them not so long ago. Now I have a job for you and you're not sure! What's going on?"

"My situation changed." She moved to sit on the bed, her gaze landing on the flowery wallpaper. "It's complicated now."

"I need an answer," Michaela said. There was a tapping in the background as though she was drumming her nails on the desk.

"I suppose I have to say no then." As soon as Josie said it, she panicked. It was like flipping a coin to make a decision and realising what you want as soon as the coin landed. "Wait," she said, terrified it was a final answer sort of situation and she'd just sealed her fate.

"What should I tell them?" Michaela asked impatiently.

"Tell them I'll take it. I want the job."

CHAPTER 33

W hat on earth had she done? She felt as though she was spinning out of control. Had she really accepted the job? Was she actually going to move to London?

When Annette asked about the phone call, Josie had lied and said they'd given her more time to think about it. She needed time for it to sink in. Telling Sam would be awful, and she was already dreading it.

He messaged to say he'd see her in the pub that evening but would be a bit later than usual. He was stuck at work. It bought her some time to gather her thoughts.

She was like a zombie when she sat down at the usual table in the Bluebell Inn with Tara and Amber.

"I would be depressed too if I just turned down the job opportunity of a lifetime." Tara patted her arm. "I hope Sam's worth it."

"She didn't turn it down just because of Sam," Amber said.

"No," Josie said, staring straight ahead. "I didn't."

"I hope you don't live to regret this," Tara said. "If I were you, I'd forever wonder what might have been."

Josie's eyes snapped to Tara. That summed up how she'd been feeling all week – that maybe this was a great opportunity, and if she let it slip away she'd forever wonder how it would have turned out.

"I didn't turn it down," she whispered.

"Didn't you speak to your agent?" Amber asked.

"I spoke to her." She looked at Tara, then at Amber. "I just didn't turn it down. I accepted the job."

"Oh my God!" Tara cried. Josie couldn't tell if it was shock or excitement but shushed her friend nonetheless.

"You're leaving?" Amber asked quietly.

"I was going to say no," she explained. "I did say no to start with, but it felt wrong so I changed my mind. But I haven't signed a contract or anything. I can still back out. But if I said no today, it would've been final, they'd have found someone else."

"So you still might turn it down?" Amber asked.

Josie rubbed at her face. "I don't think so. I really want the job." She took a deep breath and looked up at them. "I think I'd regret it if I didn't give the acting one last shot. Working at the kennels was never going to be a long-term career path. I feel like it's the sort of job you should do because you love it, and I'm not sure I do."

"Wow," Amber said sadly. "I can't believe you're going to leave."

Amber's words made Josie panic and she was filled with doubt again. "Oh God, what am I doing? I love my life here. I've never felt so settled. Why would I give that up?"

"Because this is a great opportunity," Tara said.

"I'm so confused." Josie automatically looked towards the door when it opened. Sam beamed at her from the doorway. "I'll be back in a minute."

Hurrying over, she greeted Sam with a kiss. Then she stood at the bar asking him about his day and hanging off his every word. When he asked how her day was, she shrugged and said it was the same as always. That was far from the truth, obviously. It wasn't every day she accepted an acting job in London. She ended up telling him the same as she'd told Annette – that she had more time to think about the job.

"I'll get back to the girls," she said when Sam glanced at the pool table and nodded a greeting to the group beside it. "See you later."

He gave her a quick kiss, and she went back to the table in the far corner.

"I didn't tell Sam," she said in hushed tones. "I just couldn't bring myself to say anything."

"You might be underestimating him," Tara said. "If he knows how much the job means to you, he should be understanding. And it's not like you're splitting up with him. You can still have a relationship."

Josie reached for her wine glass and twirled the stem. "He's made it very clear how he feels about long-distance relationships."

"Sam loves you," Tara said bluntly. "He'll soon change his mind about long-distance relationships when it comes down to a choice between that and losing you."

Josie certainly hoped so. "Part of me wishes they'd never offered me the job," she said. "I was perfectly happy a week ago."

To change the subject, she asked Amber about Kieron. It was guaranteed to get her talking. Josie nodded along and made the odd comment. Eventually, Tara rolled her eyes and moved the conversation on again. It was a struggle for Josie to pay attention, and she was glad when Sam finally came and sat with them. She leaned into him when he put an arm around her shoulder, and she suddenly felt like crying.

They didn't stay for long after that and walked home in an unusual silence.

He squeezed her hand as they neared the gate at Oakbrook. "Are you staying at my place?"

"I think I'll stay at home." She didn't offer an explanation. She didn't have one, other than she was feeling deceitful for not telling him the truth about the job.

"Shall we do something tomorrow?"

She tensed. "I was actually planning on a quick trip up to Oxford. Just for one night. I haven't seen my parents for a while and my friend Emily is back there for the weekend so it seemed like a good time." Actually, Emily had just messaged her that afternoon to say she was in Oxford for the weekend and asked Josie to come too. Josie had told her she was too busy, but it suddenly seemed like a good idea. It would give her some much-needed headspace. "I only spoke to Emily today," she said.

Sam looked disappointed but didn't say anything.

"Could you do me a favour?" Josie said.

"Does it involve me helping Annette with the dogs while you're gone?"

"She'll say she doesn't need any help, but I'll feel better if I know you're calling in."

She smiled sweetly as he agreed.

CHAPTER 34

J osie left for Oxford first thing on Saturday morning and arrived in time to have lunch with her parents. It was good to catch up with them and refreshing to be away from Averton. She hadn't realised how much she needed a change of scene. Conversation with her parents was neutral, and she didn't mention anything about her job offer. She wasn't ready for their opinion.

Emily was a different matter. Josie blurted everything out to her almost as soon as she saw her. They met in a pub in the centre of Oxford that was an old haunt of theirs. She'd gone to school with Emily and they'd lived not far from each other growing up, but it wasn't until after school that they really became close friends. They'd connected at an amateur dramatics club and were fairly inseparable for a while.

Emily listened intently as Josie filled her in on her news.

"It's perfect," Emily said excitedly about the job offer. "You could come and live with me!"

"What?" Josie was taken aback. She'd considered it herself but knew how tiny Emily's flat was and didn't think she'd be quite so quick to suggest it.

"Yes!" Emily reached to squeeze Josie's hand. "My rent is killing me and it'll be so much fun living together! I've missed you."

"I missed you too," Josie said slowly. What she really needed was some huge obstacle to the move, not things falling into place as though it was meant to be. "Isn't your place a bit small for two, though?"

"You'd have to sleep on the couch," Emily said. "But it would be so much fun. Didn't we always talk about getting a place together in London? You were going to be a famous actress and me a famous author!"

Josie chuckled. "I think we've got a way to go still."

"I know but it'll feel like we're at least trying to do what we planned. It'd be such an adventure. And after all those times you came crying to me because you'd got rejected from some acting job, how can you even think of turning it down?"

"I was just feeling settled at last. I'm worried I'll just turn my life upside down for what might end up being another dead-end job."

"But I thought Michaela said it could end up being a speaking part."

"It *might*," Josie said. "It also might not." She paused. "Things are going so well with Sam. I don't want to mess everything up."

"But you keep telling me what a great guy he is. Surely if he's that great he'll be supportive. You don't have to break up with him."

"I think you might be simplifying things," Josie said.

"That's because it all looks pretty simple from where I'm sitting."

"Maybe we should swap seats," Josie said drily.

She was filled with anxiety as she drove back to Oakbrook on Sunday. She really was going to take the job in London. Emily made the move sound so exciting – and easy since she'd have a place to live, at least temporarily. It was one of the hardest decisions she'd ever made, but it felt like the right thing for her.

She could find someone to take over her job at the kennels so she wouldn't be leaving Annette in the lurch. And her relationship with Sam could surely survive long distance. She was dreading breaking the news to him.

He was at Oakbrook when she got there. The dogs had already been fed, which Josie was happy about – she wouldn't miss the smell of dog food.

Sam and Annette were sitting at the kitchen table playing cards.

"I'm just gone for a couple of days and he leads you astray with gambling and drinking," Josie remarked, leaning on Sam's shoulder and kissing his cheek before stealing a swig of his beer.

"There's no money involved," Annette said, flinging a card on the table.

"Which is good for me," Sam said. "I've yet to win a hand."

"Did the dogs behave?" Josie asked.

Sam nodded. "It's a very easy job you've got here."

"She works very hard," Annette put in. "Leave her alone."

The comments stung and Josie had a wave of nausea at the thought of leaving.

"I'm just teasing," Sam said. "There's more beer in the fridge if you want one."

She declined and took a seat. Sam dealt her in on the next hand and they spent an hour happily playing gin rummy. When Annette went up to bed, Josie braced herself to talk to

Sam, but he complained about having to be up early for work the next day and said he needed to get home to bed. On the patio, she kissed him goodnight. He was just about to leave when she reached for his arm and pulled him back. Her heart was racing.

"Can we talk?"

He swallowed hard, then gave her a lopsided smile. "Can it wait until tomorrow?"

She could tell by the look in his eye that he knew what she was going to say. He just didn't want to hear it.

"Okay," she managed weakly.

He kissed her again.

The sinking feeling came as she watched him walk away. Why did it feel like she was losing him?

CHAPTER 35

J osie broke the news to Annette over breakfast the next morning. It was unnerving how calm Annette was about it. She was understanding and reassuring, even encouraging. She seemed excited for Josie. If only Josie could muster the same enthusiasm.

There was no trip to the bookshop for coffee with the girls that morning. Instead, Josie called Lizzie and gave her the news. They discussed finding a replacement for her at the kennels. That made it all seem real. She was leaving. Suddenly, she was terrified by the prospect. What if she'd made the wrong decision?

She wanted to speak to Sam, needed him to wrap her in a big hug and tell her everything would be okay. With his reassurance, she'd be able to breathe easily again.

It wasn't that simple, though.

When she perched on his couch that evening, he took the armchair. There was distance between them already.

"You accepted the job, didn't you?"

She nodded and moved to the arm of the chair. "I need to

give it a try. I feel like I'll regret it if I don't. I'll forever wonder."

"When do you leave?"

She bit her lip at the hurt in his eyes. "A couple of weeks."

There was silence for a moment before he spoke. "I thought you liked working for Annette. I thought you were happy here."

"I was … I *am*. But I—"

"You're never happy." He stood and crossed the room, turning back to her when he reached the window. "Max did try and warn me."

"Warn you of what?" she demanded.

"That you wouldn't stick around. That you never stick at anything."

She couldn't help the tears then. It was partly true, of course. She hadn't been great at sticking at jobs. She'd spent a long time drifting from one thing to another, always looking for something better.

"This is what I wanted for so long," she said tearfully.

"I thought you wanted to be with me. What was this, just a bit of fun for you?"

"No." She went to him, reached for his hand. "I love you."

"Don't," he said bitterly, snatching his hand back.

"But it's true."

"It's slightly hard to believe when you've already decided you're leaving me."

"I'm not leaving you." She took a deep breath.

"I'm not moving to London, Josie."

"I wouldn't ask you to. But we don't have to split up."

"So, what's the plan? You'll come back here on week-ends? Didn't you recently have a similar conversation with your ex?"

"It's not like with Jack," she said.

He stood rigid. "I told you I won't have a long-distance relationship."

Tears spilled down her cheeks. "You said you didn't want one. I know it's not ideal …"

"It's not just that I don't want it. I won't do it."

She frowned, biting her lip as her chin quivered. "But I love you. And I thought you loved me."

His features softened. "I do. Of course I do. I just know long-distance won't work. Not for me. I need to see you more than just a couple of times a month."

"So what are you saying, that it's over between us?"

His eyes pleaded with her. "I'm saying don't go."

There was a short pause. She knew if she stayed for Sam, she'd end up resenting him. She hated that he'd even ask. "London isn't the other end of the world. It's only a drive away."

He moved away from her and sat on the couch. "A five-hour drive."

Her brow furrowed and she could feel her blood pulsing faster. "So you claim you love me but not enough to drive five hours to see me? You don't love me enough to make that much effort?"

He hung his head and rubbed at his temples. "I don't know what you want me to say."

Tears streamed steadily down her face. Every muscle in her body was tense. He only wanted to be with her on his terms. How could he say he loved her and then ask her to give up her dreams? When he finally looked at her, there were tears in his eyes too, but she couldn't rustle any sympathy. Wiping her cheeks, she walked to the door. He called her name, but she didn't stop and he didn't come after her.

She was still crying when she got back to Annette. She sat

at the kitchen table and hugged Macy when she jumped into her lap.

Annette gave her shoulder a quick squeeze. "You talked to Sam?"

Josie nodded miserably. "He asked me not to go. Said it's over between us if I go to London."

Annette switched the kettle on and joined Josie at the table. "Give him some time to get used to the idea. Talk to him again when he's calmed down."

"I don't want to lose him." More tears appeared. "Maybe I shouldn't go? I might be making a huge mistake."

"I think you should go," Annette said.

"Really?" Josie wasn't sure whether to be happy at the support or offended.

"You're following your dreams. How can that be a mistake?"

"But if I lose Sam …"

"If you give up on your dreams for Sam, things won't work out anyway. You know that. He should never have asked you to stay."

"I know. I'm so angry with him." She sniffed. "But he looked so hurt, and that's because of me. I never wanted to hurt him. And I really can't stand the thought of losing him."

Annette patted her hand. "He loves you. You won't lose him." She stood and began to make a pot of tea. "Everything will be okay in the end. You'll see."

CHAPTER 36

J osie's stubborn side took over, and she didn't get in
touch with Sam but waited for him to contact her. It had
never occurred to her that she'd end up missing him
before she even left. She almost called him lots of times, but
every time she reached for her phone she remembered how
adamant he'd been that their relationship was over if she left.
He wouldn't entertain the idea of a long-distance relationship.
If she left, that was it. Could she really be with someone who
gave her ultimatums?

In the end, she was sure that if Sam really loved her, he'd
be supportive and do whatever it took to make things work.
He just didn't care enough. It broke her heart, but that was the
conclusion she came to.

She spent her days walking the fields with the dogs.
She'd miss all the fresh air and exercise, and Annette too.
Annette being alone was something she worried about a lot.
Of course, Annette insisted she'd be fine, but Josie felt guilty
all the same.

She'd thrown herself into finding a replacement –
someone to help Annette with the kennels. Max had insisted

he could find someone, but Josie wanted to do it. It reminded her of those first days in Averton when she'd driven to all the pet shops and vet's practices, putting up adverts for the kennels. Except now she was advertising a job. *Her* job. She trawled job sites on the internet too and put up online ads. It should be someone local who could call in every day. She couldn't stand the thought of someone living at Oakbrook like she had.

On Friday morning she drove to Hope Cove. When Lizzie wrapped her in a hug, it made Josie cry. She wiped away tears and they moved into the living room. Max was at the desk in the corner and looked up from a pile of paperwork.

"Sorry for disrupting your morning," Josie said when he left to make coffee.

"It's fine," Lizzie said. "I'm glad you came. We were planning on calling over to see you before you left."

"I can't believe I'm leaving in a week," she said. "I'm worried about Annette. I think I might have found a replacement to help her with the kennels. I've been emailing a local girl who's looking for something part-time working with animals. She's coming over tomorrow and I think she might work out."

"That's good. Don't worry too much about Annette. We'll keep an eye on her, and Sam said he'll help out as much as he can."

"That's nice," Josie said bitterly. "He's not speaking to me." Her hands covered her face as she dissolved into a blubbering wreck.

Lizzie patted her shoulder.

"I really thought that when he got used to the idea, he'd be okay with it. I never wanted to lose him. I thought he'd call and we'd work things out."

"I know," Lizzie said gently.

"And I'm angry, so angry with him!" Josie's voice quivered with emotion. "He's being unreasonable. He wouldn't even talk about it. All he says is that if I leave, that's the end of things between us."

Max arrived and put mugs of coffee on the table. "He's really upset too."

"Did he talk to you?"

Max nodded. "He's being pig-headed but he's got his reasons."

"What?" Josie said, desperately.

Max glanced at Lizzie before he spoke. "I take it he didn't tell you about his ex?" Josie shook her head, remembering a conversation where he'd brushed the subject aside. "When he moved back to Averton, he was with someone. They were living in Bristol, but Sam wanted to move and she agreed to it. Except she had a project she wanted to finish up at work, so she was supposed to be in Bristol for six months while Sam moved back first." He waved a hand as though skipping a few details. "She ended up cheating on him with one of her colleagues."

Josie sunk into the couch. At least that explained his aversion to long-distance relationships. "I live in a village. Everyone gossips. How didn't I know that?"

"I don't think he told anyone why they split up." He smiled. "Didn't want everyone gossiping about it, I suppose. He barely spoke to me about it."

"I think he had a lucky escape," Lizzie said lightly. "If you can't manage six months apart then you really shouldn't be getting married anyway."

"Married?" Josie said.

Lizzie winced. "He didn't tell you?"

"That he was engaged?" she snapped. "No. He forgot to mention that!"

There was a silence, and Josie caught Max glaring at Lizzie. They shouldn't be caught up in her and Sam's problems. Life would be much simpler if she'd never agreed to take the job at Oakbrook. She would never have got together with Sam, and getting her old job back would have been exciting rather than stressful.

Of course, she also wouldn't have become so close to Annette or met Amber and Tara. There were lots of positives to her time in Averton, and she couldn't let them be overshadowed by her problems with Sam.

"I'm sorry," Lizzie said. "I just assumed you knew."

"It doesn't matter. He obviously didn't want me to know. I'm starting to think things would never have worked out with us anyway. I thought I knew him so well, but I clearly don't."

Max cradled his coffee and sighed. "I'm sure he would've told you eventually. You've not been together long."

Lizzie scowled at him. "That's not really the point."

"Max is right," Josie said, hating the friction. "We haven't been together long. It was probably never as serious as I thought. I got carried away, that's all."

"Well, I didn't mean it like that," Max said, letting out an exaggerated sigh.

Josie crumpled into tears and sobbed as Lizzie enveloped her in a big hug. She really hadn't been together with Sam very long so she shouldn't be so upset to find out things she didn't know about him. Except that she distinctly remembered him telling her about the girlfriend he'd lived with in Bristol, and he'd made it sound pretty casual. He'd purposely not told her they were engaged. It's not like she would've cared. She just hated that he'd kept it from her.

Max moved to sit on the other side of her and patted her knee. "Do you want me to talk to him?"

"No." She sniffed and took a calming breath. "Thanks. I don't think it'll make any difference, and I don't want to make things awkward for you. I'm sorry you're caught up in the middle of my mess."

"Don't worry," Max said with mischief in his eyes. "We have pretty boring lives these days. It keeps us entertained."

"Oh my God," Lizzie said. "You're the most insensitive person in the world today! What is wrong with you?" She pushed Josie back into the couch so she could give Max a playful shove.

"She beats me up like this all the time." He chuckled. "I thought I might get away with one joke since you're here." He raised an eyebrow at Josie. "Mrs Crazy Hormones doesn't get jokes any more."

"Because all you do is joke about my hormones! It's not funny. I have two babies inside me." She paused. "And I live with an idiot!"

"See what I have to put up with?" Max said.

Lizzie glared at him. "See what *I* have to put up with, more like!"

Josie couldn't help but smile. They were very entertaining when they bickered.

"You know I love you really," Max said, leaning over to kiss Lizzie.

"All right!" Josie said, pushing them apart. "Don't go all lovey-dovey on me. It's sickening."

"How about we go down to the beach for a bit?" Lizzie said. "Swim and a picnic?"

Josie agreed, happily.

"Guess I'm making a picnic," Max said. "Beats paperwork, I suppose."

~

They spent a lovely afternoon on the beach. It was another thing Josie would miss: her spontaneous trips to the seaside to visit her sister. She tried not to dwell on it too much. She'd be back to visit as often as she could.

Alone in the car on the way back to Oakbrook, Josie's thoughts inevitably lingered on Sam. She thought of him not telling her about his engagement and was angry with him again. If he didn't think enough about their relationship to tell her about his past, then why had he made such a fuss about her leaving?

She'd worked herself into a state by the time she reached Averton, and she drove straight to Sam's house. His van was on the drive but there was no answer at the door. It crossed her mind that he was ignoring her. Well, she'd just keep knocking and see how long until he let her in. She was hammering a fist against the door when she decided it didn't seem like something Sam would do.

Then she heard the faint hum of a radio and followed the noise round the back of the house. She crossed the garden and saw him in the garage, hunched over a table with a look of concentration on his face. Her anger morphed quickly into sadness. She really did love him.

He stopped when he saw her and stood up straight, then walked casually over to her.

"Do you want a drink or something?"

She shook her head. What she really wanted was to put her arms around him and breathe in his scent. She wanted to laugh and joke with him and cover him in kisses. She didn't want to feel so awkward around him. She clenched her jaw, trying her hardest not to cry.

"Can we talk for a minute?" She gestured the patio table and he pulled out a chair opposite her. She hesitated for a moment, watching a butterfly float across the lawn as she searched for something to say.

"Max explained why you won't do a long-distance relationship. He told me about your ex."

Sam's eyes darkened. "It's nothing to do with my ex. And Max should learn to mind his own business."

"Don't be annoyed with Max," she said quickly. "If you'd talked to me he wouldn't need to fill me in. Why didn't you tell me about your ex?"

"This has nothing to do with my ex!" he said angrily. "It's about you. You get bored and move onto the next thing. How long before you get bored of having a long-distance relationship and move on? I'm guessing not very long."

"I don't have a crystal ball," she snapped. "I can't tell you what will happen. All I can tell you is that I want us to try and make this work."

"How would it even work? Would you come back on the weekends? Do you expect me to drive all the way to London—"

"Yes!" she shouted, shooting out of her chair. She gave up with her attempt not to cry. "Yes, sometimes I would expect you to get in a car and drive to see me. What's so unreasonable about that?" A sob escaped her. "I expected you to tell me important stuff like previous fiancées. And I expected you to make a bit of effort for our relationship. I guess I expected too much!"

"Will you stop turning this around on me?" he said, his voice a low growl. "You're the one who decided to move away. It's you who isn't giving our relationship a chance."

She took a deep breath. "So you want me to turn the job down? Stay here for you? How well do you think that would work out in the long run?"

"It won't," he said sadly. "We want different things. Different lives."

"I still want you in my life," she whispered.

The silence stretched out uncomfortably, and when it became clear he had no more to say, Josie walked back around the house and into her car.

She spent a week hoping he'd change his mind. Every morning in the barn, she hoped he'd creep up and wrap his arms around her and tell her that he was an idiot, and they could survive any distance. He never showed up, though. Never called or messaged her.

She kept herself busy training up her replacement, a young woman called Heather. She'd just finished training to be a veterinary assistant but hadn't managed to find a job in the field yet. She was quiet, but polite and respectful, and at least Josie wasn't leaving Annette completely alone.

Josie also met up with Tara and Amber that week and had one last night in the Bluebell Inn on Friday evening. Sam was nowhere to be seen, and she decided it was probably a good thing. She didn't want a big scene in front of the whole village. It was harder than she'd expected saying her good-byes in the pub, especially to Tara and Amber.

She was due to leave on the Sunday, and on Saturday evening she couldn't take it any more and ended up on Sam's doorstep. He was unshaven and unkempt. He looked how she felt: a mess. When he stepped aside without a word, she wandered into the living room. There was a dip in the couch where he'd been lying.

"I don't want to argue but I'm leaving tomorrow and I didn't want to leave things as they were." She sat on the couch and looked up at him with sad eyes. "I already miss you so much."

Still he didn't say anything, and she was surprised when he sat so close beside her. He put an arm around her and pulled her to him. She revelled in the warmth of him and then slowly moved her mouth to his. The kisses started slow and gentle but soon became urgent and frantic. Clothes were discarded in a frenzy, and they clung to each other desperately as they made love.

When she woke in his bed the next morning, the sun was streaming through the window. Their bodies were tangled amongst the sheets. He ran a hand through her hair and she propped her chin on his chest to look up at him.

She didn't want to go anywhere.

CHAPTER 37

For the first few days in London, it felt like all Josie did was stare at her phone. She just wanted Sam to call. Her appetite had vanished and the ache in her chest was constant. It reminded her of when Sam had been working away and she'd missed him so much. Except this was way worse. A few weeks ago things had been so good. Now she was sleeping on Emily's couch and waiting to start a job she wasn't even sure she wanted any more.

That last night with Sam had arguably only made things worse. She'd been so tempted to stay with him but knew this was something she needed to do. It hurt her so much that he couldn't be supportive.

She spent those first days wandering the streets, keeping out of Emily's way while she was writing. It gave her time to think that she could've done without. Increasingly, she felt like she'd made a huge mistake. There was nothing she could do now, though. She could hardly go running back to Sam and promise to stay forever in Averton. The desire to call him was almost overwhelming sometimes. She wanted to ask about his day and tell him about hers. But the pain of missing him was mingled with anger at his stubbornness.

Four days after she arrived at Emily's place, she got up while it was still dark and set off for her first day of work. It took an hour to get from Emily's place in Shoreditch to the TV studio in Borehamwood. The underground was busy, even at that ungodly hour, and the bustle of people annoyed her in a way it never had before.

The television studio was far from being glamorous, just an old grey building. It took her a while to find the entrance. Eventually she found a couple of other people wandering around, looking as lost as her, and they walked the perimeter together until they found a door at the back with a piece of paper flapping in the breeze. The makeshift sign read *This Military Life* in barely legible scrawl.

Josie still felt half asleep when she sat in front of a mirror at 6.30 a.m. A busty brunette applied her make-up in thick layers. The foundation felt heavy on her skin and the false eyelashes made it a battle to keep her eyes open. Once the bright red lipstick was applied, Josie felt like laughing. It was quite a transformation. Her hair had been pulled into a messy top knot.

Staring in the mirror, she mentioned that she'd had a much more natural look when they'd filmed the pilot episode. Kate, the make-up artist, insisted she was following instructions and shooed her out of the chair, then beckoned for her next victim.

Josie was ushered to a holding room to wait for filming to start. She was uncomfortable in a mini skirt and shirt that gaped at the bust. The shoes were the worst, though – strappy sandals with three inches of stiletto heel. She kicked them off and sat barefoot.

The ridiculous shoes shouldn't have surprised her. She'd worn a similar pair for the pilot. Somehow, she'd forgotten all about that, and when it did come back to her, she recalled how hilarious she'd found it last time. In fact, the first time she'd met Jack it was because he'd reached out to catch her when she'd wobbled on her heels. They'd had a great laugh about how high the shoes were. Jack had always made fun of how precarious she was in them.

Josie looked around the holding room. There were probably twenty other people, chatting in various groups. She kept her head down, looking at her phone. She wasn't in the mood to be sociable. A group of girls in their early twenties laughed loudly at the other side of the room. Back when she'd filmed the pilot it had all seemed like fun to Josie too. Of course, she hadn't given up anything for the acting job then. It had come along at just the right time and had been a big adventure. She'd met Jack on the first day of filming, while she'd been tottering round the holding area trying to get the hang of walking in high heels. Jack had made everything fun.

For the first time in a long time, Josie found herself missing Jack. *Great!* As if missing Sam wasn't enough, now Jack too. He always knew how to cheer her up. On a whim, she scrolled to his number and pressed call.

He sounded happy to hear from her.

"I'm starting filming today," she said. "I'm just sitting in the holding room."

"That brings back memories," he said. "Have you got crazy shoes again?"

She glanced at the discarded shoes. "Yes! They're awful."

"Have you fallen over yet?"

"No, but I've only had them on for about three minutes."

"Shall we have a bet on how many times you fall? I'll say five times today. And a trip or a stumble counts as a fall, okay?"

Tears stung her eyes. "I think I made a mistake, Jack."

"Splitting up with me?" he said, mischief in his voice. "I knew you'd realise eventually!"

"No!" She managed to laugh through her tears. "Taking this job. I was happy at Oakbrook. I don't know why I thought this was such a great idea."

"Has this got something to do with the guy?" Jack asked.

"Maybe," she said.

"It's okay. You can talk to me about the other men in your life. I'll probably cry myself to sleep tonight but I'll pretend to be cool about it now."

"Sorry," she said. "I shouldn't have called you. I just feel like my life is a mess." She couldn't help thinking about Sam's comment about her not sticking at anything. Why couldn't she find a job that she was content with?

There was a pause before Jack spoke. "You can call me whenever you want. And talk to me about anything. We always said we'd stay friends."

She sniffed and fumbled in her bag for a tissue, hoping she wasn't ruining her make-up. "Sam didn't want a long-distance relationship," she finally said. "He told me if I moved to London it was over between us. And now I miss him so much."

"Call him," Jack suggested. "Tell him you miss him. He was probably just upset. I bet he misses you too."

"I don't think it's that simple. He's hurt and angry. But he's also adamant that he doesn't want a long-distance rela-tionship, and I can't help but think that means he just doesn't care enough."

"Maybe he just needed some time to get used to the idea. Call him and talk to him again. Give him another chance."

"I don't know …"

"I'm not sure why I'm giving you that advice," Jack said with a laugh. There were voices in the background. "Just a minute."

"Are you at work?" Josie asked.

"Yeah."

"Are there customers waiting for you?"

"Yeah. But some of these people really need a lesson in patience."

"Jack!" She laughed. "Don't lose your job because you're chatting to me."

"I better go then. But stop worrying so much, it doesn't suit you."

"That's easy to say when you didn't just give up a lovely life in the country for a job where you have to wear crazy shoes and more make-up than a clown."

"The job will get better. I promise!"

"I hope so. Thanks, Jack."

He told her they'd talk again soon before he ended the call.

She felt marginally better. Maybe Jack was right and she should call Sam.

The door to the holding area swung open a moment later and they were ushered down to the studio. It was strange being back on the same set that she'd been on before. It was so familiar, but she felt completely different.

The afternoon dragged on. They were filming some of the main characters chatting at the bar. A few soldiers with their wives and girlfriends. Josie barely paid attention. She spent a lot of the afternoon polishing glasses and keeping her back to the camera as she'd been instructed. There was no acting involved, really. If she turned towards the action she was supposed to keep a neutral expression and not react to anything. It was pretty easy. If they'd asked her to smile, she might have had a problem.

She had plenty of time to think that afternoon. By the time the director shouted "cut" for about the hundredth time, she was convinced that calling Sam was a good idea.

.

CHAPTER 38

It was late when Josie got home and she was exhausted after such a long day. Emily briefly looked up from her laptop and asked how the day had been. After an unenthusiastic reply from Josie, Emily disappeared into her bedroom, saying she needed to get a bit more writing done before bed.

Josie sat on the couch and slipped her aching feet out of her shoes. She checked the time. Just before 10 p.m. A little late to start making phone calls, but Sam would still be up. An image of him relaxing on his couch came to mind, and then she thought about the last time she was on his couch. The tightness in her chest returned. She wanted to be there with him.

The phone rang for a while before he answered. Josie's heart was hammering so hard, she wasn't sure she could talk.

"Everything okay?" he asked wearily.

"Yeah," she said, finally finding her voice. "How are you?"

He sighed impatiently. "Fine."

"Good." She got the definite impression he didn't want to

talk to her, but she pressed on regardless. "Did you have a good day?"

"Yep." He paused. "Were you calling for something in particular?"

"No. I just wanted to hear your voice."

He didn't reply, and in other circumstances she'd have made a joke about the irony.

"I started work today," she said, desperate to fill the silence. "You should see the stupid shoes I have to wear …"

"I don't really have time to talk now," he said, speaking over her. His voice was so cold she barely recognised it. "I have to go."

"Wait," she said, sure he was about to hang up. She didn't know what to say, though. "When will you have time to talk to me? Are you going to stay angry at me forever?"

"I'm not angry," he snapped. "We want different things."

Tears stung her eyes and she felt herself losing control of her emotions. "Can you stop being so stubborn and pig-headed? We can still work things out."

He went quiet again. "I don't want to argue with you, Josie."

"Just talk to me then."

"We can't keep having the same conversation. I'm going to hang up now."

"No!" she said through a sob. "I miss you."

For a moment she could hear him breathing and hugged the phone to her cheek.

His voice was soft. "Take care, Josie."

Silence.

She wanted to call him back and scream down the phone at him. Or get in the car and go and shout at him in person. How could he be so cold? And how had they gone from things being so perfect to so awful in a matter of weeks? She was absolutely furious with him. And heartbroken at the same time.

She gripped the phone tightly, resisting the urge to throw it at the wall. Instead, she lay down and sobbed quietly into her pillow.

∽

"You're not making my job easy," Kate, the make-up artist, said as Josie took a seat at her station the next morning. She'd barely slept and felt awful. If she made it through the day without bursting into tears it'd be a major achievement. Thank goodness she had a make-up artist to make her look human.

"I don't even know where to start," Kate said. "What happened? Did you break up with your boyfriend or something? You look like you've been up all night crying."

"I have," Josie said flatly.

Kate rolled her eyes and got to work. When Josie walked into the holding room, the gaggle of young girls were huddled in a corner laughing loudly. They were always bloody laughing. What exactly *were* they so happy about? They'd probably all spend the next couple of hours in the bland holding room, waiting to be called onto set. How was that fun?

There were several groups of people dotted around, and Josie wondered whether she'd feel better if she got to know some people. She recognised one or two people from filming the pilot but it was a long time ago now, and she'd really only had eyes for Jack back then.

After scanning the room, Josie decided she couldn't face being sociable and sat alone once again.

Staring miserably into her coffee, she replayed the conversation with Sam. It was hard to believe things really were over. She blinked away tears. Her emotions were all over the place. She felt so terrible for leaving, and part of her wanted to go back and grovel and get everything back to how it was a month ago. But another part of her was angry with Sam. He was being unreasonable. It was a side of him that she wouldn't have believed existed. Maybe she hadn't really known him very well at all.

There was some bustle as a group of guys dressed as soldiers came into the room. She smiled when a couple of them asked if they could sit with her, and she managed to make polite conversation before she was called onto set. They were filming more quiet scenes at the bar before shooting scenes with the room full of soldiers. It should be slightly livelier than the previous day.

After an hour, her feet were killing her, and she was well and truly fed up. When the director called "cut", she kicked her shoes off and enjoyed the feel of the cold floor on her aching feet. The director called for quiet and she didn't have time to put her shoes back on so she stood on her tiptoes as he shouted "action" and hoped no one would notice. Typical – it was a long scene and she gradually got shorter. She was fairly sure she wasn't in shot, anyway. Cleaning glasses was getting tedious. At the back of the bar, she straightened the bottles of spirits and wiped down the counter. God, it was boring. Her mind drifted to Oakbrook and she remembered all the good times.

Recently, the images of Sam in her head were all negative, but suddenly she could see him laughing so clearly that it was a struggle not to cry. She missed him so much.

As she straightened a bottle of vodka, she caught sight of herself in the mirrored wall behind the bottles of alcohol. She moved the vodka aside. The person in the mirror didn't look anything like her. There was so much make-up.

Without much thought, she reached for a glass and poured a shot of vodka. With her back to the room, surely no one would notice. She winced as it burned her throat. What on earth was she doing? Drinking on set was surely a sackable offence. No one noticed, though, and she realised the thought of getting fired really didn't bother her at all. She wouldn't have to wear the stupid shoes any more.

The set got busy as a crowd of soldiers filed in. It was probably going to be a long afternoon.

"You need your shoes on," the assistant director told her. "You shrank three inches in that last scene. Good job you weren't in shot."

"My legs are hidden by the bar. Does it really matter what shoes I wear?"

"Yep! It does." The walkie-talkie on her belt crackled, and she muttered something into it before turning back to Josie. "Put them on, please."

"My feet are killing me. I've got about ten blisters."

"I'll get you some plasters. But keep the shoes on."

She spoke into her walkie-talkie as she walked away, and at the end of the next scene one of the runners appeared with a handful of plasters for Josie. They helped a bit but she really couldn't wait to get out of the shoes.

When the director called "cut" the next time, a cocky voice behind her asked for a drink. She grinned automatically but couldn't quite believe her ears. When she turned to face Jack, she almost cried tears of joy.

"I have never been so happy to see you!" She hugged him tightly across the bar. "What are you doing here?"

"My duty to queen and country," he said, looking at his uniform with mock pride.

"I didn't think you wanted to take the job again."

"It's just a week. They need a crowd for the scenes on location. I thought it might be fun so I took a week's holiday from work. The money's decent enough."

"That's great. It's so good to see you."

"I told you the job would get better!"

"That's what you meant?" she said, chuckling.

"You're really not enjoying it?" he asked.

"My feet are killing me and I've taken to sneaking shots of vodka … so no, I'm not enjoying it."

"Feel free to sneak me shots," he said, then looked serious. "What about lover boy? Did you call him?"

"Yeah." She bit her lip. "He doesn't want to know."

Jack muttered something derogatory and then the director called for quiet. They moved into action for the scene, and as soon as the director shouted "cut" she turned back to Jack.

"Do you want to get a drink later?" she said. "In an actual bar!"

He grimaced. "I've got a date."

"Really?"

"Yeah. That's not weird, is it? I'm allowed to date. You did dump me!"

"Of course you're allowed to date."

"Are you gonna get all depressed that your ex-boyfriend's dating while you're miserable?"

"No," she said, amused. "Who is she?"

"Her name's Lauren. If you spot a female soldier in here, there's a fifty percent chance it's her."

"She's here?" Josie asked, scanning the room.

"Yeah. The one staring at us," he said with a boyish smile. "I just met her earlier."

"Oh my God! No wonder you like this job."

"I know. Crazy, huh? We just got chatting and she asked me to go for dinner later. I can have a drink with you tomorrow night? I don't like to think of you crying yourself to sleep over a guy."

She'd have laughed if it hadn't been an accurate assessment of her evenings. "Don't worry about me. I'll get over it."

"He doesn't deserve you," Jack said.

"Shut up or you'll make me cry again!"

They were interrupted by the director calling instructions. In the scene, the crowd of soldiers were drinking and getting more and more boisterous in the lead-up to a punch-up between two of the main characters. Josie had her back to the action most of the time, only turning when the fight broke out. It was all hidden from her view by the crowd anyway.

"Maybe you'll get some lines eventually," Jack said at the next interlude. She obviously looked as bored as she felt.

"I hope so." After everything she'd left behind at Oakbrook, she really needed something good to come of her new job. It was supposed to be a great opportunity, but it had been completely overshadowed by all the negativity with Sam.

"I'll be glad when we're out on location," Jack said. "It should be more interesting."

"When's that?"

"Starts tomorrow. Five days of filming in South Downs National Park."

Josie swore under her breath. "I guess they don't need a barmaid on location …"

"Hadn't you already heard?"

"Nope. Nobody mentioned it. What am I going to do for a week?"

She hoped there'd been some mistake, but when she went to sign off on her hours at the end of the day, it was confirmed – she wasn't needed until the following week. Just when she thought things couldn't get any worse, she now had a week with no income and far too much time to think.

CHAPTER 39

Emily was working at the restaurant that evening so Josie had the place to herself. The day of filming had been much more bearable with Jack around. It was nice to catch up with him, and there was a lovely feeling of nostalgia being with him on the TV set. It was weird, though, seeing him leave with someone else.

It didn't seem that long since it was her who was happily going on dates with Jack after long days of filming. It was good to see him so happy, but at the same time, it did seem to highlight her lack of a love life, or a social life even, come to think of it. Maybe she should start dating. When she was filming with so many men, she surely wouldn't have a hard time finding a date.

Not that it was a serious thought. The only person she wanted to go on a date with was Sam. She called Lizzie that evening. Instead of telling her how miserable she was, she ended up telling her the filming was going great. It seemed to be what she expected to hear, and Josie wasn't quite ready to admit to her sister what a mess she was in. She didn't mention the fact that she'd done two days of filming and now had a week off. When she ended the call, it occurred to her that the conversation with Lizzie involved far more acting than she'd done the past two days in the TV studio.

How on earth was she going to get through a week with nothing to do? It crossed her mind to visit Annette, but she couldn't decide if it was a good idea or not. She wanted to see Sam so badly, but she didn't think she could bear it. Him being so cold towards her was agony.

She felt pathetic for being tempted to call him again. She wouldn't, though. He'd made his feelings very clear, and she needed to accept it and move on. It would be easier if she could stop thinking about him.

When she woke the next morning, it was to the sound of Emily tapping away on her laptop.

"To think I used to hate being woken by birds when I was at Oakbrook," Josie mumbled from her bed on the couch.

"Sorry." Emily swivelled in her chair at her little desk in the corner. "I end up with a stiff neck if I write in bed for too long."

"It's fine," Josie said.

"Are you working today?"

"No, I've got a few days off. But I'll get out of your way."

"Thanks," Emily said. "I've got loads to do."

"Are you sure it's okay me staying here? I don't want things to get weird. If it's a problem just say."

"It's fine … I could really use the help with the rent."

Josie sat up and stretched. "And that's a subtle hint for me to give you some money."

"There's no hurry," Emily said with a sweet smile.

"I'll go to the bank today." It was a good job she'd saved

some money while she was with Annette. Working two days a week wasn't really going to cover her living costs.

"Thanks," Emily said. "Sorry I'm no fun at the moment. I'm snowed under. Maybe we can have a night out at the weekend?"

"Sounds good," Josie said.

"How's it going with the filming?"

"It's okay. Jack was there yesterday so that livened things up."

"How's he doing?"

"He's the same old Jack. He was off out on a date last night."

"That must be weird," Emily said idly. "It's a shame things didn't work out with you two. I always thought you made a good couple. You're not tempted to try and get back with him since things didn't work out with Sam?"

"No!" Josie wrinkled her nose. "Of course not."

Emily shrugged. "Have you heard anything from Sam?"

"Yeah." She sighed at the reminder. "I spoke to him, but it seems like it's really over." The thought made her chest ache.

"He sounds like an idiot."

Josie tilted her head. "He's not."

"Don't get all defensive," Emily said. "I'm just telling it like it is. If he can't make the effort to try and make things work, he's probably not worth it anyway."

Josie stood abruptly. "I'm going to have a shower and I'll get out of your way."

"Sorry," Emily said, clearly sensing she'd hit a nerve. "I just hate you moping around because of some guy. You can do much better."

Resisting the urge to argue, Josie went for a shower and spent a long time under the hot spray. She was annoyed with Emily, but could also see her point. Sam *had* treated her badly, and it was probably time she moved on. It was so hard, though. She still had a tiny spark of hope that he'd call her, grovelling, and say he was an idiot and he wanted them to work things out. After the shower she automatically checked her phone, but of course there were no messages.

Not wanting to disturb Emily, she didn't bother with breakfast, just grabbed her bag and set off with no specific plan for the day. Wandering the city wasn't going to help. She needed something to take her mind off things.

Her stomach growled with hunger as soon as she walked out of the apartment, and she ducked into the nearest cafe. It took ages to get served but she eventually ordered coffee and toast. She needed to be frugal with money if filming was going to be so irregular.

It was the first time Josie had been into Brenda's Kitchen, which was located just a couple of buildings away from Emily's flat. She was surprised by how bad the service was. She'd only ordered coffee and toast but it took almost half an hour before it arrived. Not that Josie really cared; she wasn't in a hurry. She probably wouldn't return to the cafe, though.

It seemed like there was only one woman working, and she looked like she was about to have a nervous breakdown. Josie took pity on her and cleared her table when she'd finished, bringing her plate and mug to the counter. The poor waitress was having an argument with the cook, and the raised voices drifted out into the cafe. It was embarrassing, really.

Josie was about to leave when a table strewn with dirty dishes caught her attention. She'd worked as a waitress many times and it was almost an automatic response to clear the table. The frazzled waitress looked at her sympathetically when she walked towards the counter with her arms loaded with dishes.

"Did heaven send you?" she asked.

Josie chuckled. "No. You just seemed swamped."

"I am," she said with a sigh. "My regular waitress broke her leg yesterday and the dishwasher chose this morning to give up on me. I'm waiting for the repair guy now."

"It never rains but it pours …"

"Too right! Don't suppose you have waitressing experience and need a job?"

"My sister says it's quicker to list the jobs I don't have experience in than the ones I do." She grinned at the puzzled-looking middle-aged woman. "Yeah I have experience."

"And you need a job?"

"I already have a job." She dithered and her gaze swept over the cosy little cafe. "I suppose I could help out today."

"Really?" The woman's eyes filled with relief. "You're a lifesaver. I'll give you cash at the end of the day." She rooted in her pocket and pulled out a key. "You can put your bag in the office, then I'll tell you where to start. I'm Brenda, by the way!"

"I'm Josie," she called over her shoulder. When she came back from the office, Brenda was busy serving customers, so Josie cleared tables and took the dishes to the kitchen.

"Hi!" she said to the cook. "I'm Josie. Looks like I'm working here today."

"Good," the dark-haired woman said. "I'm sure I wouldn't last the day alone with Brenda! When she's busy she gets stressed … and when she's stressed she takes it out on me!" She shuffled eggs in a pan. "I'm Stella."

"Nice to meet you." Josie was about to start washing up when she glanced at the dishwasher. "What happened to this thing?" she asked, opening it up.

"No idea," Stella said. "The water won't drain. There's a load of dirty water sitting at the bottom of it. The repair guy should be here soon."

"Sometimes they just get clogged." Josie bent down and pulled the bottom tray out. The water at the bottom was foul.

She stuck a hand in regardless and pulled out the filter at the bottom. "Did you try clearing it?"

Stella nodded. "Brenda had a look at it but she couldn't fix it so she called the handyman."

Reaching for a spoon, Josie stuck the handle into the drain at the bottom of the dishwasher. She poked around a bit until she heard a glug and the water began to recede.

"Have you fixed it?" Stella said, in awe.

"Maybe," Josie said. "Let's give it a go." She filled it up and switched it on.

"This one's fixed the dishwasher!" Stella said when Brenda walked in a few minutes later.

"You're kidding?" Brenda said, wiping her brow. "How did you manage that?"

"It was just clogged up." At the sink, Josie scrubbed her hands thoroughly under the tap. "You should still get someone to look at it. It might keep happening."

"You really are a lifesaver," Brenda said.

"Table eight!" Stella said, plating up two full English breakfasts.

"I've got it," Josie said, jumping into action. It felt good to be needed. Plus she'd just gone a full ten minutes without thinking about Sam, which felt like a major achievement.

It was a while since she'd done any waitressing, and she was amazed by how much she enjoyed it. She liked being busy, and in the quieter moments she chatted with customers or with Brenda and Stella, who seemed an amiable pair when they weren't rushed off their feet.

"What is it you do when you're not saving cafés from disaster?" Brenda said cheerfully at the end of the day.

"I'm working as a TV extra. I play a barmaid in a new soap opera."

"Oh, exciting! What is it? Maybe I've seen it?"

"It hasn't been aired yet. We're just filming the first series. It's a military thing. But the filming is a bit hit and miss so I have quite a lot of spare time."

"Don't suppose you can help me out again tomorrow, can you? I can get someone from an agency but you never know if they'll actually turn up, or if they'll be any good."

"Well, I've got the rest of the week free and I could do with the money."

"Brilliant!" Brenda counted out a hundred pounds from the till and handed it over to Josie. She'd probably made the same in tips so she was quite happy. No need to go to the bank after all.

In the apartment, she handed the money over to Emily with a smile on her face. "That was an interesting day!"

She proceeded to fill her friend in over a glass of wine.

"You seem much more positive this evening," Emily said.

"I am." Josie pulled her feet underneath her on the couch. "It was only a day of waitressing in a greasy café, but I guess being busy did me good. I think I've been so consumed by all the drama with Sam that I lost sight of things. This move was supposed to be a positive step. I need to stop moping around and get on with my life."

And she really was determined to.

CHAPTER 40

The café turned out to be her saviour. It kept her busy, which was exactly what she needed. Six weeks passed without her having a day off. Whenever she wasn't on the TV set, she was in the café.

Stella and Brenda were great fun to work with and had become good friends too. She preferred her days working in the café to the ones on set. It was fortunate, really, since the filming was only usually two or three times a week. She hated that it wasn't working out as she hoped, but she was making the most of the situation.

Once or twice she'd spoken to Michaela about quitting the acting job, but Michaela kept insisting there were rumours about Josie's role becoming a speaking part and she'd be doing some real acting before she knew it. Of course, Michaela didn't want to lose her commission, and Josie still had that glimmer of a dream of being a proper actress.

When Josie wasn't at the café, Brenda used a temp agency to get someone to fill in for her. It was always entertaining to hear stories about the temporary waitresses. Josie wasn't sure if Brenda and Stella really hated all of them as much as they said or if it was just a joke to make Josie feel better about herself. Occasionally, Brenda would suggest Josie should take a day off, but Josie insisted she didn't need one. As far as she was concerned it was the last thing she needed. The café had saved her when she'd hit rock-bottom, and working there had been the only thing to keep her sane.

It was still an effort not to dwell on Sam, and she was sure a day to herself would only set her back on her plan to move on. She spoke to Annette twice a week and always enjoyed their chats. Only occasionally did Annette mention Sam, and Josie was always torn. It was so hard to hear about him, but she also clung to the nuggets of information like treasures. It was never anything exciting – only that he'd been for a visit or what job he was working on. With a great effort, Josie had barely reacted to the mentions and managed not to ask questions about him. The anger she felt for him was something else she clung to. He'd given her up without a fight. It was easier if she was angry with him.

She still messaged Tara and Amber too, and Amber would message her photos of little Kieron. They always made her smile.

"So you and Jack finally got together?" Brenda asked one gloomy Thursday morning. They were standing in the café's kitchen waiting for opening time. Josie was helping herself to a coffee and barely registered the question. The mention of Jack made her smile, though. What would she have done without him recently? He could make her laugh, even when the last thing she felt like doing was laughing.

"What?" she asked, looking over her coffee at Stella and Brenda.

"Oh, come on," Stella said. "Last time we saw you, you were having breakfast with Jack. We presumed breakfast came after a night of passion?"

"We like him," Brenda said casually. "He gets our approval."

"Well that's good to know," Josie said brightly. "It's not like that, though. He was just doing a couple of days' filming and slept on the floor at Emily's instead of going all the way back to Oxford."

The two women exchanged a suspicious look.

"We're just friends," Josie insisted.

"You talk about him far too much for him to just be a friend," Stella argued.

"Because he's about the only friend I've got at the moment!" That wasn't really true. There was Emily too, but she'd been so busy recently, and with the amount Josie had been working, they barely saw each other. When they did meet up, Emily had a tendency to say the wrong thing. Mostly because Josie couldn't stand to hear anything negative about Sam, even if it was true.

"He's a lovely lad anyway," Brenda said. "You could do much worse."

"We weren't right for each other. We're much better as friends." Josie glanced at the kitchen clock. "Anyway, it's about time to open up, isn't it? Come on."

"Yes, boss!" Stella and Brenda said in unison before howling with laughter.

Josie shook her head and went to flip the sign on the door to "open".

It was busy as always and the day went quickly. There was a lull in the middle of the afternoon, and Josie sat down with a bowl of pasta that Stella had whipped up for her. She was ravenous. A dog barked and Josie glanced out of the window, her gaze landing on the golden retriever tied up outside.

"I wish someone would shut that bloody thing up!" Brenda said as she walked past with an armful of plates.

The woman on the table next to Josie paused from feeding her toddler, who was babbling in a high chair. "He's mine," she said, nodding towards the door. "If you ever want to drink your coffee while it's warm again, don't have kids or dogs." She looked flustered as she rose from the chair. "Can you watch the little one while I go and shout at the dog?"

"Drink your coffee," Josie said. "I'll see to the dog."

She was halfway to the door when the bemused woman shouted her thanks. The dog stopped barking as soon as Josie opened the door and looked up at her with big eyes.

"Hello!" she said softly. He wagged his tail and she bent down, scratching behind his ears and stroking his soft coat. He reminded her of Charlie. "Aren't you lovely?" she said. "You're a good boy." She laughed as he eagerly demanded more attention, creeping closer and attempting to lick her face. "Okay," she said, pushing him down. "You need to calm down. You've got to be quiet out here. Can you manage that?" After giving his head a ruffle, she turned to go back in. He let out a high-pitched bark.

Josie held out a finger and glared at him. "Sit," she said firmly.

He stared at her for a moment before shuffling down onto his back legs.

"Lie down," Josie instructed. His front legs padded forward until he was on his belly. "Stay," Josie said fiercely as she pushed the door open.

"Can you tell me your secret?" the woman with the toddler asked. "He never listens to me."

"She used to work at a dog kennels," Brenda said, patting

Josie on the shoulder. "Now wash your hands and get back to work."

Josie did as she was told. When she returned, the golden retriever was still lying obediently outside the door. Josie smiled sadly. All that time she worked at the kennels and never managed to get the dogs to follow instructions, and now she suddenly had no problem. She made a mental note to tell Annette about it when she spoke to her.

It played on her mind for the rest of the afternoon, making her think of Oakbrook Farm and all the associated memories. She'd done so well burying her feelings, but suddenly she was an emotional wreck. Brenda found her sitting in the office at the end of the day, tears damp on her cheeks.

"What's wrong, love?" she asked, putting an arm around her shoulder. "Are you still thinking about Sam?"

She shook her head and blew her nose on the tissue Brenda passed her. "I was thinking about Macy and Charlie," she said miserably. "I miss them." It had taken a good couple of weeks to stop expecting dogs to run around her legs when she opened the door to Emily's place. She'd got so used to living with dogs around, it felt weird to go home and not be greeted by her furry friends.

Brenda looked puzzled. "The dogs," Josie explained. "At the place I used to work. I miss the dogs. I miss everything."

"Why don't you go for a visit? It might do you good to escape the city for a few days. And you've been working non-stop. You need a break."

"Maybe." She'd been thinking of visiting Annette but she was nervous about seeing Sam. It had been really tough getting over him – and life at Oakbrook – and she was nervous of undoing her hard work.

In the end she decided she would go. She'd have to face Sam eventually, and she desperately wanted to see Annette.

After spending every day with her for over two months, the absence felt strange.

She drove over on Saturday, arriving at lunchtime. The wonderful purple rhododendron flowers at the end of the drive were a welcome sight. Then there was the house with the rosebushes creeping up one side, and the barn, the fields … everything was just as it had been.

It was so good to be back.

CHAPTER 41

Annette was waiting for her and greeted her on the patio with a big hug. Tears stung Josie's eyes and she blinked them away.

"It's so good to see you. Where are Macy and Charlie?" She'd expected them to be bounding all around her by now.

"Out for a walk with Heather. I imagine she'll be back with them soon."

It was a strange feeling that came over Josie. She couldn't quite put her finger on it. Jealousy, perhaps. It was hard to think of Heather doing her job. She wondered how Charlie and Macy had taken to her then brushed the thought aside, realising how ridiculous it was.

Walking into the house, Josie was hit by the familiar smell. She'd never noticed it when she was there every day, but it was distinct, the way all houses have their own particular scent. She'd only been gone six weeks, but it felt like so much longer, and she was hit by a flood of memories.

Annette put the kettle on and peppered Josie with questions about London. Josie tried to concentrate, but she was tired from the early start and the long drive and only just kept up with the conversation. Glancing out of the window she caught sight of Heather outside the barn. She froze at the sight of Sam. He was bending to stroke Charlie but looking up to chat to Heather at the same time. So not only did she have Josie's job, but she'd befriended Sam too. It was like Heather had taken her life. Josie felt sick as she watched them. They looked so relaxed as they chatted together.

"Sam's here," she said quietly.

Annette moved beside her at the window. "Have you spoken to him much since you left?"

Josie shook her head and couldn't take her eyes off him. "We don't speak."

"He'll have seen your car. No doubt he'll come in and say hello."

Josie wasn't so sure and stayed at the window while Annette made tea. She suspected he wouldn't hang around when he realised Josie was there. It was agony just seeing him from afar. When he moved away from Heather and headed to the house, Josie ducked away from the window.

Her pulse sped to a rate which she was sure put her at risk of a heart attack. The hammering on her chest was powerful and overwhelming. Quickly, she took a seat at the table and tried to control her breathing. Surely he'd leave pretty quick. It would be far too awkward between them.

His knuckles rapped on the doorframe as he walked in. Josie felt faint at the sight of him. She shouldn't have come back. There was a sparkle in his eyes when he smiled at her. It reminded her of the day they'd met at Lizzie and Max's wedding.

She felt so uncomfortable, but he seemed completely relaxed. With a breezy hello, he kissed her cheek and told her it was good to see her. She mumbled a response and felt her cheeks heat up.

He didn't leave quickly as she'd expected but helped himself to coffee and took a seat opposite Josie.

"So Annette tells me everything's going well with the new job? She reckons you'll be a big star before we know it."

"I don't know about that." She sipped at her coffee.

"You're enjoying it, though?"

"I love it." What else could she say? That she hated the acting job but had a nice job at a café. It was hardly what she'd planned when she left. Chasing her dreams and her career wasn't quite working out as she'd hoped. There was no way she was going to admit to that, though.

"I'm glad." Sam's smile was warm and genuine.

She'd been so sure that things would be awkward between them, that he'd be angry and uncivil. And now he was looking at her like they were old friends catching up.

"How's work?" she asked to fill the silence.

"It's good." He leaned back in his chair and she was amazed by how casual he was around her. Why did she feel such a jittery mess when he was so confident? "I've had a few orders for furniture recently so that's keeping me busy."

She forced a smile.

"Keeps me out of mischief," he added.

Heather walked in then. Charlie and Macy bounded in too and went straight to Josie. She slipped off the chair and crouched to them, hugging and stroking them as they eagerly bounced around her. She finally relaxed and giggled as the dogs vied for her attention.

"Looks like they missed you," Sam remarked.

"I missed them too." She hugged Macy to her and then ruffled Charlie's coat as he panted in front of her.

Heather hovered awkwardly in the doorway, and Josie dragged her attention from the dogs to say hello.

"How's everything going here?" Josie asked. "Are you enjoying it?"

263

She nodded shyly. "It's going really well." She was hardly going to say anything else. Her gaze drifted to Annette. "Do you need me to do anything else before I leave?"

"You could just check the emails and all that internet stuff."

"Okay." She slipped off her shoes and headed through the house in the direction of the study.

"She's working out well, then?" Josie asked casually once she was out of hearing.

"Yeah," Annette said. "She gets the job done."

"That's good."

Heather appeared again a moment later. "There's an email enquiring about a booking," she said to Annette. "It's for a week in October. For their Dalmatian. Should I reply?"

Annette smiled at her. "Yes, please, love. You need to check the diary but I'm certain we're not booked up in October."

"Okay." She didn't move. "There's also a Twitter notification. Someone tweeted to say thanks for taking care of their dogs." She glanced at Sam, who gave her a reassuring smile.

Josie shifted in her chair. "Like the tweet, reply to it and retweet it." Surely she was stating the obvious. "Do you want me to come and give you a hand?"

"That would be great, if you don't mind. I'm still getting the hang of things."

Josie smiled sweetly. "It's no problem." Anything to get Heather away from Sam. Why was she looking at him with big pathetic eyes? He better not be falling for the shy and helpless act.

Josie took a deep breath as she followed Heather through the house. She was being paranoid. Sam was far too old for Heather anyway. She'd probably never once thought of him that way. Josie certainly hoped not.

It was strange to sit in front of the computer in the small study. She flicked through the diary, checking the bookings. Things were looking steady.

"Do you want me to just do it?" she asked Heather, who hovered at her shoulder. She moved the mouse to click on the Twitter notifications.

"If you don't mind. I'm terrible with social media. I never know what to reply. And I'm always nervous that I'll make a mistake with the bookings."

"I can do it." Josie was increasingly annoyed. She could get it all done in a few minutes if Heather wasn't leaning over her shoulder. "I don't mind at all."

"Thanks," Heather said. "Sorry for getting you to work when you just came for a visit."

"It's fine." Josie glared at her and hoped she'd leave.

"I'll get going then. It was good to see you again."

"You too." Josie forced a smile and felt bad as soon as Heather had left. She could've been nicer to her. It was hard seeing her here, though, doing everything that Josie used to do.

Sam and Annette were chatting in the kitchen when she returned.

"No rest for the wicked, is there?" Annette said. "You're only back five minutes and you get put to work!"

"I don't mind." She reached for her coffee and finished the lukewarm liquid quickly.

"I should probably get off." Sam stood and Josie felt uncomfortable under his gaze. "I'll see you again before you leave. How long are you around for?"

"Just until tomorrow afternoon."

"Okay." He patted Charlie gently on the back. "Have fun."

She watched him go, then sank into a chair. Her head automatically dropped to the table.

"What's wrong?" Annette asked when she lifted her head.

"It's so awful seeing him."

"I thought it was all very relaxed."

"*He* was very relaxed! Does he even miss me at all? Tell me that was all an act and he's usually completely miserable!"

"Of course he misses you. We all do."

"He didn't need to look so bloody happy."

"Maybe he was just happy to see you."

Josie sighed. She'd been wanting to visit for weeks, but she'd put it off because she was sure it would be awkward. Apparently it was only her who was uncomfortable. She almost wished there was an atmosphere between them. Sam carrying on as though nothing had happened between them was just weird. And he'd said he'd see her before she left. So now she was going to spend the whole time wondering when he might turn up. Wouldn't it be easier if he stayed away and avoided her? She wanted to have a relaxing weekend with Annette, not spend all her time panicking about seeing Sam.

"Are you going to see Amber and Tara while you're here?"

"Yes." She'd messaged them as soon as she knew she was coming and was excited to see them. "I said I'd catch up with them tomorrow. I wanted to see Lizzie and Max but they're at some family do. His mum's birthday or something."

"Oh, yes." Josie watched Annette's reaction with intrigue. There'd been some feud between Annette and her sister-in-law, Max's mum, years ago. Josie always thought it was odd that Annette was only really in touch with Max. She'd asked Annette about it once but didn't get much of a response. Max didn't even seem sure of what had happened. "You'll just have to visit again soon. When Max and Lizzie are free." Annette's voice was light, not reacting at all to the mention of her estranged extended family.

"I'd definitely like to get some more beach days in before winter arrives." She glanced outside and caught the sway of branches in the breeze. It was gusty but bright and sunny. "I might take Charlie and Macy out for another walk. Get a bit of exercise and fresh air after being stuck in the car for so long."

"I've made lasagne for later." Annette stood and put the mugs in the dishwasher. "I wouldn't mind a breath of fresh air too. If you don't mind the slower pace."

Josie insisted she didn't and they spent a good hour wandering the familiar hills and fields. She couldn't help but glance in the direction of Sam's house when they were down that way. She wondered what he was doing and imagined him working on some furniture project with that intense look of concentration on his face.

By the time they got back to the house, she was ravenous and devoured a huge portion of lasagne. In the evening, she curled up on the couch with Charlie and Macy and told Annette tales of working in the café. She tried very hard to drop the TV work into the conversation, but she was happier talking about Brenda and Stella and the regulars who frequented the café.

She was exhausted when she crawled into her old bed that night. After six weeks on Emily's couch it was absolute bliss, and she was asleep within minutes.

CHAPTER 42

J osie woke with the birds and smiled as she got up and dressed. In the kitchen she stretched her neck and felt utterly refreshed. "I haven't slept so well in ages."

"Still no luck finding your own place?" Annette said. Josie had told her on the phone that she was trying to find alternative living arrangements. Somewhere she had a bed would be good.

"It's hard. Everywhere is so expensive, and I really want to stay in the same area so I'm close to work."

Annette looked puzzled. "I thought you said it was an hour on the train to work."

"No, it's —" She stopped short, realising Annette was thinking of the TV studios. Josie had been referring to Brenda's Kitchen. "It's a bit less than an hour," she said quickly, "which isn't far by London standards."

They ate breakfast together and then Josie stood automatically. "I'll see to the dogs."

"Don't be daft." Annette clicked her tongue. "You're here for a visit. You don't need to work. You should put your feet up."

"I'm happy to walk the dogs," she insisted. "I'd like to. It doesn't feel like work."

Annette shook her head in amusement, and Josie pushed her feet into her shoes and set off to the barn with Macy and Charlie running happily around her. She did a quick walk-through, checking how many dogs there were and if she knew any of them. At the fourth kennel she stopped and stared. There was a grey two-seater couch that she'd never seen before. Surely Heather hadn't taken over her furniture hunt? She smiled to herself, suddenly sure that it was Sam's work. She'd ask him when she saw him. It made her anxious thinking about seeing him again. Her emotions were all over the place. She loved the thought of seeing him and hated it all at the same time.

Pushing Sam from her thoughts, she spent a pleasant morning walking the dogs. The fresh air and peaceful surroundings made a refreshing change to city life. It was almost lunchtime when she arrived back at the house. Amber and Tara were waiting for her on the patio.

"I thought we were meeting in the pub for lunch," she said as she hugged them tightly.

"We just couldn't wait to see you!" Tara said. "And Annette's offered to make us lunch now."

Josie turned her attention to little Kieron, who was patting the dogs with slightly too much force. "Look at the size of you!" Josie said, tickling him. "He's grown so much."

"Calm down," Tara said. "You've not been gone that long. You sound like some elderly aunt! Come and tell us all about the celebrity life."

"There's not much to tell," Josie said. "It's long hours and a lot of time waiting around doing nothing."

"It's going well, though, isn't it?" Amber asked.

"Yeah. It's all fine."

Tara frowned. "No red carpet events yet?"

"You'll be the first to know," Josie promised. "What have I missed around here then? Fill me in on the gossip."

She was hoping the conversation would come around to Sam. Someone would surely mention how miserable he is without her. They didn't, though; he wasn't mentioned at all. The girls talked about some of the locals, and Tara talked about work and the latest saga with her boss, James. Apparently he'd been flaunting his new girlfriend and Tara was sure it was an attempt to make her jealous. She claimed it didn't work, but Josie wasn't so sure that was the truth. There was a glint of vulnerability in Tara's eyes that vanished as quickly as it appeared. It didn't escape Josie's notice.

Annette whipped up sandwiches and salad for them and they ate lunch together on the patio.

"Where did the new couch in the barn come from?" Josie asked eventually.

Annette chuckled. "Sam found it at one of his car boot sales. He said it was a bargain and he couldn't resist."

Josie's thoughts drifted to the day she'd done the car boot sale with him. It had been so much fun. That was also the day Jack had turned up with the letter from StarSearch that had set her on a course away from Sam. She automatically glanced around. He'd said he'd see her before she left, and she kept expecting him to casually wander over and join their little get together.

"Are you driving back tonight?" Amber asked.

"Yeah." With a sinking feeling she checked the time. "I should probably get going before too long. It's a nightmare drive. I've got to be up early tomorrow too."

"What time do you have to be on set?" Tara asked eagerly.

"I need to be in make-up at six. Filming won't start until a bit later." Hours later, in fact, and Josie was sick of all the waiting time. Thankfully, it looked like she'd only have one day of filming for the week and could be at the café for the rest.

Tara was suitably impressed by talk of the TV studio. It made Josie feel like the biggest fraud ever but she indulged her nonetheless, giving her snippets of info, dropping all the right jargon and buzzwords that she knew Tara would enjoy.

The afternoon flew by, and suddenly Amber was talking about getting Kieron home for dinner. Tara left at the same time, after a round of hugs and goodbyes.

Josie stayed on the patio after they left, staring out over the fields. She should really be on the road already.

"I can feed the dogs before I leave." She stood purposefully as a couple of dogs howled in the barn.

"Leave it," Annette said. "I'll do them."

"It's fine." She didn't stop to argue but set off to the barn. She'd leave as soon as she'd fed the dogs. Auto-pilot seemed to kick in, and the dogs were fed in no time. For a moment she imagined Sam wandering in to see her, like he'd done so many times before. After convincing herself she was over him in the last weeks, being back at Oakbrook and seeing him again had set her back. She still missed him so much. Again, she looked for him as she made her way back to the house and was disappointed that there was no sign of him.

"I better hit the road," she told Annette when she arrived back in the kitchen. She declined the offer of staying for dinner, but Annette insisted on making more sandwiches for the journey.

She set off back to London with a heavy heart and spent the long drive contemplating what a mess she'd made of things.

CHAPTER 43

The weekend at Oakbrook had been bittersweet, and Josie spent the following days feeling sorry for herself.

"Can't you just go back if you miss it so much?" Stella asked on Wednesday morning.

"No, she can't," Brenda hissed. "What would we do without her?" She beamed at Josie. "You're not going to leave us, are you?"

"No. I'm not going back. I can't."

"But if you love this Sam fella" – Stella chopped vegetables as she chatted – "and he was happy to see you again, can't you just go back and work things out?"

Josie shook her head. She couldn't, even though part of her wished she could. "I can't go back to him. I miss him but I'm still angry with him. He should have been supportive about my job offer. I hate that he wouldn't look at it from my point of view and wasn't willing to make any sacrifices. It's not the sort of person I want to be with. Even if I do love him."

"And you do love him?" Brenda said.

Josie slouched against a kitchen unit. "It's irrelevant.

Relationships don't always work out. Ours didn't and I've moved on."

"Really?" Stella asked. "Because you spent all day yesterday looking like the world was coming to an end."

"Not because of Sam. I moved to London for my career but I hate the TV work. It's not the career I wanted it to be and it's never going to be."

"Oh, hang on," Brenda said playfully. "It sounds like you are thinking of leaving us."

"I love working here," she said. "I just want something more fulfilling. Something where I can grow and develop."

Brenda squeezed her arm reassuringly.

"What about doing a college course or something?" Stella suggested.

"I've no idea what I want to do, though. I was so sure I wanted to be an actress. Now I need to find a new career path."

She was still mulling it over that evening when her phone rang. Sam's name flashed on the screen. To say she was surprised would be something of an understatement. She answered hesitantly.

"Is it a good time?" he asked. "I didn't know if you'd still be at work."

"I just got home." Why was he calling? What did he want?

"How was filming today?"

She rubbed her eyes. Did he just want to chat?

"Work was fine." She didn't want to lie but she also didn't want to tell him that she actually worked in a café most of the time. "Tiring. I was just about to go to bed. Did you need something?"

"Heather logged herself out of the Twitter account and couldn't find the password. I told her I'd ask you."

She pressed her lips together. Either Heather was

completely useless or Sam was making up excuses to call. "It's on the corkboard in the study. All the passwords are up there. Heather knows that."

"She must have forgotten."

"She could also have called me herself," she said tersely.

"Aren't I allowed to call you?"

She paced the room. "I'd rather you didn't, to be honest."

"I thought we could still be friends."

She gave a short humourless laugh. There was no way she could be friends with Sam. Being in the same room with him felt like torture.

"No. We can't be friends. And I find it really weird that you'd call and ask me about work since you didn't want me to take the job and broke up with me when I did." She swallowed hard and hated the tears which pooled in her eyes.

"I'm sorry." His voice was full of emotion.

"I don't care if you're sorry." She couldn't help crying and her words were muffled. "You didn't want to be with me any more. You don't get to be my friend. I don't need friends like you."

"I was an idiot," he said quickly. "And I miss you—"

"I don't want to know!" She stopped pacing and wiped tears from her cheeks. "Don't call me again." She spat the words out and then ended the call with trembling hands. Sinking onto the couch, she sobbed. It was the last thing she needed. Every day it was an effort not to think about him, to push away thoughts of going back to him. Knowing that he missed her too, and that he wanted her back, made it so much harder.

She needed to look forward and think about her future, not dwell on the past.

~

In the following days she forced herself not to think about Sam. It was made more difficult by his daily phone calls. She didn't answer them and focussed on figuring out how to get her life back on track. She knew she needed to make some big changes, she just wasn't sure what.

It was a week later while opening the café that she saw the woman with the toddler and the noisy golden retriever stop outside. Josie went out and made a big fuss of the dog and then held the door while the woman lugged the buggy inside. The dog obeyed when Josie told him to sit.

"Did it take you long to learn that?" The woman parked the buggy next to a table and took a seat. "The dog training stuff."

"Not really," Josie said vaguely.

"You just did a course or something, did you?"

Josie looked slightly confused. "I just learnt on the job when I worked in a kennels."

"That's good. I thought you'd have to do some sort of training if you were working in a kennels."

"No," Josie said thoughtfully. It had never even occurred to her.

"I keep thinking I'll sign up for one of these doggy schools. You know the ones, they meet in the park and teach you how to control your dog. I just never get round to it."

Josie took her order and wandered back to the kitchen. The day passed in a bit of a blur, and the conversation with the dog owner played on her mind. Josie got her laptop out as soon as she got back to the apartment that evening.

"Did you know you can do courses in dog training?" she mused aloud as Emily flicked through the TV channels beside her.

"I can't say it's something I ever thought about much. But I suppose that makes sense. Why?"

"It just never occurred to me that you could train in this

kind of thing. I always thought it was something you were either good at or you weren't." She scanned the course list for a small local college which specialised in animal care. "There are courses in dog grooming, dog nutrition, health and well-being. All sorts of stuff."

Emily mumbled a vague response, clearly unimpressed by the revelation.

Josie's mind raced.

Her phone lit up and vibrated round the coffee table.

Another call from Sam.

She ignored it.

CHAPTER 44

Quitting the acting job became Josie's obvious next step. She'd really come to hate it, and even the thought of it made her anxious. She was nervous about telling Michaela but she resolved to do it.

Unfortunately, Michaela called her first. It was the middle of August but you'd never know it was summer given the grey sky and drizzle. Josie looked out of the living room window of Emily's apartment as she answered the call. It wasn't much of a view, just a busy street filled with traffic and people hurrying through the rain.

"You're going to love me!" Michaela said excitedly.

"Really?" Josie replied sceptically. "What's happened?"

"They're finally giving you some lines to say! I was just talking to Sally at the studios and she told me. Didn't I tell you it would end up being a speaking part?"

"I was going to call you today," she said flatly. "I'm quitting. I don't want to go back there."

"Don't talk crazy. You were the one who always wanted a speaking part. Don't run away now you've got it. It's not stage fright, is it?"

279

HANNAH ELLIS

"No! I just don't like the job. It's not enough hours. And I'm thinking of a career change."

"But you're expected on set first thing tomorrow."

"I wasn't planning on going." She should have let Michaela know sooner, but she didn't really care.

"Of course you're going. It reflects badly on me if you fail to show up without warning. You'll at least have to go in tomorrow."

"I don't have to," Josie said, swirling the dregs of coffee in the cup. "But if you ask nicely I might."

There was a loud exhalation of breath. "Fine! Please will you go to work tomorrow?"

"Hmm. Okay. Only tomorrow, though. Then you'll have to tell them I quit." She'd been adamant she'd already done her last day of filming, but she was a little intrigued by the fact that she'd have lines to say, and one last day wouldn't hurt.

The next morning as she sat in the holding room, she even felt a little nervous. What if they were actually giving her character a storyline? Would she really walk away now if it was finally becoming a real acting job? She decided she probably would.

Eventually, the assistant director came to talk to her. She seemed distracted and kept glancing over her shoulder as she spoke to Josie. "At the start of the scene, if you can just lean over the bar and ask whoever's in front of you what they want to drink. Not too loud or anything. Just be natural. Okay?"

Josie's eyebrows shot up. "That's it?"

"It's not a problem, is it? You can manage that?"

Josie was about to tell her where she could shove her one measly line, but Jack appeared and slid into the seat beside her. She smiled and the woman went away again.

"I didn't know you'd be here today," she said cheerfully.

She hadn't seen him for a couple of weeks, but he was quite good at calling her or sending the odd message. He hadn't mentioned he'd be working with her again.

He shrugged. "I quite enjoy it. And work are happy for me to have the odd day off. It works quite well. What did she want?" he asked, nodding at the retreating assistant director.

"They've finally given me something to say."

"Great!"

"Not really. One crappy line. I wasn't even going to come today. I'm going to quit."

"What will you do? Keep working in the café?"

"I don't know." She couldn't find the energy to discuss it and glanced at the door when it opened. "Lauren's here," she said quietly. It was the woman Jack had been on a date with. Jack took a sudden interest in his coffee until she'd passed. "She hates you," Josie remarked.

"She's a psycho!" He shook his head. "I really know how to pick 'em, don't I?" She gave him a friendly shove just as they were called down to the studio. "What do you have to say then?" Jack asked as they walked. "Have you got it all memorised?"

"I hope so." Josie rolled her eyes. "I have to ask someone what they want to drink. Let's hope I don't mess up! Ooh, if you stand at the bar, I can ask you. That'd be exciting."

He laughed as they filed onto set with everyone else.

As it turned out, Jack did manage to scoot into position across the bar from her, and she couldn't help but grin as she turned to him to deliver her line.

"What can I get for you?"

"A shot of whatever's convenient," he replied loudly.

Her eyes went wide and she whispered out of the corner of her mouth. "I don't think you're supposed to talk."

"It's a bar," he said loudly. "And I want a drink."

She bit her lip in an effort not to laugh at him. "Jack!" she hissed, trying to sound stern.

"Quick," he said, breaking into a grin. "We'll get thrown off set any second now. Get me a drink!"

"You're an idiot." She reached for the nearest bottle and poured clear liquid into two glasses. She glanced up as the director called "cut" and started shouting something in their direction.

Jack knocked the drink back and she did the same. "Sambuca," he coughed. "Thanks a lot. I think it's time we ran!"

"I think you've just got us both fired," she said, as the crowd parted and an assistant director headed over to them.

"That was the plan. Come on!"

She hurried round the bar and grabbed Jack's hand. He led her quickly through the throng while the director shouted after them. She couldn't make out what he was saying, but he didn't sound happy.

"You're such an idiot." She kicked her shoes off in the hallway and ran up the stairs with Jack as though they were fugitives. No one followed them, but they raced back to the dressing room anyway and hastily changed back into their own clothes. They were still running and laughing as they burst out of the building onto the street behind.

"I can't believe you just did that."

"You said you were quitting anyway. I thought we might as well have some fun."

"I think I need another drink!"

It felt like a weight had been lifted as she sat in the dingy corner pub down the road from the TV studios. It was too early to be drinking, really, but it seemed like one of those days, and she felt the need to celebrate the end of her job.

"So what's your plan now?" Jack asked.

She took a long swig of her beer and then set the glass on the stained beer mat. "I think I want to do something with animals."

"Go back to the kennels?"

She shook her head. "I've been looking into doing some courses. I know it sounds a bit crazy, but I was thinking about dog grooming. I could be a mobile dog groomer and offer it as a service to boarding kennels. I could run some obedience classes … Are you laughing at me? It's stupid, isn't it?"

"I'm not laughing." He was definitely laughing. "Sorry. I just had an image of you tying ribbons in a poodle's hair!"

She gave him a friendly slap on the arm and let out a sigh.

"I'm only teasing." Jack's features turned serious. "If that's what you want to do then do it. Why not?"

Since she couldn't think of a reason why not, she decided that's exactly what she would do.

CHAPTER 45

Once she'd made some decisions she felt much better. She was going to continue working for Brenda but take some courses too. With some training under her belt, she could start her own small business offering obedience classes and dog grooming. It wasn't the most ambitious of plans, but she was sure it would be good for her. She'd also started looking for a new place to live with renewed vigour. She'd found a few possibilities for flat-shares and had lined up appointments to view them.

Lizzie had called a couple of days after Josie had left the acting job. Apparently Lizzie and Annette had been discussing Josie's birthday and were insisting she go down to Oakbrook for the last weekend in August so they could celebrate with her. Josie was turning twenty-nine and wasn't convinced it was something she wanted to celebrate but agreed nonetheless.

Sam still popped into her head with annoying regularity. The phone calls didn't help. Her willpower seemed to be diminishing, and she was sure she'd break down and answer if he kept at it. Surely his persistence would wane soon.

It didn't, though. On Saturday, Josie was busy unloading the dishwasher at the café when Brenda shouted through that she had a visitor.

She was wiping her hands on her apron as she walked out and then stopped dead at the sight of Sam.

"I tried calling." He looked at her woefully. All she could do was stare.

"How did you know where I'd be?"

"I spoke to your friend, Emily. She said you worked here on the weekends."

Josie silently thanked Emily for not mentioning that the café was now the only place she worked. She'd not got round to telling many people that news.

"Can we talk?" he asked.

Brenda placed a hand on Josie's shoulder. "Take a break if you need to."

"Thanks." She untied her apron and beckoned for Sam to follow her out of the café.

Up in Emily's apartment, she switched the kettle on and turned to find Sam looking around the place. "So this is where you live?"

"Not for much longer. I'll be moving out soon. Somewhere bigger." Or so she hoped.

"I miss you," he said flatly.

She hated the way her stomach went all fluttery. It took a lot of self-control not to tell him she missed him too.

"I've moved on," she said instead. "I have a life here. And you were right – long-distance would never have worked for us. There's no point dwelling on it."

He stared at her like he was some sort of human lie detector. Her heart rate increased and she looked away, moving to gaze out of the window onto the busy street below.

"I wasn't right," he said. "I'm not sure I've ever been so

wrong about anything in my life." He paused and she felt him moving nearer to her. "But I really want to fix it."

"We can't fix it. You couldn't be supportive and I don't want to be with someone who asks me to give up my dreams. I need someone who'll push me to take chances." Tears welled in her eyes and she turned away from him.

"Sit down for a minute." He took her hand and pulled her gently to the couch. She didn't have the energy to protest. "I loved you from the moment I met you at the wedding."

A smile flashed onto her face and disappeared again. She opened her mouth to speak but he talked over her. "When we got together I thought that was it for me. I planned a whole life for us in my head. Then you said you wanted to take the job in London and I realised you wanted something completely different. I didn't know what to do, and I stupidly thought a clean break would be the best thing."

"I never wanted to lose you," she said.

"I know. And I should never have let you go."

"What were your plans?" she asked seriously. "You said you planned a whole life for us …"

He leaned back into the couch, biting his lip. "Marriage, kids, dogs, old age." His eyes finally met hers. "But I always planned on living in Averton. London was never in my plans." He paused briefly. "Now I don't really care where I live as long as I'm with you. I've been asking around and I think I can get a job in London—"

"What?" She couldn't quite believe what she was hearing.

"I'll move to London," he said. "We can get a place together."

"You can't move to London." The idea of it almost made her laugh. "You've got your lovely house and your life. You can't just leave."

"Of course I can. You need to be in London, and I don't want to hold you back from your career. It makes sense for me to move. Just say you still love me and we'll figure the rest out."

"It's so expensive here," she mused. "We'd have to live in a tiny apartment."

"I don't care." He reached for her hand and looked at her hopefully.

"I don't know if it's what I want," she said slowly. His grip loosened on her hand and she grabbed onto him, not wanting to let go. She hadn't meant that she didn't want to live with him, just that she didn't know if she wanted to live with him in London. It didn't make any sense. What she really wanted was to live in Averton again, but that meant admitting what a huge mistake she'd made. She was embarrassed that her dreams of an acting career had vanished after all she'd talked about it.

"I need time to think," she said. "This is all so out of the blue. I'm supposed to be at work and you've just sprung this on me." Part of her wanted to jump into his arms and go back to how things had been between them, but after so long trying to get over him, it felt like a step in the wrong direction.

"Okay." He squeezed her hand and stood up. "I'll leave you to get back to work."

She was aware of how far he'd driven to see her and was tempted to say he should hang around and she'd meet him after work. That didn't give her much time to think, though. And if there was one thing she was sure of, it was that she needed to start taking more time to think things through properly instead of making rushed decisions.

"I'm visiting Annette next weekend." Her birthday celebration. "We could get together then and talk things through."

He paused at the door and nodded. "That sounds good."

She lifted onto her toes and gently kissed his cheek before telling him to drive safely.

CHAPTER 46

M ax and Lizzie were sitting on the patio at Oakbrook when Josie arrived on Saturday lunchtime. She looked Lizzie up and down. "You're massive!"

"Careful," Max said. "The last person to say that almost ended up with a black eye."

Lizzie frowned. "It's not a very nice thing to say!" She hugged Josie regardless and wished her a happy birthday.

"Good thing she's so slow these days." Max flashed a boyish grin. "Black eyes don't suit me at all!"

Josie chuckled and bent to stroke the dogs.

"There you are!" Annette stepped outside. She had an apron on and flour smudged on her cheek. "Happy birthday!"

"Thank you." She didn't sit down, feeling the need to stretch her legs after so long in the car. When Charlie brought her a tennis ball she threw it across the lawn for him to chase.

"How's city life?" Max asked.

"It's okay," she said without enthusiasm.

"We saw your TV show," Lizzie said excitedly. "We found it on some random channel." Josie had told her a couple of weeks ago that it was now being aired. She hadn't quite got round to mentioning that she no longer worked there. No time like the present, she decided.

Max spoke before Josie had a chance. "We think we saw the back of you. I thought it looked too tall to be you and the hair was funny, but Lizzie thought it was you."

"I'm sure it was," Lizzie said.

"Sounds like it. I had to wear shoes with three-inch heels."

"Wow!" Lizzie laughed. "I'm surprised you lasted more than a day."

"Not much more." Josie finally took a seat with them. "I quit a couple of weeks ago." She felt tearful and hoped she wasn't about to start blubbering.

"What happened?" Lizzie asked, putting her hand over Josie's.

"It didn't turn out how I thought it would. I've been working at a café." She smiled sadly when no one said anything. "Did you have bets on how long I'd last at this job?"

Lizzie shook her head. "I thought this one would last. It seemed like you were finally doing what you loved. And nobody's judging you for changing jobs."

"I'm not sure that's true."

"I think it's very brave," Annette put in. "Most people stick at jobs they hate because they're too scared to take a chance."

Lizzie moved her hand to stroke her swollen belly. "Eventually you'll find something you love, and you'll know for definite it's what you want to do."

Their kindness made Josie's eyes fill with tears. She couldn't believe she'd put off telling them everything because she'd been embarrassed. She'd assumed Lizzie would roll her eyes and tease her. It seemed like it was only Josie who was judging herself harshly.

"I already found something I love." Josie glanced at Annette. "I want to work with dogs. I found there are all these courses you can do to work with dogs and I thought—"

"You want your job back?" Annette jumped in.

"Well I know you've got Heather now, but I thought that maybe I could help out a bit. I know Heather hates all the computer stuff."

Annette waved a hand in front of her face. "Of course you can have your job back. Heather walks the dogs once a day, that's all. Sam's been teaching me to use the computer. It seemed easier than standing over Heather's shoulder telling her what to write every time."

"You couldn't fire Heather. I'd feel terrible."

"I can keep her as well. I told you, she doesn't do many hours. And if you're serious about doing some courses, you'll only work part-time anyway. I think it'll work brilliantly."

"I'm going to learn about dog grooming so we can offer that as part of the stay. I've got more ideas too. I'll earn my keep. I promise."

"You always do!" Annette said happily. "I suppose I better run a duster over your room."

Josie reached down to stroke Macy. "I might not live here," she said as casually as she could.

"Where would you live?" Annette asked, bemused.

Max grinned. "Am I allowed to guess?"

"You're going to move in with Sam?" Lizzie asked with wide eyes.

"Maybe." Josie grimaced. "I'll need to ask him first …"

"Are you going to ask him today?" Max said. "Because that could really put a damper on your birthday if he says no!"

Lizzie and Annette swiped at him at the same time.

"I'm joking," he said, laughing.

Josie looked at Annette. "You wouldn't mind if I lived next door instead, would you?"

"Of course not."

"I should probably go and find Sam then." Josie stood. "Wish me luck!"

"Just hurry up," Annette said. "The rest of your guests will be here soon!"

Josie gave a quick salute and hurried in the direction of Sam's house.

～

He opened the door wearing the same blue shirt he'd worn on their first date, and the smell of his aftershave took Josie straight back to that night.

"I was just about to come up to Annette's." A smile spread over his face as he looked at her.

"I thought about everything," she announced.

He opened his mouth to speak but stopped when she leaned close. Gently, she brushed her lips against his, then closed her eyes as she kissed him. He relaxed into her, his arms snaking around her back and pulling her to him.

When they broke apart he beamed at her. "I take it I'm moving to London then?"

"No!" She pushed the door shut and pulled him into the living room. A gift bag sat on the coffee table, and she was intrigued as to what he'd have chosen for her.

"I'm going to move here," she said.

"What about your job …"

"It's a long story. Can I open my present first?"

She reached for the gift. It was a big box, so definitely not jewellery like she was used to getting from Jack. She never even wore jewellery.

"I might have made a huge mistake." Sam looked

suddenly worried. "I'm ninety-nine percent sure you'll hate it. I should have got you something romantic."

Even more intrigued, she tore at the wrapping paper. She stared at a shoebox.

"I'm concerned that this doesn't say Converse …"

Opening the lid revealed a pair of grey hiking boots.

Sam frowned. "I thought they'd be useful when we come and visit."

Josie's eyes filled with tears and she bit her lip to stop her chin trembling. "I love them."

"Really? Because I won't be offended if you return them. The receipt's in the box."

Shaking her head, she pulled the paper from inside the shoes to try them on. She pushed her feet in, wriggling her toes and then pulling the laces tight. They were sturdy but not uncomfortable. "I really do love them. And I love that you care about my feet being cold and wet." Her eyes locked on his. "And they're perfect for my new job!"

"What new job?"

"I'm going to work for Annette again," she told him happily.

He looked confused. "But I meant what I said about moving to London."

"I know you did. And I love you for it. But I know you want to be here really, and I do too."

He still looked sceptical. "What about your career?"

"I'm working on a new career. I have lots of plans to improve the kennels. And I had an idea about doing consultancy work with other kennels. I proved I can build up a business, so I thought I could help other places do the same. I have so many ideas." She took Sam's hands in her own. "But I want to be here."

"Are you sure?"

"Definite."

"So you'll move in with Annette again?"

"Probably." She tilted her head to one side. "Unless I get a better offer …"

"You could live with me," he said, smiling uncertainly.

She beamed and moved to kiss him. "I was hoping you might say that."

End of book two …

SUMMER AT THE OLD BOATHOUSE

HOPE COVE BOOK 3

Emily Winters would do anything for her best friend **Josie**. Every week they meet for a catch up at the Old Boathouse - an idyllic little café by the Thames where Josie's boyfriend **Jack** works.

As the summer draws on, life seems perfect. Emily's writing career is taking off and she's throwing herself into the dating scene.

There's just one problem: she compares all the men she meets to Jack.

And none of them measure up.

Now all she needs to do is figure out how to fall out of love with her best friend's boyfriend. Because even when Josie moves to the countryside, and her relationship with Jack crumbles, Emily knows there are rules to friendship that you should never break.

But can they be bent in the name of love? Is there a way Emily can get the man of her dreams without ruining her friendship with Josie? One thing's for certain: when you're in love with your best friend's guy, the course of true love will be anything but smooth…

ALSO BY HANNAH ELLIS

Hannah has also written a series of children's books aimed at 5-9 year olds under the pen name, Hannah Sparks.

ACKNOWLEDGMENTS

Many thanks to the people who read and gave feedback at the various stages: Anthea Kirk, Nikkita Blake, Sarah-Jane Fraser, Michele Morgan Salls, Sarah Walker, Sue Oxley, Kathy Robinson, Hazel Baxter, Dua Roberts and Stephen Ellis. You are all amazing!

Thanks to Katherine Trail for a great editing job. It was a pleasure working with you again.

Aimee Coveney: I'm so glad I found such a fantastic cover designer. Thank you!

Again, thanks to my Mario for everything you do.

Last but not least, a big thank you to my readers. You're the best!

Printed in Great Britain
by Amazon